MW00619207

THE BILLIONAIRE'S LIST

Praise for The Billionaire's List

The Billionaire's List is a creative and fun story set at one of my favorite places, the New Jersey shore. Cortney Donelson captured me with the prologue and didn't let go.

Christine Dorfler, CFO, NBC Sports

Cortney Donelson spins an exciting tale that will keep readers turning the pages late into the night. When her rich uncle dies, Greta is in line to inherit a fortune, but she must first meet the demands of her uncle's last unusual request. Readers follow her to the Atlantic City addresses made famous by the classic board game Monopoly as she visits the eclectic group of people who have, for different reasons, been important in Uncle Richard's life. Something about these visits seems off, and the anxiety intensifies as random murders punctuate the story. The author's clues throughout the novel are nuanced, and readers will find themselves returning to re-read earlier passages after concluding the book. Well-written and clever, *The Billionaire's List* is an outstanding debut novel.

E.A. Coe, award-winning author of multiple novels, including *The Other Side of Good*

What an engaging and intriguing tale of philanthropy, redemption, and murder! After writing several non-fiction books, Cortney Donelson's debut novel, *The Billionaire's List,* is a wild and inventive story that grabbed me from the first page. If you like mysteries or board games, this one's for you.

Terri DeBoer, meteorologist/lifestyle show host, WOOD-TV, Grand Rapids, MI, author of *Brighter Skies Ahead: Forecasting A Full Life When You Empty The Nest* and *Grieving Well: A Healing Journey Through The Season of Grief*

THE BILLIONAIRE'S LIST

Cortney Donelson

Copyright © 2023 Cortney Donelson | vocem LLC

All rights reserved. No part of this publication may be reproduced, distributed, or transmitted in any form or by any means, including photocopying, recording, or other electronic or mechanical methods, without the prior written permission of the publisher, except in the case of brief quotations embodied in critical reviews and certain other noncommercial uses permitted by copyright law. For permission requests, contact the publisher via the contact page at www.yourvocem.com.

This is a work of fiction. Any resemblance to persons, living or dead, or actual events is either coincidental or used for fictive and storytelling purposes. Some elements of this story are inspired by real places, including street names located in Atlantic City, New Jersey. Other places are products of the author's imagination.

ISBN: 978-1-7375641-3-3 (paperback)

ISBN: 978-1-7375641-1-9 (ebook)

Front cover design by Hannah Linder Designs

Interior layout by Catherine Posey

Printed by KDP Amazon Services

First printing edition 2023.

vocem LLC

Huntersville, North Carolina

www.yourvocem.com

To my kids,
I pray you always be leaders for what is right
and not followers of the world.

Author's Note

The Billionaire's List was inspired by Monopoly, the classic board game of wealth-building by Hasbro. As you move through the story, I hope you enjoy picking out the references to each stop on the board as you try to unravel this not-so-cozy mystery. I had a blast weaving them in there!

Prologue
Three years ago

Nashville, Tennessee

The killer pulled the black hoodie over her shaved head, tightening the strings enough to conceal part of her face, and maneuvered the short tactical knife inside the front pocket of her sweatshirt, positioning it within her right hand and gripping the wood handle as she walked. Number one was sitting alone on a bench a hundred yards to the northeast. He smoked a Camel cigarette as he read a manuscript, oblivious to his upcoming demise.

The park buzzed with people enjoying the crisp air and pacifying October sunshine. The murderess saw everyone, anticipated every move in her periphery before it happened. A rollerblader who made a sharp turn toward the pond. The geriatric couple, walking hand-in-hand, bird-watching as they strolled away from her. And her target, who was inhaling his last puff on his last cigarette.

As the woman passed behind the bench, there was a quick movement, the sound of a wet pop, then nothing. The hooded figure kept walking, never looking back as she discreetly returned the knife to her pocket. To anyone else, it looked as if she was warming her hands, protecting them from the chilly wind blowing off of the pond.

Back on the bench, movie director Charlie Garrison slumped forward in the appearance of sleep. A small wound at the base of his head leaked red, his brainstem fatally punctured. His cigarette fell to the pavement and the manuscript he had been reading to his lap, left hanging from his right knee as his arms relaxed at his sides. He felt nothing. Death crept in a few seconds later.

The woman with the hoodie and crimson-stained knife ducked out of the park through a narrow exit at the north end created by a pair of trimmed hedges. She hailed a taxi at the corner and gave the driver the address of her next destination. It was not the location of her home or work, nor the address of anyone she knew. It had been randomly selected that morning, one that would lead no one to her.

As she relaxed in the back of the taxi, she assumed she'd feel something. But no discernable emotion knocked on the door of her heart. Instead, thoughts of how the twists and turns of her life had led her to that day rocketed through her mind. Disappointments and loss had littered the path. But she didn't care about any of that. She only cared about one thing.

No one could have guessed the reason she ended Charlie Garrison's life. Few had the knowledge that could explain the violence surging through her veins. And she liked it that way.

Once the cab stopped and the hooded figure stepped out, she and her knife disappeared, as they always would.

It was time to plan for number two.

Part One

House Rules

1

Present day, Wednesday
I-95 North between Woodbridge, Virginia, and Washington, DC

The smell of the bus's fumes wafting through the rear vents makes Greta gag for the second time. She stares out the window and watches the sun set behind the trees lining I-95 just south of Washington, DC, wondering if she'll ever overcome her fear of flying. As the miles add up, she reminisces about a man who's life seemed larger than any life had a right to be.

Greta's great-uncle was famous and not because he sported a stovetop hat or carried a white metal cane—though those fashion choices left no doubt about his offbeat personality. Her great-uncle, *the* Mr. Richard M. Goldman, was the wealthiest man in New Jersey. He had called Atlantic City his home for seven and a half decades, a place where he labeled a variety of individuals *friend*. From the down-and-out junkie with puncture scars on his arms to the high-rolling executive with diamonds fanning her neckline, Great-Uncle Richard enjoyed a robust network of *who's who* and *who used to be,* even a few *never to be*. He certainly had a way with people. Everyone loved him. Or so she'd heard.

Great-Uncle Richard was murdered two days ago. Now,

Greta makes her way to the AC—Atlantic City. She wonders, as the lights of the nation's capital glow in the distance, if anyone else calls it *the AC*. It's not meant as a kind nickname.

An attorney, who introduced himself as Brian Gogh, had called Greta yesterday, notified her of Great-Uncle Richard's brutal passing, and tasked her with the job of deciding what to do with the pieces of his empire, his monopoly of real estate holdings. She's learned there are many pieces to gather. Richard Goldman owned nearly half of the beach-front city, and as the dice have been rolled, it's now her responsibility, as his named heir, to wrap up his life and put it back in a box, so to speak.

Greta, an unhitched and reclusive oddity herself, continues to stare out of the bus window to avoid eye contact with the bus-goers around her. Introverted is probably the most polite description for Greta. She's a novelist with an imagination as vivid and unique as her six-foot-one frame. Growing up, most people assumed she'd become a famous track and field or basketball star, given her long legs. But Greta doesn't like to run. And she can't dribble a ball.

It's been six years since Greta even spoke to good ole Great-Uncle Richard. As the wheels below her turn on the pavement, thoughts about why he chose her as his benefactor tumble inside her head. Greta detests everything her great-uncle treasured: fame, parties, even people to some extent. According to the countless professionals she sat opposite during her teens and early twenties, that last one is not her fault.

Through cautious eyes, Greta peeks at her fellow passengers. She's grateful no one sat next to her. Small talk is not something she ever learned to handle well. Greta prefers deep relationships—if only she could maintain one. Her *quirkiness*, a term her high school and college classmates used, serves as a deterrent for connection. Being a loner has certain advantages. As long as she stays away from crowds and out of the spotlight, she is invisible. And that's how she likes it.

The bus seat, into which Greta's lean and lithe legs folded

before dawn, is now causing her butt to go numb. She's been sitting far too long, traveling up from her tiny town in North Carolina, the place she calls home, on her way to the AC. *It's not as bad as say, LA or Vegas,* she thinks. Greta plans to sell all of her great-uncle's holdings, tidy up his life as quickly as possible, and return to her refuge so she can finish her next book manuscript before her publisher's deadline, now five weeks away.

After five stops and eighteen long hours, the bus finally slows as it nears her destination. Greta stretches her legs underneath the seat in front of her, having recently woken from a nap.

In a half-cough, half-shout, the driver yells, "Next stop! Atlantic City Boardwalk!"

Greta glances at her watch. The hands had moved past midnight while she slept. *Wonderful. Let's do this and get out,* she thinks as she eyes the door as it slides open.

Greta steps off the bus, her sling purse over her right shoulder and her only other bag in her left hand—an extra-large teal-colored duffle sporting a deep red stain the size of a grapefruit, making it seem as if she has murdered some poor soul and is trying to hide the evidence. She inhales deeply through her nose, which promptly crinkles as the scents of funnel cake, diesel fumes, and the cheap cologne from the man ahead of her intermingle in her nostrils.

Gross, she thinks as she spies the offending food truck half a block down on her left.

Greta moves swiftly toward the rental car window, passing Old Stetson in two strides, arriving in time to stand on the second *X* painted on the ground. When she reaches the counter a few minutes later, the Black woman behind the divider stares at her, making no effort to smile or ask what she can do to assist her. The woman's glasses remind Greta of the enormous white sunglasses popular in the 1960s, over three decades before Greta was born.

"I reserved an oversized car for three days. My name is Greta Goldman." As someone who stretches as tall as some men, larger cars or SUVs are something Greta always reserves when traveling.

The timeworn woman, whose name tag reads, "Precious," seems startled by Greta's words. Her eyebrows pinch together. "Who'd you say you are?" she asks, her words dressed in traces of doubt.

"Greta Goldman." Greta tries not to shout through the thick, plastic window pane. She drums her knuckles in short bursts on the counter, hoping Precious will get the hint and hurry up. Greta's stomach growls its displeasure at the lack of food she has ingested over the many miles of travel. And her nerves are putting a damper on her appetite.

"Are you related to Richard?" Sweet Precious hasn't deciphered the hint.

Greta pauses. "Yes, I'm his great-niece." Her heart races as she looks at the people in line behind her. She isn't interested in revealing too much about herself or making new friends. Even the word *friend* makes her shudder. The only priorities on her list tonight are food, hotel, shower, and bed, in that order. Attorney Gogh has scheduled an early meeting with her at a local breakfast café.

"He's gonna be missed around here," Precious continues. Greta detects moisture behind the woman's white frames. "He was a nice man, that Mr. Richard. I'm sorry for your loss. I dunno who would have killed him." The woman blinks rapidly, then gathers the required paperwork and slides it under the window. "Sign at the bottom. I need to make a copy of your driver's license."

As Greta turns to leave after the rental agreement and other paperwork are completed, Precious whispers one last sentence: "Richard gave me my name." Then Precious promptly waves the next customer in line over to the window, as if she had said nothing at all.

Greta shrugs and faces the small lot of parked cars, searching for space number eight.

As Greta squeezes behind the wheel of the Jeep Compass, she uses the lower bar to slide her seat back another six inches. Using her right hand to pull her seatbelt across her body and buckle it, she promptly speeds off as the GPS announces, "Starting route to Caesar's Atlantic City. Turn left on North Michigan Avenue . . ."

2

Thursday

Brian Gogh, one of the most respected lawyers in Atlantic City, steps out of his sleek Cadillac SUV after his chauffeur opens the rear door. Brian's navy Gucci necktie flies sideways in the wind, and his right hand presses it back down in one fluid motion as he thanks his driver. They smirk at each other, sharing an unspoken, inside joke forged through a decade of working together.

"That early April wind will get you every time, Antonio," Brian warns. His driver smiles wider and nods his understanding.

Many of Brian's clientele boast eight- or nine-figure empires. Richard Goldman had been his favorite one, though. While exceedingly wealthy, Richard's philanthropic heart elevated him to the level of those like J. K. Rowling, or perhaps Bill Gates—people who give away more money than they spend.

Brian had wanted to be an attorney almost from birth. Certainly, from the time his younger brother and sister fought over slices of apple at their kitchen table and he'd stepped in to mediate their arguments. It was a better option than having Mom or Dad hear about all the bickering from their nanny.

Just before 8:30, Brian sits down at a corner wooden table at The Extra Egg café, facing the door to watch for Greta Goldman. He runs his fingers through his dark blond hair, hoping the gel is successfully holding down the cowlick that popped up after his last haircut.

The smell of every kind of breakfast meat travels to his corner of the restaurant. Brian's mouth fills with anticipatory saliva. He speculates about what Greta might be like. He wonders if she will take after her great-uncle and hopes so. To be abundantly rich and authentically kind is a rare combination. Richard Goldman epitomized both qualities. As his throat tightens with these thoughts, he stuffs his grief down into the bottom compartments of his heart for another time.

The front door to the café swings open and a towering young woman with flowing dark brown—almost black—hair enters, ducking to avoid the top of the door frame. Her eyes dart around the café as she searches for a companion.

Brian chuckles inwardly, knowing that Richard had been possibly a whole foot shorter than his great-niece. He waves to Greta and stands as she approaches the table. The two shake hands as five-foot-eleven Brian looks up slightly to meet Greta's eyes.

"I'm Brian Gogh. It's nice to meet you, Ms. Goldman. I'm so sorry for your loss."

"Nice to meet you too. Call me Greta." Greta hates the last name *Goldman*. So pretentious—as if the whole family legacy is about Great-Uncle Richard's billions.

The irony is that Greta is not unwealthy herself. She carries the Goldman name, and because of that, she has netted above-average royalties as an author, particularly with her last novel. However, her parents willed most of their savings to local charities upon their deaths in a horrific accident when she was twenty. They had set up a trust for her to access some money to finish her education and get her life started on the right foot, but they had always believed that children should learn the value of money by earning it, not by receiving it free.

Greta never minded what most believe was an obvious slight, a parental slap to her face. She understood the lesson, and anyway, she distrusts the wealthy, their treasures, and everything else having to do with the entitled life. As a best-selling author, Greta lives comfortably. Though when unexpected expenses creep in, which seems to be often, there are occasions she wishes she had a few million dollars in her bank account. She knows she'd spend it wisely.

"Can we get started, then?" Greta asks, always aiming to get any new social interaction over with quickly. Her peculiar personality is of no help when meeting people for the first—or even the fifth—time. She's nervous, and it shows.

"Of course. Would you like any coffee or breakfast?" Brian replies, aware Greta arrived on the bus late last night. He assumes she's hungry and, at the very least, needs everyone's favorite morning pick-me-up, a cup of dark roasted caffeine. He knows he does.

"If you insist," Greta answers just as a middle-aged, aproned man with gray hair covering his temples arrives at the table, a notepad and pen at the ready.

"What can I get for you this morning?" he asks, somewhat loudly, the clank of dishes in the kitchen prompting the unnecessary volume.

Brian looks at Greta, always the gentleman, and nods for her to start.

"I'll have two poached egg whites, rye toast, no butter, and a black coffee," Greta says as she hands the server her unopened menu.

Brian lips turn up. Richard always ordered rye toast too. "And I'll have the special—eggs over medium, turkey sausage, potatoes, and a black coffee as well." The server finishes writing the order down and scurries off. "How was your trip?" Brian ventures.

Greta is in a hurry, though she has no reason for rushing. She sighs. "Long." Greta offers no further explanation, avoiding Brian's gaze. After a few awkward seconds, her cobalt-blue eyes look up toward his chin and soften. "I'm sorry. I am not a fan of the AC . . . uh, Atlantic City. I prefer small, rural towns, and the bus ride was stuffy and cramped—and long." She realizes she has already said *long*. "But we're here now."

Brian nods his understanding. "Well, let's get to it, then. Okay?" He pulls out his caramel-colored document bag and unzips it, retrieving some official-looking papers, then gently lays the bag on an extra chair at their table. Greta notices the authentic and expensive leather case right away.

Of course, she thinks with a bit of contempt.

"First, I want to say I'm really going to miss Richard. The community is heartbroken over his passing, especially such a violent one." Brian clears his throat.

Greta nods. He had told her on the phone that Richard had been killed while strolling along the beach a few evenings ago. His body had been discovered early the next morning by a pair of fishermen. The news reports failed to mention—and Brian doesn't know—that Richard was lying face down in the sand with the waves lapping at his socked feet, and his sneakers and white cane lay half-buried beside him. A peculiar hole was later found on the back of his upper neck.

"He was a client but also a friend. Several years ago, he profoundly supported my family. Your great-uncle was a force to be reckoned with, but also made a tremendous impact on this community over the past five decades." Brian's voice catches, and he takes a sip of the coffee their server has just delivered to collect himself.

Is he going to cry? Greta wonders.

"As I mentioned on the phone, your great-uncle left everything he owned to you to decide how to handle." Brian watches Greta carefully for a reaction. He could not detect any surprise or sorrow when they had spoken two days ago on the phone. No reaction when he had notified her of her great-uncle's untimely death.

Though he isn't a fan of gambling, Greta provides him with one of the best straight faces he has ever seen. Not even a flicker shows in any of her facial muscles. His curiosity blooms. When he doesn't get any verbal response either, he continues: "There's a small catch, though. Richard wants you to follow a list he created before his death that will take you to the streets where he owns property. He wants you to spend at least one day and one night on each street, getting to know the people he knew and respected. He's provided either hotel or host family contact information, and everyone knows to expect you at some point."

Brian stops talking as the server arrives, places a couple of plates of food in front of them, and refills their waters.

Greta stares at her eggs, then looks up at Brian, her shimmering eyes seeking his nose to avoid direct eye contact, which makes her uncomfortable. If she could make eye contact, she would bore into his like drills. "Are you serious?" It is all she can muster. "How many streets are we talking about?"

Given her reaction, Brian is hesitant to answer. For the first time, he spies a two-inch scar on Greta's upper lip, barely noticeable through her rose-colored lipstick. Hoping for the best, he softly says, "Nearly two dozen."

"What!" Greta's voice explodes through the café. She looks around, feeling ashamed and conspicuous. After a beat, she complains in a quieter tone: "I can't stay here that long! I have a book deadline with my publisher. I assumed I'd be here for three days—tops!" Greta's cheeks flush, and she grips the edge of the table. Then she whispers, "I can't do this . . . for too many reasons to list."

"Ms. Go—Greta, look, Richard and I spoke at length about this a couple of months ago. I know it's unexpected. It was his last wish, recorded in his most recent will. To take control of his estate or sell it off and dissolve it—to do anything really—this is the only way. I'm sorry. Nobody expected him to be gone so soon, including him."

"There is no other family to do this?"

Brian's head tilts to the side. "Well, since his brother Bill and his wife have no kids and they are getting on in age . . ."

"Right." Greta sits back in her chair and frowns at Brian, despite knowing full well he is only the messenger.

A plate crashes to the ground behind the door leading to the kitchen, and all the patrons reflexively look in that direction except for Greta. Her eyes drop to the paperwork in front of Brian. She wishes she could set it on fire, erase its contents, and jump on the next bus back to North Carolina.

3

Later that same afternoon, Greta stands outside Caesar's Palace, leaning on one of the iconic Roman-style columns, with her great-uncle's list in her hands and baby blue running shoes covering her feet as she waits for Brian Gogh. After leaving the café, Brian recommended she go back to her hotel to pack up her things and put on comfortable shoes. She had been wearing two-inch wedges and form-fitting jeans earlier. Brian said he'd handle the rental car Greta used to get to the hotel, ensuring it was returned to the airport location.

Greta had benefited from the few hours' break to lower her heart rate, get herself together, and rearrange the next month of her life. Thankfully, as an impulsive choice, she had packed her laptop into her sling bag, assuming she might work on her novel while riding the bus to and from New Jersey. She hadn't felt compelled during the trip up, but now, she would have to finish the manuscript while staying in Atlantic City *for who knows how long*.

A large black Cadillac SUV pulls up, and an Italian man slides out of the driver's seat. His wavy jet-black hair nearly matches Greta's long strands in color.

"Miss Goldman?" he asks, as he passes the rear bumper and

puts his hand on the rear door handle to open it for her. "Welcome to Atlantic City. My name is Antonio Rossi. Mr. Gogh is waiting." Antonio waves her inside the SUV to where Brian sits.

"Greta," she corrects the too-formal driver. *And look at this car!* Brian's multiple flashes of wealth irritate her.

Greta pauses before handing Antonio her duffle bag. She doesn't know the man from Adam. Unsure but relenting with a sigh, she hands him the bag, bends in half to slide inside the car, and sits beside the attorney.

"How are you feeling?" Brian asks with sincerity as Greta buckles up.

"Better. I don't like this, but if this is what we have to do, let's do it." She catches a whiff of his cologne, a fir balsam and coriander-infused smell that, when it hits her brain receptors, makes her feel more comfortable, like being in the woods near her home in North Carolina.

She glances at Brian's face and tries to smile before glancing out of the window again. A peace offering, she supposes. Before she looks away, Greta notices his eyes' steel-gray hue, pulsating yet calming, like a storm moving off over the ocean.

The car inches away from the curb as Brian gives Antonio the name of the first street. "Mediterranean Avenue, Antonio . . . address 1225. Thanks."

As Greta stares out the window, thinking she'd rather travel via Uber by herself than in this Cadillac, her left knee bounces. On one hand, she feels obligated to talk to Brian who sits a few inches away and still smells wonderful. On the other hand, she doesn't care what he thinks about her. She assumes he wouldn't like her if he got to know her, anyway. In three weeks, she is hoping to never see, or smell, him or this city again.

"So who is at this first stop?" she asks a minute later. On the other side of the tinted windows, she spies rows of dilapidated townhouses, dotted patches of thin grass, and few people.

Brian had called ahead and made the arrangements with the owner of the house. "It's an older woman in her mid-nineties, and they both assumed Richard would outlive her. Her name is Edith Moore. She played an integral part in Richard's life, but I'll let her tell you the details. She's feisty, but I think you'll like her."

Greta nods but doesn't respond verbally. As an introvert, she knows this entire adventure will be torturous, zapping more of her energy with each passing day. She just hopes she gets to the end of the twenty-plus-day escapade without going insane.

The car slows, and Greta squeezes her fingers around the rolled-up list in her lap. The townhome they stop in line with is an end unit with white siding peeling in places, and instead of a proper front railing, a metal bicycle rack sits, serving as the boundary between the sidewalk and porch. The front door is embraced by black bars, which cover its small square window, and there is an empty lot on the left side of the building where a semi-covered motorcycle and a random boat sit on cement blocks.

Greta's heart rate ticks up. This is all just too much. If she had known she was required to take a tour of the worst parts of the city, she would have asked them to bury Richard and donate everything, sight unseen. Though, if she understands Brian correctly, that isn't even possible.

"Here we are!" Brian seems overly excited given the condition of the neighborhood. Greta sighs and reaches for the door handle. Before she can pull it, Antonio is there on the other side, opening the door and stepping away.

She and Brian walk up to the bike rack and step around it to ring the doorbell. No sound can be heard when Brian pushes the button, so he knocks loudly on the door frame. Greta notices a gold bracelet as it jangles against his watch on his left wrist. She can't make out the inscription, but she thinks she spots angel wings engraved on the surface. She primes herself to ask him about it when the door opens.

Greta blinks at the delicate woman standing before her. She first notices the oxygen cannula in her nostrils, pumping breath into her lungs through a portable machine that sits in a bag, which hangs on her walker. The woman's umber-colored eyes squint, and her lips part into a smile as she focuses those eyes on Brian.

"Ms. Moore, it's so nice to see you," Brian says. "Is this still a good time?"

"Of course, dear. Come in!" Edith Moore reverses her steps to make way for Brian and Greta.

As they step inside, Greta finds herself in the middle of Ms. Moore's kitchen. It is as ancient as its host, with a peeling linoleum floor and two of the ugly-brown cabinet doors hanging from their hinges. The scents of lemon and baby powder become more prominent as Greta moves further into Ms. Moore's home. Her nose wrinkles.

Brian starts the introductions. "Ms. Moore, this is Greta Goldman, Richard's great-niece. As I mentioned last evening, she's going to spend the next twenty-four hours here, if that's still okay with you?"

"Oh, please sit, dears. Can I get you something to drink?" Ms. Moore peers at Greta through her thick glasses.

"No, ma'am," Greta answers. She is afraid the woman might trip and fall while trying to manage her walker with the oxygen tubing and two or three drinks, especially in this tiny space.

"Ma'am? I love it! Come, let's move to the living room." Ms. Moore takes off into the dark hallway that leads from the kitchen. Greta waits for a beat and follows Brian, glimpsing the framed photos that line the hall. The last photograph stops her.

"Is that you and Uncle Richard?" Greta asks. She stares at the black-and-white photograph of a white, rotund teenager standing next to a slim and polished Black woman wearing a polka dot dress—no doubt Ms. Moore in her prime. The boy has on a cap and gown, and Ms. Moore is staring at him with her arm around his shoulders and a look of pride, obviously not realizing the cameraperson was already snapping the shot.

"Oh, yes, dear. That was a long time ago. Richard's high school graduation, in fact. He was such a smart boy. And such a wise man . . ." Ms. Moore takes a tissue from the end table next to her and dabs her eyes.

Greta moves into the room and sits next to Brian on a flowered couch, facing Ms. Moore who has found rest in a canary-yellow wingback chair that looks like it cost her two dollars at the local flea market. Multiple holes dot the chair, and a large gray stain was evident on the seat just before Ms. Moore sat on it. Greta drops her bags on the floor next to her feet.

"So how did you know my great-uncle, Ms. Moore?" Greta ventures, ready to get past the superficial small talk and out of this twenty-four-hour prison.

Ms. Moore smirks. "Not so fast, dear. First, call me Edith."

She is feisty!

"Tell me about yourself. I want to get to know the person Richard entrusted his entire estate to. The Lord knows I don't have much longer, but you, my dear, are young . . . and tall!" Edith laughs at her own words.

Greta feels a small measure of unexpected gratitude. *This old woman is entertaining! Maybe this stop won't be so bad.* She glances at Brian who has turned to face her on the sofa. He looks as if he is settling in for a long movie on a Friday night.

"Well, okay. I'm twenty-nine years old—"

"Oh, gracious, dear. Don't give away your age!" Edith places a crooked finger against her lips and points at Brian with her other hand. Then she winks and nods for Greta to continue.

"Right. I'm a writer . . . a novelist. My next manuscript is due soon. I live in North Carolina. I have a cat?" Greta looks at Edith for permission to be finished with her mini-biography.

"And when was the last time you saw Richard?"

"About seven or eight years ago. He came to my college graduation at UNCC." Edith's eyes seem to betray a question. "It's the University of North Carolina in Charlotte. And the time before that was at my parents' funeral." Greta waits for the next barrage of questions. None come. Edith stares at her for a long time, and Greta fidgets in response.

"Well, I'm going to get going now," pipes in Brian to break the silence. "Ms. Moore, thank you for your hospitality. I know Greta is going to have a fantastic stay. Greta, good luck!" He chuckles as he stands. "I'll let myself out, Ms. Moore. Please don't get up."

"Edith," Ms. Moore reminds him. He nods an apology.

And with that, Brian leaves. Greta watches him walk back down the dark hall and around the corner until she can no longer see him. She hears the kitchen door open and close, and then she looks back at Ms. Moore. Edith is rubbing her hands together as if her fun is just beginning.

4

That evening, Edith and Greta sit down to dinner in the metal chairs on either side of the white plastic table in the kitchen. Greta can't believe Edith still lives alone, let alone cooks her own meals. She can't imagine doing such things when—*if*—she makes it to ninety-six years old.

The pair had spent the afternoon walking along Mediterranean Avenue. With Edith's slow pace, it had taken them over ninety minutes to go five blocks up and then return to the house. On the way, Edith pointed out friends' and neighbors' homes and shared some of their more poignant stories. Greta tried to listen as best she could but couldn't focus, her distractibility a trait that had cost her many friends and jobs in the past. The entire time, Greta had constantly wondered what the woman's connection to Great-Uncle Richard had been. It was apparent that Edith wasn't giving away anything until she was good and ready.

Now, the two are sharing a pot of meatballs doused in a red sauce and a salad overflowing with vegetables taken from Edith's garden in a corner of her tiny backyard. Greta feels appreciative of the simple food. She was afraid she'd have to force down something horrible on the first night of this agonizing journey.

Finding some courage, Greta asks, "Ms. Moore, when are you

going to tell me how you knew Uncle Richard?"

"Alright, dear. I'll spill the beans. And it's Edith, remember? But let's clear the plates and go in the living room where it'll be more comfortable." Edith sits back and takes a large sip of the red wine from her glass. She adjusts the oxygen in her nose and then stands and carries her plate toward the sink with one hand as her other hand pushes her walker forward.

Greta jumps up and tries to intervene, but Edith waves her off. So Greta picks up her own plate and carries it to the sink, purposefully leaving her wineglass on the table. She hopes to refill it before they retire to the living room.

Once the dishes are clean and the glasses full, the two relax in the living room, a space not much larger than the kitchen but with a fireplace and cozier chairs. Greta races to the couch to avoid the stained wingback chair. Once seated, Greta looks around as she waits for Edith to get comfortable and notices for the first time that the tiny flowers on the wallpaper don't match the flowers on the sofa. The colors are completely different.

Edith begins with a question. "Do you know anything about Richard's childhood?"

"No, ma'am," Greta replies. "My parents died when I was twenty, and they never shared much of anything about Uncle Richard."

"Well then. It's time you learn! Richard was kicked out of his house when he was sixteen. He had two brothers. The older one, named Bill, was nineteen and long gone from the home. The younger, your grandfather, Henry, was in boarding school. Richard, who wanted to stay behind and go to high school here, had been making some poor choices and going against his parents' wishes. They just couldn't take it anymore.

"I was in my mid-thirties. I met him on the boardwalk one day. He was sitting there, burning in the nasty mid-day sun, playing an old guitar that was missing a string. He had a ball cap on the ground next to him with a few coins in it. He was playing that guitar pretty well, so I walked over and threw two dollars into the hat—a lot of money at the time." Edith pauses and gets a faraway look in her eyes, then continues.

"He said, 'Thank you, kindly, madam,' and I couldn't believe his manners. He was certainly not like the other destitute kids on the streets who didn't have a good education. So I sat with him for a bit, asking him why he seemed to be alone and playing guitar for spare change."

Greta's mouth, which has been hanging open for the last few seconds, closes so she can speak. "Was Uncle Richard homeless?"

"He sure was. He somehow kept going to school, never telling the administration or his teachers that he had been kicked out of his house and was sleeping on the beach in a tent, showering at a friend's house—whenever his friend could sneak him inside, that is."

"Wow. I had no idea."

"Well, that's just a part of the story." Edith's grin touches her ears. "I thought Richard was mighty smart to be so sly to fool that school and mighty creative to be playing guitar so well, so I invited him to my house to spend the night. He slept in the very bedroom you will stay in tonight." Edith points up the stairs, and Greta again notices her fingers, which are bent with advanced arthritis.

Edith stops talking. Greta waits but soon becomes impatient. She bites her lower lip to stop herself from being rude. Finally, Edith speaks again.

"It's getting late. I'm tired, and I know you must be too," Edith surmises. "I put two clean towels on the stairs to take on your way up. Goodnight!" And with that, Edith stands and pushes her walker into the downstairs bedroom off of the hallway.

Well then, thinks Greta. She, too, stands up, helps herself to a glass of water in the kitchen, retrieves the towels, and heads to her room for the night. As she ascends the steps, she hears each one creak and wonders if anyone replaced them in all the years the house has been standing.

She doesn't notice the figure, dressed to match the night, standing across the street, watching through the open curtains.

5

Friday

The next morning, Greta wakes to the sizzle of someone cooking in grease and the air carries the aroma of freshly brewed coffee. She stretches her arms over her head and shoves her feet into one of the few pairs of socks she packed.

Wish I had my slippers. Contempt sits just at the surface.

Then she smells the bacon. "Great," she says out loud. *I'm going to gain fifteen pounds in these next few weeks.*

When she reaches the bottom of the stairs, Greta finds Edith in the kitchen with the table already set for two. Bacon is not the only offering. Ms. Moore has put together a spread of pancakes, strawberries, syrup, blueberry muffins, and two kinds of juice.

"You didn't have to do all this," Greta says incredulously. "I rarely eat breakfast." She winces. *Probably didn't need to go that far.*

"Nonsense, dear. You need your energy. And I miss cooking for people. Richard used to come here every Sunday morning after church for a home-cooked brunch. I'm happy to do it. . . . I want to do this."

Greta pulls out the metal chair she used last night and sits down as Edith places a hot mug of coffee and some creamer in front of her. Greta can't believe how fast Edith moves in the kitchen—wouldn't have believed it if she wasn't seeing it with her own eyes.

"Thank you."

Once they are both seated and Edith says grace, Greta ventures another question to get some answers.

"So Richard stayed here for a night, then?" She stabs a pancake with her fork.

"Oh, no, dear. He stayed for years. I adopted him!" Edith responds with a gleam in her eye. She winks at Greta as she stirs nearly a half-cup of creamer into her coffee.

Greta's fork stops halfway to her mouth, and she looks at Edith with suspicion.

"You adopted him?"

"Why, yes, dear. Unofficially, of course. Race was a big issue back then. Still is, I guess. . . . His family had abandoned him, but they were still around. He needed a home. A good home. And I needed him too. You see, I lost my son shortly after giving birth to him. SIDS, they told me. He just didn't wake up after a nap one day." Edith takes a bite of bacon and chews slowly. After she swallows the piece, she adds, "Oh, I was devastated. My husband at the time—he couldn't take the grief. He walked out about a month later. I had been alone for about eight years when I took in Richard. He saved my life."

"How?" Greta can't bring herself to take another bite of food. Her stomach is warning her she's been eating way more than usual. She sets her fork down and waits for Edith, who hasn't answered her yet. "Edith?" Greta asks.

"I was so depressed, dear. I had lost every reason to live, or so I thought. Then the good Lord brought me Richard. He filled a void for me, and me for him. It was like a match made in heaven. He needed guidance, a mother figure. I knew I couldn't replace his mama, and he couldn't replace my Stevie, but we were a good fit. He finished high school while living here, and I was so proud of him when he graduated. That photo—the one in the hallway—it was the proudest day of my life."

Greta notices streams of wetness on Edith's sunken cheeks. She looks around for a box of tissues, action coming easier than verbal condolences, but she doesn't see one.

"Oh, I'm fine, dear." Edith offers a sad smile. "Just didn't think I'd outlive Richard, that's all."

Greta nods, her lips a pinched line across her face. Her knee bounces under the table. She has never been good at handling sadness, especially others' sorrow. She never knows what to say and often ends up saying the wrong thing. And she feels no sorrow herself, as much as she'd like to. So she keeps her mouth shut and folds her napkin on top of her leftover food. She can't take the sight of it anymore.

AT TWO O'CLOCK SHARP, the Cadillac pulls up outside as if Brian and Antonio were waiting down the street until it was time to arrive. Edith and Greta had spent the rest of the morning looking through photos and news clippings of Richard from age sixteen through his early seventies. Greta had gleaned a lot about Edith's feelings for him and learned that for most of Uncle Richard's and Edith's birthdays, the two of them had spent time together, even if just an hour or two to chat over tea or coffee.

Greta realized they had a special bond that extended far beyond an adoptive mother and child. That idea left her with mixed feelings and tugged on the fibers of her heart. What she did not learn, though, is what Uncle Richard had done to earn his billions or take ownership of half the city. Edith hadn't wanted to talk about money. Greta had even asked her why she still lived in an old, dilapidated townhome, despite Richard being so wealthy.

"Didn't he want to get you a new house?" Greta had asked.

Edith explained how she refused to accept his multiple offers to re-home her. This house shelters all of her memories, she'd told

Greta, and she never thought money could buy better ones. Greta doesn't understand that last part, even though she doesn't like all that comes with money either. She would still want to live in a house that isn't falling apart.

"How'd it go?" Brian asks as he enters through the front door into the kitchen and accepts a glass of lemonade from Edith.

"Wonderful!" Edith exclaims. "Thank you, Greta, for listening to all those stories about Richard and me." Edith beams. It's obvious talking about Richard serves to ease some of her grief.

Greta nods and looks at her feet, feeling uncomfortable. She still doesn't harbor any sadness over Uncle Richard's death, and she doesn't want anyone else to know that. "Ready?" she asks Brian after a few seconds. She isn't purposely being rude, but she knows the faster she can move to the next place, the quicker she will be finished with the list.

"I sure am," Brian replies. He gulps the rest of his lemonade, sets the glass in the sink, and hugs Edith, thanking her for her generosity.

"Anytime, dear," Edith answers. "Bye, Greta. It's been an absolute pleasure. Will you two please close the door? I'm going to take a nap." And with that, she turns and pushes her walker into her bedroom, shutting the wooden bedroom door behind her.

ANTONIO GETS behind the wheel after Greta and Brian are settled in the back of the Cadillac and pulls away from the curb to drive to the second location on Greta's list: Atlantic Beach Community College.

In the SUV, Greta smells Brian's cologne again and wishes she could just go back home today rather than only to stop number two on her list. While her visit with Edith was enlightening and went by faster than she imagined it would, she feels low on energy. It is taking all of her internal resources to act appropriately and politely with so many strangers. *And this was only the first place on the list.*

"How are you doing?" Brian asks, breaking into her wishful thinking.

"Fine."

"Fine?" he presses. "Did you learn about Richard's teen years?"

"Yeah, I did. I had no idea."

"The next location will pick up where you left off with Ms. Moore. You'll be staying at Atlantic City Fire Station Number Two on Baltic Avenue, but we're visiting Atlantic Beach Community College first."

Greta stares ahead with tired eyes.

"The fire station has an extra bedroom you can use." He winks at her when her eyes skip to his face.

What's with the winking?

Greta nods and looks away as the car speeds on.

6

Greta follows Brian through the front doors of the community college's main building. It is a weekday afternoon, and the foyer buzzes with students and staff. They make their way toward the glass doors marked "Main Office," and again, when Brian holds the door for her, she spies his gold bracelet.

Definitely angel wings on there.

As they walk into the brightly lit business hub, Greta notices the framed picture of Uncle Richard, hanging to her right above two side chairs. The caption on the metal plate reads:

"Never underestimate education. It opens doors of opportunity, teaches you to think, and brings you a host of friends for life."
(Richard M. Goldman, 1999)

Greta moves toward the picture and stares at the words, then raises her eyes to Richard's goofy, albeit iconic, top hat. His smile looks genuine, and she notes his dimples, set into his pudgy cheeks. She shakes her head and turns toward Brian who is talking to a receptionist.

"Oh, wonderful!" the auburn-haired thirty-something

woman says to Brian. "Let me get President Schafer. Wait right here." She hurries through an open door on the opposite side of the partition behind the main desk. Greta can hear her heels clicking down an unseen hallway and cringes.

"The president?" she asks Brian. "Isn't that a bit much?" Her voice carries across the office, and this time, she notices her volume. The admonition of teachers from her past rings in her mind. *Greta, please use your inside voice . . .*

"No. Not too much at all. You'll see." Brian smiles at her with his steel-colored eyes, and a part of her stomach flutters, surprising her. She turns to face the opposite direction.

As Greta continues to survey the space around her to avoid more conversation, they wait. A bizarre painting hanging on the wall opposite the photograph of Great-Uncle Richard grabs her attention. On the print, an obscure figure rises out of what looks like sand, and two figures embrace in the background. The metal plate below it reads, "The Enigma of My Desire by Salvador Dali."

"Richard actually donated that Dali to the college a few years back."

"Really? Why?" Greta asks, knowing full well what a Dali is worth.

"He loved Dali's artwork, and the college meant a lot to him. That's why we're here. Oh, here comes President Schafer."

"Mr. Gogh! Good to see you, sir!" President Schafer is a tall Black man with a square face, salt-and-pepper hair, and a matching silver-flecked goatee. He beams, filling the room with his positive charisma. He shakes hands with Brian and turns to Greta.

"Ms. Goldman, the pleasure is all mine. It's so nice to meet you." President Schafer's tie is filled with tiny flowers that remind Greta of Ms. Moore's couch. "We are so sorry for your loss. Though it's different, and I mean no disrespect to compare, the loss of Richard is ours too. He was an incredible part of this school for over five decades. We miss him so much."

"It's nice to meet you too," Greta replies as she shakes the man's extended hand. His grip is warm, his fingers soft as he covers her hand with both of his.

"Come on. Let's find a quiet place to chat." President Schafer opens the glass doors and Brian and Greta lead him out into the main hallway. They wait for him, then follow him to a state-of-the-art conference room, equipped with technology the likes of which Greta has never seen. The three sit in plush, black leather chairs around a mahogany table stretching twelve feet long. She feels as if they've entered a Fortune 100 company conference room.

"Thank you for seeing us, President Schafer," Brian starts. "As I mentioned on the phone last week, we're here so Greta can learn a bit more about her great-uncle."

The president clasps his hands across his stomach and leans back, making himself appear not only comfortable but relatable. Greta instinctively relaxes but only a bit. Formal educational institutions always make her nervous, especially since her trek through academia often led to social dilemmas, unsympathetic teachers, and sleepless nights as she maneuvered through classes she cared little about. Except for creative writing. That class had always been her favorite.

"Richard attended Atlantic Beach Community College for two years in the sixties. He studied business, and he excelled. Of course, I wasn't here then, but I got to know Richard in the late eighties when he stopped by one day to make a donation to the school." President Schafer chuckles as he recalls the memory. "I was new here, and when I unfolded the check, I got a little light-headed. He had given the school five million dollars and then kept donating more through the years." He waves his hand toward the wall of computers and video equipment in the room. "Richard is the sole reason our campus is as state-of-the-art as it is. He wanted only the best for ABCC, and we couldn't be more grateful for his generosity."

Greta looks again at the technology equipment that her great-uncle funded. She shakes her head and forces a smile. "That was very kind of him. I don't know what to say—except I'm surprised he didn't leave you all of his money. This school obviously meant a lot to him."

"Oh, no. That's not why you're here," the president says. "I didn't mean to imply that I am hunting for more. Richard met with me about two months ago to explain that he was making his final general donation. He faithfully supported this school for decades, and then he was finished, aside from a few scholarships he continues to fund. I believe he had another project up his sleeve, and we respected that. Again, we couldn't be more grateful for the way he has lifted and enhanced our educational programs and campus." He smiles at Brian with knowing eyes, and Greta detects a hint of something, but she's not sure what. *Maybe comradery?* It seems more than that. She wonders if it's about her. That thought causes a couple of beads of sweat to form under her arms.

"I think your uncle put us on your list so you could see a part of his heart. He was a firm believer in education and several scholarships for at-risk kids coming out of high school with great promise but zero resources. He also funded scholarships for future teachers, the educators he felt were so important. He had such a philanthropic soul."

"Yes, it seems he did," Greta replies, somewhat confused about why everyone thinks this should matter to her. Her leg bounces under the table. She turns to Brian. "How did he make his billions?"

"We'll get to that shortly," Brian says with a wink.

Greta's face flushes, and her leg movements become more erratic.

"Well, President Schafer, it's been a pleasure." Brian senses Greta's discomfort. "We don't want to take up all of your afternoon. I'm sure you're busy. Thank you so much for seeing us," Brian says as he stands and reaches for the president's hand. The two shake goodbye, and Greta steps forward to offer her hand as well.

"Again, I'm so sorry for your loss. Richard was like family here . . . I'll never forget his laugh. A real, authentic belly laugh. He touched the lives of so many." The president frowns with his last statement. "I hope you don't mind me asking. Have they figured out who did this to him?" President Schafer can't seem to say the word *killed*.

Greta looks at Brian, who shrugs his shoulders. "Not yet, I guess."

Greta removes her hand from President Schafer's grip and aims for the exit. Brian opens the door and waits for her to step through.

They weave between the students still milling around the hallway, making their way toward Brian's Cadillac parked in the guest lot just beyond the front doors of the building, where they find Antonio waiting.

"You okay?" Brian asks as they slip inside the SUV.

"Yeah. Sure. And thanks for the save," Greta says. "It felt stuffy in there." Greta waves at her face, attempting to cool herself off.

"Yeah. Okay."

Brian watches her with curiosity, wondering if losing Richard is finally hitting her.

7

As Greta and Brian stroll through the twelve-foot-high, open garage doors of Fire Station #2, the alarms blare. Where there was no activity a moment ago, there's now chaos. Firefighters run into the garage while donning jackets and helmets and climb into two of the three trucks parked in the bays. Greta and Brian step to a corner to get out of the way, and Greta slaps her hands to her ears.

As the trucks pull out and the alarm is silenced, Greta turns to Brian and shrugs. "Now what?" Her idea of spending the night in a place where bells and whistles may sound at any hour is not appealing, and her attitude turns even sourer.

"Hello there!" A husky voice calls from the other side of the garage. "You must be Ms. Goldman!" A sixty-something-year-old man with smoke-colored hair and tanned skin approaches Greta and Brian. "Sorry for all the fuss. There's been an accident down by the boardwalk. Don't think it's too serious. Everyone will be back soon, I'd guess. My name's Sully. Captain Sully Palmer." Captain Palmer sticks a calloused hand out toward Greta.

Good thing I brought hand sanitizer for all of these handshakes, she thinks, a germaphobe if there ever was one.

"Hi. Call me Greta."

"We don't mean to intrude if it's a bad time," Brian offers as the two men grab each other's arms as they shake hands, obviously friendly with each other from past interactions.

Brian seems to know everyone!

"Oh, no, not at all. It's probably good all the guys are gone. Gives you a chance to get settled before all the questions come . . . I can't believe I'm staring at Richard M. Goldman's great-niece," Captain Palmer says. "You sure are taller than he was," he adds with a chuckle.

"Yeah, I've heard that a lot," she answers, wishing the captain would quit staring at her. "My parents were on the taller side."

"Well, Captain . . . Greta, I have a meeting I need to get to, but I'll be back tomorrow around one o'clock." Brian turns to Greta. "Have a good time and make sure you ask these guys any questions you have. They spent a lot of time with Richard."

Brian exists through the gigantic doors and slides into the waiting Cadillac. A few seconds later, Antonio speeds off down Baltic Avenue.

CAPTAIN PALMER SHOWS Greta to her room where she'll stay for the night. There is a small, private bathroom attached to the concrete brick space, which is painted a light blue to soften the stiff atmosphere. She sees a single bed, a desk, and a small, draped window facing the main street. Greta throws both her duffle bag and sling bag onto the bed and faces Captain Palmer, her mouth a tight line and her eyes silently asking him what she's supposed to do now.

"I'll let you get settled. Say ten minutes? I'll come back and give you a tour of the firehouse. I can't wait to tell you all about Richard and his shenanigans here!" He laughs more to himself than anything and ambles down the hall. Greta still hears the echo of his laughter as she steps toward the bathroom to freshen up.

Ten minutes later, Captain Palmer starts his tour, leading

Greta through the station, showing her the kitchen, recreation room—which hosts a gigantic TV and a foosball table—and the main offices.

"We're set up for eight firefighters to stay overnight, and we have all our meals here," he explains as they pass a long wooden kitchen table with benches tucked underneath each side. "This is where we'd sit for hours with Richard when he visited. We're sure gonna miss his jokes and stories. He was always the life of the fire station when he was here."

"How did you meet him?" Greta asks.

"I'll let Jason tell you that. Sounds like they're back," Captain Palmer answers as they move toward the garage bay, where the noise of returning trucks and excited firefighters filters through the space.

As they enter the bay, they see five men circled up around the ladder truck, shucking off their gear. One man is readying the truck for the next call.

"Guys, hey! I want you to say hi to someone special!" The men stop talking and turn toward their captain. "This is Greta Goldman, Richard's great-niece. Remember, I told you she'd be coming?"

Greta stands still, caught in the stares of too many eyes, and immediately notices their fit physiques. "Hi. It's nice to meet ya'll," she ventures, her Southern drawl slipping out with her nervousness.

"Wow! Richard's niece! I can't believe it!" One guy with dark hair and stubble on his face steps forward. "I am still shocked and sad to hear about his death." His voice is now quieter to match his sympathies. "My name is Jason, by the way. Nice to meet you." Jason steps even further from the circle and lays his hand on Greta's arm as he offers his condolences. She sees fine wrinkles on his forehead and around his hazel eyes and guesses he must be in his mid-forties.

At least it's not a handshake, she reminds herself as she pulls away slightly. Physical touch is not her thing.

"Have they found out who killed Richard yet?"

The men all stop talking to hear her answer. Greta shakes her head. "No, the police are still looking into it," she replies.

"It's just such a crazy thing. Everyone loved Richard. It doesn't make any sense." Jason shakes his head, his eyes downcast.

The other guys come over to offer their condolences.

After, Captain Palmer asks Jason to take Greta to the kitchen to see if there are any drinks or snacks to be had. "And Jason . . . she's wondering how we know Richard. Maybe you can tell her the story of when we first met good ole Mr. Goldman." The captain nods to Jason and then ushers the rest of the brotherhood back to their chores.

As Jason and Greta nibble on a microwaved soft pretzel that they dip in mustard and drink from cans of Diet Coke, Jason shares the story of how the firefighters knew Richard. As he talks, Greta can't believe what she hears.

"Many years ago—Richard must have been in his mid- or late-twenties or something like that—he was driving down the street, over on Oriental Avenue, when he witnessed a horrific car accident right in front of him. A young woman was crossing the street, and the driver of a pickup truck never saw her. They hit her in the crosswalk at nearly full sp—"

"That's awful," Greta interjects.

"Yeah, it was horrible," Jason continues. "The driver fled the scene, a hit and run. Richard pulled over and jumped out of his car. He raced over to the woman as other bystanders found a phone to call 911. Our alarm went off, and four of our guys, including my dad—I was a toddler at the time—hightailed it to the scene. When they got there, Richard was talking to the semi-conscious young lady and putting pressure on a deep puncture wound to keep her from bleeding out."

Greta doesn't even wince at the gory details, her interest piqued.

"My dad heard Richard say to her, 'I'm going to call you Precious' before he took over the care, and the ambulance arrived about a minute after that. When the medics got her squared away and took off for the hospital, my dad introduced himself to Richard—after Richard had given the officers who had arrived on the scene the information they needed about the pick-up truck and what he had witnessed." Jason talks quickly as his mind takes him back to the night his dad shared the tale. Back to when he was a stubborn high-schooler intent on joining the fire department, just like his old man.

"I'll never forget the story, especially since I met Richard shortly after hearing it," he adds.

"Did they catch the guy?" Greta asks.

"Girl, actually, and yes. She was a fifteen-year-old that had taken her dad's truck out for a joy ride."

"Yikes!" Greta says, "And Precious—that's an interesting name—she survived?" Greta thinks she knows the answer.

"Yeah. She and Richard became close friends, though nearly a decade apart in age. They continued to see each other every once in a while throughout the years. She works—"

"Over at the bus station." Greta finishes for him. She lowers her eyes and slowly shakes her head. She recalls the strange words from the woman at the rental car window. *Richard gave me my name.*

"At the rental car agency! How did you know?"

"We met briefly." Greta offers without further explanation. "So why did Uncle Richard give her that name?"

"Apparently, while she was lying on the ground and Richard was trying to keep her awake and alive, he asked her what her name was. She couldn't remember. Some kind of amnesia from the trauma. So he gave her that name, and lo and behold, it stuck! Turns out her given name was Gladys, but she had never liked it, anyway. So Precious it was from that day forward. The local paper even ran a story about it a few months later, when she finally left the hospital."

"Wow. That's quite a story. So you and Uncle Richard kept in touch, too, I guess?

"Yup. The guys invited him over to thank him with a big spaghetti dinner at the fire station, and that turned into a weekly meal that continued over the years. Richard would bring the stories, and we'd supply the food. We have shared many laughs between these walls. When my dad retired, Richard was there." Jason bows his head as memories flip through his mind like a picture book.

"After Richard made his first few million, he donated some of it to the station. It was enough to help us buy a new ladder truck we had been saving for. He was such a generous guy. But mostly, we loved him for who he was on the inside. We miss him. I'm sure you do too." He offers Greta a sympathetic look, which she waves away.

"We didn't know each other that well. I haven't seen him for seven or eight years, but yes, I keep hearing what a wonderful person he was. I wish I had known him better," she says earnestly. "By the way, how did he make his billions?" Greta asks, hoping Jason will provide more information than Brian has.

"I know he got into commercial real estate development as a twenty-something, which is lucrative if you do it well. Eventually, he earned enough to buy a pair of smaller casinos. But honestly, I don't know the rest of it. Billions is a lot of money. There have always been rumors, though."

"What kind of rumors?"

"Oh, silly ones. Gambling success, a lottery win, you name it."

"Interesting." Greta's mind is working overtime.

As they make their moves to stand up, Greta suddenly remembers the list. "Wait!" she says. "Did you say Precious was hit on Oriental Avenue?"

"Yeah, why?" Jason asks.

"That is the next place Uncle Richard wanted me to visit. I have to go there tomorrow."

"Hey, why don't we go over there after dinner? I could show you the place where Richard saved Precious's life," Jason offers helpfully. He's enjoyed reminiscing about Richard and also sees how easy-on-the-eyes Greta is, even if she is a decade and a half younger.

"That would be great!" Greta feels a measure of elation. She can tell Brian when she sees him tomorrow that she's ready for stop number five instead of four on the list. *If I can move through this journey faster, that would be fantastic!* she thinks with newfound hope, oblivious to Jason's motive for wanting to spend more time with her.

8

After dinner with the guys at the station, where Greta hears tales of her great-uncle's best jokes, childish dares between him and the firefighters, and their collective fascination with Uncle Richard's billions, Jason and Greta are sitting in his cherry-red Ram truck, heading toward Oriental Avenue. The radio is tuned to classic rock, and the sounds of Queen and David Bowie's "Under Pressure" drift from the speakers. Without realizing she's doing it, Greta taps her foot to the beat of the music. Hyper-focused on her goal, she's eager to cross off another street.

"So tell me about you. Who is Greta Goldman?" Jason probes, glancing toward Greta, then moving his eyes back to the road.

Talking about herself is Greta's least favorite activity. Her lips disappear as she thinks about how much information to offer.

"What do you want to know?" she asks after a few seconds.

"I don't know. You said earlier you're an author. What's that like?"

"Oh, it's . . . you know. It's great," she starts. "I can sit in my house by myself and just tell stories."

"Sounds good, I guess. Seems lonely, though. You're not married? No kids?"

He sure is nosey.

"No. No husband. No kids. I do have a cat . . . hopefully he's okay at my neighbor's house."

"Oh, what is your cat's name?"

"Marqués." Jason looks over, his eyes begging for further explanation. "That was the name of the mastermind behind the theft of the Mona Lisa back in the early 1900s. I've always been fascinated by stuff like that," she explains.

"Oh! Is that what your novels are about? Crime and mystery?"

"Yup," Greta answers as she nods, ready to be finished with this conversation about her and her work. After a beat, she adds, "But not the gory kind. More mystery—who-done-it kind of stuff —than murder."

Jason slows his truck as they pass the Ocean Resort & Casino and pulls to the side of the road at the next intersection, S. Rhode Island Avenue.

"This is it," says Jason.

It's 8:12 p.m., according to the truck's dashboard clock, and there's only moderate traffic, despite the location being so close to the resort and it being a Friday night. Greta opens the door and slides out, then slams it behind her. Jason walks around the back of the truck to join her on the sidewalk. The smell of fried food from a corner take-out restaurant called Rafters moves through the humid air. The temperature is hovering near seventy, an unusually mild spring evening, and the sea air is muggy.

"So Richard was driving toward us from that direction," Jason explains as he points north. The truck the teenager was driving came down this road," he continues as his hand sweeps to the street sign marked, S. Rhode Island Avenue. "She never stopped. Precious was hit there." Jason points to a spot on the asphalt about ten yards from where the two are standing. Greta can envision the scene, and she frowns.

"Interesting," she says in response. "Of course . . . I mean, terrible."

"Yeah. Richard was a hero." He looks at Greta. "Do you know when his funeral will be?" he asks, suddenly realizing no one has mentioned the plans for laying his friend to rest all evening long.

"Not yet. They're still investigating his death."

"It's just so crazy," says Jason. "I don't know why anyone would want to hurt the guy who helped so many people in this city."

"That's the inquiry of the week."

"Neither the news nor police have mentioned the details about how or why he was killed," Jason ventures cautiously. "They haven't told you anything?"

"I don't know either. I have a meeting with the lead detective in a few days," Greta replies. "I'm not sure I need to know any of the details, but I'm curious where they are in the investigation. I've heard nothing since Brian Gogh, the attorney handling all this, called me with the initial news and invited me up here."

Jason looks at Greta closely, wondering if she's grieved yet. *She seems so calm.*

To avoid his stare, Greta glances across the street and spies a young man in a torn flannel shirt and stained baggy pants bent over a cardboard box, train tracks of powder lining its surface. She shakes her head at the audacity. *Right out in the open and no one cares,* she thinks.

The two walk back to Jason's truck in silence, the unanswered questions about Richard's death hanging over them. Jason drives back to the fire station as Greta stares out the passenger window, watching the AC and its grunginess fly by.

THE NEXT MORNING, Greta sits on the bed in the firehouse bedroom, typing on her laptop. She had awoken with a fresh idea for her novel swirling in her head, a surprising path for her protagonist to journey through the final chapters. Not wanting to waste any time getting it from her brain to her computer, she didn't get up and sit at the desk in the room. She simply grabbed her laptop from her duffle on the floor by the bed and went to work. She snuggles under the weighted blanket Captain Palmer gave her the night before.

Greta smiles as she writes, believing this may be her best book yet. Earlier, she had answered an email from her publisher asking about her progress and reminding her of the looming deadline. Her stomach had clenched with anxiety, given how her New Jersey story was unfolding and taking up all of her time, but now that her creative juices are flowing again, her anxiety is receding. All she's ever wanted is to be a world-famous novelist.

And I'm nearly there, she thinks.

There's a soft knock on her door. Greta glances at her phone's clock. *8:53.* She's been writing for nearly three hours.

"Greta? It's Jason. We're cleaning up from breakfast. Do you want anything to eat?"

"No, thanks. But I'll be down soon!"

"Okay," he says, and she hears his footsteps as they move away from the door.

At that instant, the fire alarm blares, drowning out Jason's footfalls. Greta jumps and her computer falls out of her lap and onto the tile floor. Covering her ears with her hands, she squeezes her eyes shut.

"Great!" she says under her breath. Her brain rings with the sound of the alarm. Her face flushes as her heart pounds faster against her ribcage.

There goes the quiet and my creativity, she thinks, ignoring the positive thought trying to emerge through her sour attitude—the thought that at least it didn't happen while she was sleeping.

THE LUNCH HOUR is spent chatting with the fire station crew after their return from the house fire three blocks away. They still smell of smoke, even though most have showered and changed clothes. Greta listens to the continuing stories about Great-Uncle Richard but soon grows tired of them. They all tell the tale of a generous, likable man who was bigger than the wealth he held.

Then one story makes her perk up.

"Hey, did you all ever hear about Richard's meeting with Charlie Garrison before that guy was killed—probably a few years ago now?" A fireman nicknamed Cheetah throws out the question, and Greta's eyes go wide at the mention of the murder.

"Killed?" she asks at the same time hoping for a change in topic.

"Yeah, yeah," answers Captain Palmer. "I remember that. Richard came in here the day after the story hit the papers. The guy was a movie director from the Midwest or somewhere, right? I think Richard had met with him about doing a documentary about Atlantic City or his life . . . something like that." Captain Palmer shakes his head. "Then, *bam,* the guy is murdered, and Richard dropped the idea. Kinda weird Richard was killed too, huh?" Everyone grows quiet at the coincidence.

"Maybe it's something the police should know?" Jason offers.

Greta listens to the back and forth between the guys and their theories and feels her stomach somersault with their conversation. She cannot wait for Brian to arrive so she can get out of this concrete cave, skip the next stop, and be on her way.

Just then, Greta's phone dings, notifying her of an incoming email. She taps the screen and scans the subject line:

Time to make general repairs on your property . . .

She scrolls down and continues to skip-read to get the gist of the message:

The public easement on your property requires general repairs to meet new code requirements. . . . each homeowner with an easement . . . pay $25 . . .

Greta stops reading and flags the email for later.

"Hey, Greta," Jason says. Her head pops up. "Do you have any last-minute questions about your great-uncle before you leave?"

"I don't think so," she replies. Then an idea hits her. "Wait. One question: Did Richard ever date anyone or bring anyone here for you to meet? He never got married, I guess?"

"Nope. Richard never married. That's likely why you're here. No spouse to inherit everything. He always said he was happy just being friends with everyone. Of course, many women wanted to marry him! But he figured at least some of them weren't really impressed so much with him but with his money." Jason smirks at the memory of Richard's wisdom in this area. "He was friends with and loved so many people—and was loved back. I don't think that left room for just one special person."

Greta nods at Jason's assessment. That's what she had guessed. *Too bad,* she thinks to herself.

9

Saturday

Just after nine o'clock in the morning, the hooded murderess watches number four enter PNC bank from across S. Boston Avenue in the center of Atlantic City. The portly man carries a black briefcase in his left hand. From her research, she knows he is about to withdraw a half-million dollars. Gabe Riley, normally so self-controlled and shrewd, often falls prey to impulsivity, prone to becoming irresponsible with his money when collecting high-priced art, a habit-turned-addiction. She knows he has his eye on a rare Gerhard Richter that dock workers are unloading from a container ship in Miami at this very moment. She also knows art dealers don't risk taking checks and for various reasons, many buyers don't want the paper trail left by electronic transfers. She's done her homework.

The killer walks southbound, anticipating the direction Gabe will take when he exits the bank with his briefcase full of cash. She casually flips the tactical knife between her fingers, her heart barely registering the upcoming kill. Her respiration remains steady at ten breaths per minute.

The hooded woman tucks herself against a building, hidden

from the street cameras she scoped out earlier, and waits. Twelve minutes later, Gabe Riley approaches. She scans her surroundings and finds the lack of pedestrian traffic suitable. As Gabe steps just past her position, the killer lunges behind him, cocks her right wrist, and plunges the knife into the base of his skull. Immediately, she catches his limp body and props it against the building, leaving his briefcase where it fell. Gabe's eyes stare ahead, and the woman with no conscience closes his lids with her fingertips before turning and crossing the street to head west.

To passersby, Gabe appears to have succumbed to a drunken stupor, his head lolling to the side. No one notices the red wound seeping down his posterior neck, turning the back of his gray sport coat a deep burgundy color.

AFTER THE LUNCH HOUR, Greta is standing in the open bay of the fire station, enjoying the sunshine as it warms her face when Antonio pulls Brian's Cadillac up to the sidewalk. In typical fashion, Antonio jumps out of the driver's seat and bends around the rear of the car to open the door. Then he faces Greta and smiles.

"Hello, Ms. Goldman. How was your stay at the fire station?"

"Fine, thank you," Greta replies as she considers handing Antonio her duffle bag. "And it's Greta, remember?" Antonio smiles and nods. "Just got back from a walk. I think I know this city better than you do now." Her comment comes out snarky, but she doesn't notice.

"This morning was chilly, but it's warmed up nicely," Antonio replies.

Greta pats her duffle. "Glad I brought some warm clothes." She hands it over to him.

Brian steps out of the car with his phone to his ear and signals Greta to wait *two minutes* as he holds up the universal peace sign.

As much as she wants to avoid the awkward goodbyes, she

steps into the garage bay to thank her hosts, especially Jason, for their time. Brian joins her a minute later.

"Thank you, Captain Palmer," Greta says with a bit of animation. Brian stares at her. It's the first time she's shown any gratitude to someone she's met.

"And Jason, I owe you. Brian, this is Jason," Greta says as she glances back at the attorney. "He already took me to the next street on the list, so we can skip it. Isn't that great?"

"Oh?" Brian asks as he looks at the tall fireman Greta is referencing. The man's piercing eyes unnerve Brian when he notices them linger on Greta longer than Brian would like.

Jason turns to Brian to answer him. "Yeah, it turns out the street was the one where Richard saved Precious's life, and since that was part of our story with Richard, too, I thought it would make sense to show Greta the place her uncle became a hero." Jason's gaze once again reaches back toward Greta, and Brian notices her grinning back, a smile that travels to her eyes.

A twinge of jealousy erupts from a place in his soul that Brian didn't think existed until now—at least not for this unusual woman. He shakes it off and offers Jason a firm handshake. While simultaneously telling himself to grow up, he offers a "Thanks, Jason" to the fireman.

The rest of the guys wave goodbye from across the bay as they prepare to wash a truck. They tell Greta to stay in touch. Greta stifles a chuckle at the request. *Once I leave, I will never return,* she thinks.

"Well, are you ready to go?" Brian asks.

"Ready," Greta replies, and they walk outside toward the open door of the Cadillac.

"Keep in touch, Greta!" Jason calls out. She turns and blows him a kiss. Brian's eyes go wide behind his Salvatore Ferragamo aviator sunglasses.

"So . . . sounds like you had a productive visit." Brian can't believe his tone sounds clipped, and he wonders what's going on.

"It was fine. There was only one alarm this morning, but it

startled me, and I dropped my laptop on the ground. Thankfully, it's okay. The best part was crossing off two more streets." Greta looks toward Brian. "You know, you and Jason have the same color eyes."

Brian flinches. "No, we don't."

"Yeah, you do . . ."

Brian lets it go. There is a bigger issue to handle.

"You know Richard wanted you to stay overnight at each street, right? We have a room for you at The Oceans at Boardwalk Apartments. All expenses were covered by Richard before his death."

"Seriously?" Greta can't believe it. Her empty fist balls at her side. "Look, Brian, I'm doing my best, but spending all this time here is affecting my life, and we've *just* started. Who or what am I supposed to learn on Oriental Avenue that isn't related to Precious? I figured that was the story ya'll wanted me to know."

Brian finds her Southern drawl intimately attractive, and something stirs in his chest. He clears his throat. "Richard owned The Oceans at Boardwalk. It was one of the first buildings he bought, renovated, and flipped."

"Well, now I know that. Yes, my great-uncle was a stand-up guy, perhaps the savior of the world, and was super business-savvy. I get it. Can we skip it, please?" Greta implores, interrupting Brian. She sighs as her harsh retort produces a fleeting twinge of guilt, something for which she is not used to feeling. She buries the twinge. "I have a life of my own, you know."

Brian empathizes with Greta's situation.

"Okay," he relents. He wonders if he's giving in so quickly because of those gut flips he's been experiencing and the interaction with Jason he just witnessed. *She is a stunning woman, but she's as frustrating and off-putting as can be,* he thinks. The dichotomy leaves Brian confused, perhaps even tired.

"Thank you. Before we move on to the next stop on . . . Vermont Avenue," Greta says as she checks her great-uncle's list,

"I need to get some more clothes or wash mine or something. I'm running out."

"Of course! And I'm sorry I didn't think of that. We'll cover those costs." Embarrassment washes over him because he hadn't planned for this before it came up.

Greta's mouth forms a smirk, but she holds in the snide comment that floats to the forefront of her mind. "Is there anything around here? A mall or something?"

"Actually, yes, there's an outlet mall right here on Baltic. How's that sound?" When Greta nods, Brian gives Antonio the destination. Seconds later, the car takes off down the street.

After a quick purchase of three tops, another pair of jeans, a sundress, leggings, and some unmentionables using a credit card Brian gave her, Greta and Brian sit side-by-side in the Cadillac as Antonio drives toward Vermont Avenue. Brian hangs up the call he had made while Greta was shopping.

"Working on the weekend, huh?"

"I suppose so." Brian shrugs. With Richard's death, his life has taken a detour too. "Do you want to call the police and check on the status of Richard's investigation?"

"No, why?"

Brian studies her. "Just curious. I haven't heard anything."

"Me either."

Brian leaves his phone in his lap.

Greta notices he is dressed more casually. His attire, including tan chinos and a navy and white striped T-shirt, the ladder peeking through his linen jacket, caught Greta's attention the second she laid eyes on him at the fire station. His dark blond hair lacks the usual amount of gel, giving him more of a surfer's look than an elite attorney's look. Greta ignores the warm feeling swirling inside her.

"Where to now?" she asks to break the silent impasse.

"Eastern Pines Nursing Center," Brian answers. "And before you scoff, let me just say one thing." He eyes Greta, begging her not to complain or interrupt. "I imagine visiting a rehab facility, slash nursing home, isn't high on your priority list."

Greta shakes her head. His eyes narrow into a warning.

"But this place means something to me too . . ." He looks away.

Realizing he's gathering his thoughts, she braces herself for whatever he's about to say, coaxing herself to remain cordial.

"My uncle passed away there two years ago," Brian admits.

"I don't know what to say." And she truly doesn't. All of this loss, which she's been expected to hear about and respond to is too much for her to handle. She feels the start of a stomachache.

"It's okay. He was my father's brother, and really . . . more of a father to me than my dad ever was. My parents travel a lot. My uncle was always someone I could run to when I needed a father figure's attention and my dad was MIA when I was young, before I met Richard."

"I get that," Greta answers. "I had someone who served the same purpose for me growing up."

Brian smiles, but it disappears quickly. "My uncle had ALS. I visited him every week, then every day for the month before his death."

"That's a tough disease." Greta's leg bounces, and she shifts her body.

"Richard visited my uncle too . . ." Brian clears his throat and takes a deep breath. "The two had met in one of Richard's casinos, and they had become fast friends. But that's not why we're going to Eastern Pines. I'll leave that as part of the suspense for—"

"Great. Where will I sleep?" Greta asks, aiming to change the subject. Comforting people isn't one of her strong suits. Brian is half relieved and half taken aback by the sudden detour in the conversation. He quickly recovers, remembering Greta's quirky communication style, and chooses not to be offended. He imagines there are many people who choose differently and distance themselves from her.

"You'll be staying in the director's office. She has a pull-out couch and a full bath in her office. Hope that's okay."

"Beggars can't be choosers."

The Cadillac slows and makes another turn into a parking lot. Greta feels the bump as the back tire jumps the curb.

"Sorry about that!" Antonio yells from the front.

Brian laughs. "No worries, man."

After they exit the car, Brian and Greta walk through the sliding glass doors into the lobby of the nursing center. The odors of disinfectant and cooked eggs fill the space. Greta is not surprised. *Why does every old people's home smell like this?*

Brian leads them over to the main receptionist desk near a wood-paneled wall on the right side of the lobby.

"Brian! So good to see you! And a day early!" An elderly woman with wire-rimmed glasses stands up. Her black short-sleeved dress shows off the liver spots dotting her arms. Her red lipstick is the focal point of her face, and her smile grows as they approach the desk.

"Yes, Virginia. Hi! I called Dawn to let her know we're ahead of schedule. I should have called you too." Brian apologizes.

"Oh, hush. I don't care." Virginia laughs. Greta notices a smudge of red on Virginia's front tooth when they reach the desk.

"You have lipstick on your teeth," the no-holds-barred Greta tells Virginia.

"Oh, thank you, sweetie." Virginia chuckles and grabs a tissue from the desk. Brian's widened eyes find Greta's, and he holds them. She shrugs and mouths, *What?*

"I'll call Ms. Dawn now and let her know you're here." Virginia is now back on task.

Greta turns to Brian. "Who's Dawn?"

"Dawn Marshall. She's the director. . . . And here she comes now," Brian says as he steps around Greta to shake hands with a tall, auburn-haired woman with straight bangs and a narrow nose.

While not quite the same height as Greta, Dawn is taller than average and looks like a director of something—anything. Her polished salmon-colored pants suit fits well, and she wears a colorful scarf around her neck.

"Brian, it's so good to see you." The fifty-nine-year-old director's voice is like gravy, warm and soothing. The perfect trait for a nursing home executive who must deal with disgruntled or grieving family members in difficult times. "How's your family?" she asks Brian.

Greta internally jerks at the question. She had never asked Brian about a family. *Of course, he's married,* she thinks. *How could I be so stupid?* She looks for the ring on his hand.

"Oh, Mom and Dad are great. I have no idea where they are at any moment in time. My brother and sister-in-law are still living out of state, but there's talk of them moving back to New Jersey. We'll see," Brian says.

"Oh, I hope so for your sake! Well, let's go find a place to relax and talk," Dawn says.

No wife? Greta wonders. She cannot find a wedding band and reads between the lines of Brian's answer.

10

The trio sits comfortably in Dawn's office where the old wood paneling from the lobby continues as a full wall in the rectangular space. There's a window past her desk where only minimal natural light enters. Otherwise, the space is lit with various floor lamps, and Greta detects the scent of vanilla. It's cozy and reminds Greta of her writing space at home.

"I'm so excited to meet you, Greta."

"Thanks for hosting me on my little journey through the city." Greta doesn't hear the patronizing tone in her voice. She winks at Brian in jest. *See, I can be nice.* "How did you know my great-uncle?"

"Simply put, he was my best friend," Dawn answers. She sits in a side chair and motions Greta and Brian to a couch against the front wall next to the door.

My sleeping arrangements, I presume. Greta thinks.

"Best friend?" Greta repeats as her body sinks into the cozy fabric, and she wonders if she'll wake up with back pain in the morning.

"Yes, I loved Richard."

Greta's eyebrows rise, and Dawn laughs. "No, not like that. He and I were each other's most trusted confidantes. I went to him for advice and vice versa. We knew each other probably better than we knew our—ourselves." Dawn's voice catches.

"How did you meet?" Greta asks. She realizes this woman is more upset about her uncle's passing than she could ever be.

Dawn takes a sip of her coffee on the table next to her, and a lightbulb seems to click in her head. "Oh, my goodness! How rude of me. Can I get either of you something to drink?"

"No, thanks," Greta and Brian say in unison.

"Okay . . . I met Richard at a community meeting when I was in my late twenties. He had graduated with his associate's degree a decade before and had already started to build a name for himself in commercial real estate. I had just moved here from central New York to become the assistant manager of family relationships here at Eastern Pines. We hit it off instantly."

Dawn sips on her coffee again and smiles at a memory only her mind's eye can see.

Greta, uncomfortable with the silence, speaks up, "I think I will have some water."

When Dawn returns with a bottled water, Brian continues the conversation.

"So Dawn, as Richard's best friend for all this time, he wanted me to ask you three questions when you and Greta met. You up for it?"

"Of course. Any questions Richard planned in advance must be good ones." Dawn chuckles, but the tentacles of sorrow cling to her short-lived humor as a sad smile punctuates the moment.

Brian pulls out his phone and scrolls through an app. "Okay, first, what was the promise Richard made to himself and spent his whole life trying to fulfill?"

Dawn shakes her head as she looks upward, and Greta suspects Dawn is not surprised by this question. "Funny. I should have known," she starts. "Richard's life goal was to ensure that any person he met who needed something, he would provide it. Over the years, it meant setting up scholarships for at-risk youth, stocking the local food pantry, sending a woman to rehab, even opening up his home. Once, he took in a stray dog because of this promise."

"That seems like a lofty goal. What made him so generous?" Brian asks.

"You know, I think some people are just born with a predisposition for generosity. Like an innate gift or something. But with Richard, I think he was so grateful for the way he was supported in his earlier years that he wanted to return the kindness. He loved this city, even with all the problems it has. Most of all, he loved people," Dawn stares at her lap. "He was truly one-of-a-kind. I can't imagine anyone wanting to harm him. He left us way too soon."

Greta nods, not able to formulate words, worrying she'll say something inappropriate.

"He really was one-in-a-million," Brian agrees. He shifts in his seat. "Dawn, the second question is 'What do you think was Richard's biggest regret?'"

Dawn blinks back tears. She faces Greta directly, reaches for her hand, and whispers, "Not knowing you better, Greta. That was his biggest regret. It's why he changed the beneficiary information in his will from me to you."

Greta instinctively pulls her hand away. "What?" Her heart stutters.

"Oh, it's okay! He was so excited when he returned from your college graduation all those years ago. I think he loved the idea of family, and he didn't have many people in his life who bore that title. Of course, he loved Edith—you met her, right?" Dawn asks.

Greta's head moves up and down as she fights the urge to flee the room.

"He loved Edith and his brothers—your grandfather, rest his soul—and their wives, but I think the idea of supporting and encouraging a new generation of Goldmans who would carry on his philanthropic legacy held a lot of meaning for him. His parents abandoned him, so to have a great-niece living on the eastern side of the country and not knowing her—you—well . . .

it was a hole in his life, in his heart, that he often spoke with me about. I understood and gave him my full blessing."

Greta was speechless. In essence, her parents had abandoned her too. She knew her great-uncle had tried to reach out on many occasions, but for the most part, she had ignored him, particularly in the last few years. She wasn't comfortable with his fame and fortune and was content with living her own life.

As soon as she feels the twinge of guilt, she pushes it out of her mind. *He just wanted another pet project, someone else to save, something else he could be proud of himself for.* But her argument sounds weak, even to her.

Brian saves the moment. "Dawn, the last question is, 'What is the main thing he would want people to continue to do in this city now that he's gone?'"

Dawn sighs. "That's a hard one," she admits. Her eyes crinkle in thought.

Greta leans forward. On one hand, she doesn't want to know because it might involve her, and she is involved enough with the crazy list he left. On the other hand, she's curious what the one thing a billionaire would want to have the world continue upon his death. After all, Brian told her she'd be taking over his entire estate to do what she wants. She wonders how different his thoughts and plans were from her plan, which is to offload everything and disappear.

"He always said," Dawn muses, "if each of us chose one person to support in whatever way they needed, the problems of a lack of opportunity, the high school drop-out rate, homelessness, and the number of orphans in the world would dissipate. *Just one person* was kind of his mantra. He convinced me to become a mentor over at The Hope Floor. It's changed my life. He certainly made me a better person. I think he wants that for everyone."

Dawn's answer leaves Greta with mixed emotions. She is beginning to understand why everyone liked Richard. With all of this new information and the stories from the fire station—and Edith's story of Richard's unofficial adoption as a teen—pieces are slowly falling into place. In one word, she feels she might now know how to describe the man she barely knew: *selfless*. And that's not a typical description for someone with such an extravagant amount of money. It's certainly not a word she could use to describe herself. She has enough self-awareness to know that.

"Yes, I think that would trump any plans to continue to develop the city and make it cleaner and safer," Dawn continues. "He desperately wanted to give Atlantic City a facelift, but he believed the heart of the matter was its people, not the buildings or the businesses." Those words seem to trigger a thought, and Dawn stands up and walks to her desk. She retrieves a plaque from a drawer and hands it to Greta.

Greta reads the engraving that's centered below the etched picture of a heart surrounding two people on what appears to be the Atlantic City Boardwalk.

Not for the cumulative charitable giving, nor the beautifying city development, but for seeing people, all people, the way they should be seen . . . From this point forward, May 5 will be dubbed "Richard M. Goldman Day" in Atlantic City.

May 5, 2002

Greta stares at it and swallows, fighting off the feeling of her throat tightening beneath her chin. *What in the world?* She wonders what's happening to her and her stoicism as she places the plaque on the couch next to her. As she reminds herself that Richard meant nothing to her, she stands up and gives Dawn a forced hug. When she turns to sit back down, she notices Brian looking at her, mouth slightly agape. Greta winks at him and, at that moment, feels a vague and surprising connection to him that she hasn't felt with anyone else—perhaps ever.

11

Sunday

"Can you take me to the police station tomorrow afternoon?"

Greta and Brian are sitting in his Cadillac on their way to the next street on the list, Connecticut Avenue, also known as Ocean Beach Boulevard. Greta's dark hair sits twisted up on the top of her head, pulled into a messy bun. Her eyes appear smaller with pockets of puffiness underneath. She hadn't had time to shower or apply any makeup since she and Dawn had stayed up most of the night talking, so the only priority this morning had been coffee.

Greta rather enjoyed her stay at Eastern Pines. Dawn had turned out to be an incredible source of comfort, almost like a fairy godmother—*truthfully, like the mother I never had.* Dawn's perspective on life, and even death, made an impression on Greta, but Greta isn't certain why. It is as if there is some "it factor" that Dawn possesses, something which no one else Greta has ever met exudes. *Deep hope mixed with a lot of humility?* She isn't sure. As she considers it, she looks out of the car window, waiting for Brian's answer.

Greta senses a shift in the atmosphere and turns to see Brian staring at her with wide eyes.

"What?" she asks.

"The police?"

"Oh. I have a meeting with the lead detective on Richard's case and the police chief at two-thirty." Her flippant answer is pure Greta. "What? Did you think they'd call you or something?"

"Actually, yes. I didn't even know they had your number."

"Well, I guess they do."

She is both anxious and curious about the meeting. She wants to know what they've discovered during their investigation into her great-uncle's murder, but she is not a fan of police stations—or hospitals or schools or nursing homes. They all overload her nerves and carry germs, especially police stations. The rules. The noise. And people. All the hallmarks of any institution.

"Absolutely. Happy to go with you. Have you heard anything at all? I haven't seen much in the media about it, which is odd," Brian says.

"Nothing." Greta looks at Brian's face, and the wall she's built up around her heart for nearly three decades melts a little more. Maybe it's the way the corners of his eyes crease with compassion or that his clean-shaven chin hosts a deep dimple, which she finds strangely appealing even though it makes his chin look like someone's rear end. He's the first person who has been patient with her peculiarities, someone who isn't assuming she's a terrible person because she's so *weird*, a label she accepted from others at an impressionable age. Even teachers bullied her in elementary school, withholding cupcakes during birthday parties or making her sit in a "thinking chair" in the corner of the room.

Sitting there in the SUV, Greta wonders if there is a mutual physical attraction, and in her wondering, she panics. She spins her head and looks back out of the window. Brian clears his throat and shifts a few inches away in the seat.

"Antonio, are we nearly there?"

"Yes—about three more minutes to the Ocean Resort & Casino."

"A casino?" Greta grumbles under her breath. Her grumbling eases her discomfort by shifting her back into her typical mindset. She feels safer when either cynicism or judgment sits just at the surface. But the name of the casino rings a bell. She pauses and thinks for a moment. *Oh, from when Jason took me, near where Precious was hit.*

"You don't like to gamble?" Brian smiles as he elbows her in the ribs.

Oh my gosh, how dare he! Greta can't decide if she's appalled or thrilled.

Antonio weaves the Cadillac into a space in the parking garage reserved for VIPs. Greta quickly escapes the back of the car before Antonio can make it around the bumper to open her door. She takes a deep breath to clear her head and refocus on the task at hand, namely getting through these streets as quickly as possible.

As they cross the street, Greta spies Precious, of all people, exciting the casino, sunglasses covering her eyes. When the woman sees Greta, she hurries over to where Greta stands.

"Greta Goldman, right?" she asks when she is a few feet away. Greta nods.

"Any news on poor Mr. Richard?" Precious inquires with a tilt of her head.

"No, ma'am."

"You know what he tol' me once? He said he'd take care of me forever. I need to know who killed him."

It's Greta's turn to tilt her head. Brian reaches the pair after chatting with Antonio for a minute. The three stand in silence for a few seconds. Finally, Brian speaks. "Hello."

"Sorry." Greta seems to jump awake. "Brian, Precious. Precious, Brian." Greta waves at one, then the other with each name she says. She's still wondering why Precious is leaving the casino resort on a Sunday.

"Oh! Precious! I've heard so much about you. I can't believe this is the first time we've officially met." Brian sticks his hand out. Precious grabs hold and gives it a slight shake.

"Well, I must be going." Precious steps past them and turns the corner.

A granny with a gambling problem? Greta wonders.

Greta follows Brian through the enormous glass doors leading to the main lobby of the resort and casino. She stands in the middle of a million lights and looks around, listening to the sounds of people laughing and talking, the slot machines spinning their temptations, and glasses clinking. Her world swirls. The next thing she realizes, Brian is by her side again.

"You're all checked in."

Greta snaps back to herself. "This place is crazy! It's a Sunday morning!" Greta says loudly so Brian can hear her over the chaos.

Brian and Greta enter an elevator tucked into a niche on the left side of the lobby. Once inside, Greta notices the noise dissipate, as if someone has closed the door to a child's birthday party. Brian hits the button with the "13" on it. There are thirty buttons, thirty floors.

"What? Not the penthouse?" Greta says with sarcasm. Brian only smiles at her, which infuriates her.

They exit onto a blue carpet with tiny white diamond shapes woven in a straight-line pattern, and Brian leads her to room #1337. As he uses an app on his phone to unlock the hotel room door, Greta hears the now familiar jangle of his bracelet. He hands her two keycards since she doesn't have the app.

"You're not going to enter my room uninvited in the middle of the night with that app, are you?"

Brian's face goes slack. Greta doesn't notice her faux pa.

"So I keep meaning to ask you—" Greta continues as they walk through the doorway into a spacious room with a king-sized bed. The ocean fans the horizon just outside the window, its blue-gray waters stretching as far as her vision can travel. "Wow! What a view!" Greta interrupts herself.

"Yeah, it's really beautiful, isn't it?"

Greta drops her duffle and sling on the cream-colored comforter covering the bed and moves toward the window. Not one cloud dots the blue sky.

"What were you wanting to ask me?" Brian ventures.

"Oh, right. Your bracelet. Are those angel wings engraved on it?" Greta turns to face Brian.

Brian looks at his wrist and instinctively pulls his shirt sleeve down to cover the bracelet.

"Um. Yeah." But there is no further explanation.

"Oh, come on," Greta pries. "If you don't want to talk about it, why do you wear it?" Greta knows she's picking on Brian; she's putting up safeguarding walls to protect herself from her blossoming attraction to him. She can't help it.

"I just don't want to talk about it right now. Why don't we meet for dinner later? I can share more then," Brian offers.

Greta hesitates. "Sure. Just nothing fancy. I don't have the clothes for it. I'm talking sweatshirt attire."

"How about Villain and Saint? It's inside the resort. Say, seven o'clock?"

"What's it called?" Greta is sure she misheard the name.

"Villain and Saint. It's a rock-n-roll pub with a big menu—a little something for everyone."

"If you say so. Seven o'clock it is." *Sounds like it's named after us,* she muses to herself.

"Okay. Last thing." Brian hands her a business card. "You have a two o'clock meeting with the manager of The Hope Floor."

"Hope Floor? Where have I heard that before?"

"Dawn is a mentor there. It's in the resort. Go to the elevators, hit the up arrow, and then press the button with the cursive *H.* You'll be prompted to enter a code on the elevator's keypad. It's written on the card." Brian nods toward the card in Greta's hand. "See you tonight," he says and then abruptly leaves her room. Greta stares after him until the latch clicks. She sighs and sits on the bed.

At 1:55 p.m., Greta hits the up arrow at the bank of elevators on the thirteenth floor and waits. The ding alerts her to the pending opening of the elevator on her right. Once inside, she follows Brian's instructions and presses the *H*, followed by *9141* on the keypad. As the doors slide closed, she pulls her sling further up onto her shoulder. *Wonder what's coming now,* she thinks.

When the door opens, Greta is met with a different atmosphere. Gone is the blue-diamond carpet and low-level lighting of the hotel's typical hallways. As she steps out, her foot lands on beautiful gray hardwood floors. The space is lit up with bright bulbs, and instead of the quiet and calm of her floor, there are five or six kids on scooters, zipping down the halls. One woman, who seems in charge of the youngsters, calls out, "Henry! Chloe! Slow down!"

The children race into a room at the end of the hall to Greta's right, and the floor immediately grows quiet as the woman follows them and disappears inside. Greta looks around, trying to decide which way to go. Suddenly, the first door on the left side of the hall opens, and out walks another woman. With her black hair, olive skin, and almond-shaped eyes, Greta guesses she's Chinese. She stands at least a foot shorter than Greta.

"Hi, you must be Greta Goldman," the woman says as she stretches out her arm for a handshake. Greta nods and clasps the woman's hand, which feels frigid.

"Sorry. I just washed them," the woman explains as she raises her hands, palms out, in front of Greta. "I'm Hong Shu, the manager here. You can call me Shu. It's so nice to meet you! Thanks for coming up to our special haven here."

Greta simply nods.

"Come on, let's go to the library where it will be quiet," Shu says with a wave of her hand.

Greta follows Shu down the hallway and notices right away the floor plan differs from the floor where her room is located.

The left hall isn't a hall at all; it immediately opens into what looks like several common areas, with a large room in the middle and several arched doorways into additional spaces. On one arch, the word *Library* is painted in a rainbow of colors. Shu leads Greta there.

The two sit down facing each other in zebra-printed chairs on top of a colorful floor rug. Bookshelves line the perky room. Books of all reading levels are piled on them, and they look well worn. Greta wishes she could organize the books. She decides she might.

"I hope you're enjoying your stay. Have you been to Atlantic City before?"

Greta's attention refocuses on Shu, and she shakes her head, looking off to the side. "This is my first time here. But I'm certainly getting to know the city quickly."

"Do you know anything about Ocean Resort & Casino or your great-uncle's role in it?" Shu asks.

Greta relaxes into her chair. She seems to be getting used to these meetings. "No, I don't know anything about the resort, except that my great-uncle owned it. What is this floor? Why are there kids here? My attorney referred to it as The Hope Floor." The questions seem to keep spilling out, so Greta bites her tongue.

Shu grins. "Yes, Richard owned it all, and The Hope Floor was his idea. It started about fourteen years ago when the local homeless shelter was at capacity during a really cold snap one winter. A family with two children was denied entrance into the shelter. One of the adults and a child ended up freezing to death in an alley."

Greta sucks in some air and shakes her head.

"Richard was outraged. I think it was more that his heart broke. He knew he had to do something. So he blocked off this floor of the resort and brought in designers and construction crews to remodel it. It took seven months. He wanted to create a fun and safe space for families. But it's not just a place for families who find themselves homeless to stay. The resort provides free childcare for kids not yet in school and, during the summer months, for all kids under fourteen, as long as at least one parent works in the resort. . . . They just can't work on the casino side because Richard didn't want to create or inflame any issues with gambling or addiction. Most work in hotel management or one of the restaurants. On top of that, Richard provides on-the-job training for the parents who work here and a scholarship to attend classes at a local community coll—"

"Let me guess. Atlantic Beach Community College on Baltic Avenue?"

"Yes! How did you know?" Shu looks at Greta with surprise, ignoring the interruption. Brian had warned Shu yesterday that Greta might come off a little abrasive.

"I know Uncle Richard served on the board and created scholarships there," Greta admits.

"Richard was such a great visionary, looking at the whole person, not just one aspect of them. He knew he had to have that holistic approach to effect change. He also limited the time the families could stay here to eighteen months. By then, he wanted the working parents to have saved enough and built a network strong enough to move out on their own."

Greta nods her understanding.

"We have space for fifteen families with the assumption of one to four children per family. We have family-style suites with two or three bedrooms and a kitchenette. Then, on this side, there are common rooms, like this library, and a bigger dining area and kitchen for when multiple families want to eat together or hang out.

"That's fantastic," Greta says earnestly. She likes the idea of keeping families together, especially through a crisis like homelessness. Her family was never close, and that still causes her some sorrow, even many years later.

Shu smiles at Greta's comment. "It is," she agrees. "We've successfully graduated seventy-one families so far. One graduate, a father, is a mentor for one of the young boys who stays here now. The boy is being raised by a single mom."

They had been talking for about twenty minutes when Shu glances at her watch. "I have about five more minutes. Do you have any questions about The Hope Floor?"

"I don't think so. Thanks for meeting with me," Greta says as she stands up and moves toward the bookshelves. Grabbing one, she glances at the cover, intent on organizing the books by author.

Shu remains quiet as she watches the woman before her.

Greta gives up about a minute later, realizing it would take hours to accomplish her goal. "I can show myself out. . . . . Nice to meet you," she calls over her shoulder as she makes her way to the elevators.

Shu laughs to herself, undeterred by Greta's social awkwardness. *It takes all kinds, I suppose.*

12

When Greta returns to the quietness of her hotel room, she sighs deeply, feeling exhausted from the last couple of days. *And it's been less than a week,* she laments. She lies down for a nap.

Nearly three hours later, she awakes, grateful she didn't sleep through the entire night. Pulling out her laptop, she sits at the faux wood desk to work on her book, but her mind just isn't into it. Creativity is lacking. *The AC is ruining me.* She reaches for the remote and turns on the TV.

". . . in for the five-thirty news. Gabe Riley, owner of several high-end car dealerships in the Atlantic City area, was found dead on South Boston Avenue near PNC Bank two days ago from a knife wound. The police believe his murder is related to several others around the country by someone targeting wealthy men. They're now calling the perpetrator the 'Millionaire Club Killer.' There have been no witnesses to these crimes, which have all occurred outdoors. Authorities are asking the public to come forward if they know anything or if their South Boston Avenue business cameras caught any suspicious activity. The tip number is on the screen. Casey, back to you . . ."

Gabe Riley? Peering at the image of Gabe on the screen, Greta realizes she knows the man. Or rather, knew him. She met him at an art show a couple of years back. *Small world,* she thinks. *And too bad.*

Greta clicks the TV off and shakes her head at the name the authorities came up with—"The Millionaire Club Killer"—for the person responsible. She heads toward the bathroom to shower and get ready for dinner with Brian. As she does, she wonders what it is about him that has her reeling. He pushes all of her buttons—good and bad. He's attractive and empathetic. A gentleman, for sure. But he's almost too nice. A goody-double-wingtip-shoes type of person. And she can't help but wonder: *How can such a successful attorney with such prominent clients still be so kind, especially in a gambling town?* She assumes there's another side to him, and she wants to know what that side entails. After all, everyone has another side . . .

INSIDE VILLAIN AND SAINT, the host steps aside as Brian pulls the chair out for Greta. Their table is in a quiet corner of the restaurant, far from the wall of gold-plated refrigerators, filled with beers of every kind, and matching gold taps along the wooden bar, where a dozen patrons sit and talk with the bartenders and each other.

Greta eyes Brian, trying to communicate her annoyance at his chivalry, but sits down anyway, hoping he doesn't think this is some sort of date. She doesn't have time for the complications that would certainly erupt with a relationship, whatever it might entail. After her shower an hour ago, Greta had decided she should just move forward through Great-Uncle Richard's list and keep Brian at an arm's length, avoiding any drama that would destroy her status quo kind of life.

Brian sits opposite her. Before he picks up the menu—Greta has already sunk her eyes into hers to avoid any small talk—he asks, "How was The Hope Floor? Pretty amazing, yeah?"

Greta lifts her eyes and lowers her menu as she sighs. *Well, I don't have to be rude,* she thinks.

"It was amazing. Saw some of the kids scootering down the hallways and whatnot. I guess my great-uncle was a pretty charitable guy. I do like how they keep families together." Before she finishes the last word in her sentence, Greta sticks her face back behind the menu. Brian chuckles.

Greta lowers the menu. "What's so funny?" she asks.

"I thought I was getting used to the way you end—or cut off—conversations," he says playfully.

"I don't know what you're talking about." Greta blinks in apparent innocence, but they both know what Brian is referring to. Greta has been chastised many times in her life for her lack of social etiquette.

"Nothing. It's endearing. I'll wait until you've decided what you want to order to say anything else. Deal?" Brian smiles, but what Greta notices is his chin dimple. She nods in gratitude.

After a couple of minutes of silence, Greta pipes up. "I know what I want."

"Great!" Brian puts his menu down as the server approaches the table with two glasses of water, a basket of peanuts, and an empty tin canister, presumably for the shells.

"Can I get you two any drinks to start off?" she asks. Her purple-dyed hair is striking under the lights of the restaurant, all part of the rock-and-roll vibe.

"I'll have an IPA, whatever is on tap," Greta says.

"I'll take a Yuengling," chimes Brian.

"You got it." The server speeds off in the bar's direction.

Without preamble, Greta asks a question weighing on her mind. "Brian, how did Richard earn his billions? No one has really said. Was he a successful gambler or something?"

Brian's body bounces up and down with suppressed laughter. "No, nothing like that. Though the rumors must have reached you." Greta shrugs. "At ABCC, Richard met someone, a teacher or professor or someone—I'm not sure who—gifted in real estate development. He mentored Richard in his late teens and early twenties, taught him everything he knew. Richard had an innate gift for risk-taking. And his visionary thinking didn't hurt either. After he graduated, this mentor helped him get a few loans from the bank, and other friends he had met along the way chipped in too, as investors. Richard amassed a few holdings, sold them for more gains, the whole bit. With his charisma, people jumped on board early. He turned old sections of town, where vacant buildings were falling apart, into thriving rental properties, particularly for businesses that paid him huge sums of money . . . some old drug houses became high-dollar boutique hotels. He fixed a couple of them up and sold them outright, and that generated him a lot of money too.

"Once he started doing all that, he saw how it changed the face of Atlantic City, turned it from run-down to modern, how it made it more appealing, and that's what ignited his passion for more change. He paid off his early loans and kept growing. I think the icing on the cake came when he diversified into the gambling industry. His first casino solidified him as the wealthiest man in Atlantic City in his late thirties. It just went on from there. He earned his first billion in his early forties."

Greta sips her water. "And the angel wings?" she asks with a smirk.

"What?"

"Don't play stupid. Your bracelet? What are the wings for? Why are you embarrassed by them?"

Brian wiggles in his chair. "I'm not embarrassed. President Schafer's wife, Mona, gave me the bracelet ten years ago," he explains. "My sister Bethany was killed by a drunk driver when she was eighteen. She was a first-year student at ABCC; she had always wanted to be a teacher—ever since I can remember . . ." Brian wonders how far to take it, but when he feels Greta's full attention, he continues. "When we were young, my brother and I had to play school with her. We'd sit at the mid-point of our staircase with Bethany perched at the top, looking down on us, and she'd teach us all sorts of subjects." Brian holds his wrist out for Greta to see the engraved angel wings. "On the inside is Bethany's name and the Scripture, 'He will wipe every tear from their eyes.' It's from Revelation 21:4."

Greta nods, though she has no idea what Revelation is. Not wanting to continue the conversation in this direction, Greta says, "So tell me about you."

"I will. But first, I want you to know that this is how I met Richard and became his attorney. He already had one, obviously, but when Bethany died, Richard heard about her from the Schafers and wanted to meet my brother and me to offer his condolences. He ended up creating a scholarship at ABCC in Bethany's name. It's for students who want to become teachers. Then, after that, Richard and I kinda hit it off. We talked, and he ended up retaining me as his *legacy attorney*. At least, that's what he called me. It's why I'm so interested in taking you to the police station tomorrow. I want to know what happened to him. I want to know who would take him from this community. Who could have d-done—" Brian stops abruptly when he realizes his voice is cracking with his emotions, and he remembers who is sitting across from him. "I'm sorry. I guess I'm taking it harder than I thought."

"It's okay. I'm sorry about—" Greta doesn't know what else to say, her discomfort blossoming like the spring flowers outside. She stands up and excuses herself to freshen up, even though the server has returned with their drinks and is ready to take their food order.

"Can you give us a few more minutes?" she hears Brian say as she makes a beeline to the safety of the restroom.

13

Monday

Greta awakes early to her smartphone's alarm growing louder with each passing second. She had set it the evening before, once she returned from her dinner with Brian. After her escape to the bathroom, the rest of the night had been uneventful. Neither of them spoke about Richard or Bethany again. They talked of sports and favorite professors. Brian had graduated from Yale Law School. Greta had not been surprised. Brian told her he's surprised, now that he's met her, that Greta ever attended a four-year university. He knew from Richard that she had studied architecture. He hadn't known she was an author too.

"I don't know," she had said with a shrug when he asked about architecture and now writing.

"How did you survive the people?" he had asked about her college experience. They had both laughed.

Greta smiles as she recalls the evening with Brian. *He is easy to talk to. Just like Dawn.* Then she remembers her promise to herself not to get involved with him. Reminding herself to get on with the list and get home, she crawls out of bed and pads over to the desk where her computer—and novel—are waiting. After awakening her screen, she makes herself a black cup of joe with the small coffee maker on the dresser. As the scent of the cheap instant coffee fills the room, Greta tries to prepare herself for her visit to the police station.

Maybe I can think of it as research for a future book, she encourages herself. The anxiety remains, and she grabs a pill bottle from her purse and tosses her morning encouragement into her mouth. She sits at the desk and prepares herself for writing with some deep breathing techniques she learned from a former therapist. The deadline with her publisher is now only a month away.

Three loud knocks shake her from her thoughts. "Open the door. Police."

Greta panics and looks around the room. *What do I do?* She takes a deep breath and opens the door.

Two uniformed officers stand in the hallway. The short, dark-haired one speaks first. "Miss, there's been an incident. May we ask you a few questions?"

"Um. Sure." But Greta makes no move to let the two male offices into her room. She holds the door open, waiting.

"What is your name and when did you arrive at the resort?" the same officer asks as his counterpart scans a list in his hands.

"Yesterday. And . . . Greta Goldman." This prompts a second look at her from the officer holding the list.

"Ms. Goldman, can you tell us where you were last night around nine o'clock?" The first officer asks.

"I think I was at Villain and Saint. Downstairs."

"You think?"

Greta nods.

"With anyone or alone?" the short officer asks as he jots down her answers on a notepad.

"With someone." Greta's heart pounds in her chest. She grips the handle of the door.

"Ms. Goldman, what is the name of the person you were with?" Frustration spits through the officer's overly white teeth.

"Did something happen?" She avoids his question.

"Yes, and we're verifying the whereabouts of guests." Greta stares at the shorter officer, who seems to be the one in charge.

"I was with Brian Gogh, an attorney. What happened?"

The white-toothed officer sighs, placated by the name of her companion. "Did you see anything suspicious yesterday at the resort?"

"No." Greta offers as few words as possible. Sweat beads and runs down her back.

"Okay. Can I have your contact number in case we need to reach you?"

"Um. Sure." Greta gives the officers her number and then abruptly shuts the door as they turn to leave.

She spins around and leans against the door, breathing deeply, trying to calm herself down.

A COUPLE OF HOURS LATER, Greta hears another knock on her hotel door. Despite the earlier scare, she practically skips over to open it, energized by her afternoon of writing. She had conquered two full chapters—even started editing the first chapters of her novel, knowing that isn't ideal in the eyes of book coaches, but also not caring what anyone else thinks of her methods.

As she pulls open the door, she sees Brian standing in the hallway, dressed in a sleek medium-gray slim-fit suit and sky-blue dress shirt. The suit accentuates his narrow hips. His medium-gray tie features lobsters in the same blue color as his shirt, and a silver tie clip rounds out the outfit.

"Wow. Fancy," Greta exclaims with a chuckle.

Brian smiles at what he hopes is a compliment and not a dig. "I had several meetings this morning and didn't have time to change. Are you ready for the police station?"

Greta's smile turns downward. "I guess so. Let's get this over with," she replies. She elects not to tell Brian about her earlier encounter with the rude cops.

DETECTIVE WALKER REED arrives out of nowhere and greets Greta and Brian with a handshake as they sit in a couple of metal chairs in the lobby, where they've been waiting since giving their names to the front desk receptionist. The lobby is encased in white tile, making every voice and the sounds of the squeaking, flapping, or clicking of every shoe echo wildly throughout the space. When Detective Reed, a stout man with a mustache and snake eyes, offers to move to a conference room, Greta quickly accepts, her ears and brain unable to tolerate much more of the clamor. She's fully aware of what she might say or do as a result of too much noise. And this is not the place for those types of things.

The three sit in a quiet and dark room with a full glass window on one wall and a camera secured in the top corner of the other. Greta's nerves fire some more warning signals, and her heart rate jumps. She looks to Brian who smiles and puts his hand on her upper back, guiding her to yet another set of metal chairs on the opposite side of a metal table. His touch sends a comforting sensation through her.

"Police Chief Reynolds is in a meeting—with the FBI, actually. We'll wait here and then move to his office later," the detective offers in way of explanation.

Brian kicks off the conversation. "Detective Reed, can you tell us anything about the investigation? Greta hasn't heard anything . . . nor have I. And we haven't seen much on the news, which I find interesting, maybe even odd, given Richard's influence in Atlantic City."

Detective Reed smirks. His nostrils flare, and Greta decides she doesn't like him. The detective turns to her to answer Brian's questions. *They must know each other,* she thinks. *And not in a good way.*

"We are still investigating your uncle's murder," the detective begins.

"Great-uncle," Greta corrects him. She can't help it.

The detective eyes her. "Right. Anyway, there have been few news reports and updates because we've withheld most of the information we've discovered, and we've asked the media to sit on what they do have. In this case, they've mostly obliged—aside from a report that aired yesterday," he finishes in a huff.

"Why? I mean, why hold the information?" Brian asks.

"We believe Richard was the second victim in a series of related murders," Detective Reed admits. "In fact, there was another one at the Ocean Resort & Casino last night. A guy from Maine." He looks between Greta and Brian to gauge their reactions.

"You mean like a serial killer?" Brian asks, giving Greta a discrete side glance at the mention of the hotel where she stayed and they ate.

Greta fidgets while trying to come up with any benefit to speaking up. In the end, she remains silent about her visit from the police.

"Yes, we just pulled the video footage from the hotel. See if we can't ID the guy. There have been five victims now. We've found slim to no connections between them. FBI has the case."

Brian notices Greta's leg bouncing under the table just like it had when they were meeting with President Schafer at ABCC.

"FBI?" Greta asks quietly. She glances at the camera in the corner.

The detective ignores her and continues, "We believe someone is targeting wealthy men, but we haven't determined why. Your uncle may have become one of this guy's victims simply because of his wealth. But what we can't figure out is *why*. I mean, it's not like the killer is getting these guys' inheritances, right?" He looks at Greta with questioning eyes.

Greta squints at the detective. She misses his insinuation completely, but what she does realize streaks through her like lightning.

"What about me? If I am the named heir to Richard, am I in danger?"

Brian puts a hand on Greta's staccato knee. "Detective, no other heirs or family members have been hurt after these murders, right?" He tries to calm Greta's fears.

"Not a one," the detective confirms. "It's all very strange. But we're working all the angles. Don't worry; we'll catch 'im. And he may have already moved to another city."

There are two loud bangs on the door, making Greta jump, and Detective Reed stands and leaves the room. Greta turns toward Brian with a look of panic.

"It's okay," Brian reassures her. "They said everyone else has been fine. You're safe," he continues, though inside, his brain is in overdrive.

Greta is about to say something but looks at the camera on the wall and freezes. "I want to leave."

At that moment, Detective Reed barges through the door. Gruffly, he says, "The police chief will see you now."

They walk single-file past a few desks where officers are typing on laptops or chatting on phones. A musty smell, like what you'd find in a fitness center, permeates the space. Greta and Brian are shown into a small office with a pine desk and several accolades and photos hanging on the walls. Right out of a bad movie, Greta spies a cheap, gold-colored desk lamp, two old but recently upholstered chairs in front of the chief's desk, and yellow-stained walls behind the plaques and framed certificates. The chief sits behind his desk but stands to greet them when they enter. He is tall and lean, with pockmarks on his face and yellow teeth that match the walls. His clothes, or maybe his breath—or both—reek of cigarettes. His navy tie sits askew on a white-collared shirt. And underneath, Greta notices his undershirt's collar is stretched out at the neckline.

"Ms. Goldman. Mr. Gogh. I'm Chief Ryker. Nice to meet you. Have a seat." He speaks with clipped sentences. "Sorry about your loss. We'll find the guy. Right now, I want to talk logistics. And about the media. We need to remain tightlipped. So you can't tell anyone what Detective Reed told you. We have several leads, though." Chief Ryker seems to realize he's babbling. He's never had this high a profile murder before with Richard Goldman's death, let alone three victims of a serial killer in his city. "The FBI have arrived, and we'll tag-team to stop this before anyone else is hurt."

Right, tag-team, Brian thinks. He rolls his eyes.

Greta is stunned. She's finally met someone as socially awkward as she. *He made it to this level in the police department?* She's not sure how.

Brian clears his throat. "Chief Ryker, what do you need from us?"

"Nothing at this point. We just wanted you to know we're on it. And that Richard's murder was likely committed by someone he didn't know. We believe he was targeted because he was wealthy. And we cannot release his body yet. I'm sorry. Definitely soon."

"You haven't told us any details anyway," Greta blurts out. Her anxiety prevents her from simply thinking the words, and they spill into the room. "And you'd release his body to me?"

Chief Ryker stares at Greta for a few seconds before shrugging his shoulders.

"Okay, thank you," Brian says. With that, Greta and Brian stand up and turn to leave.

After Greta exits the office, Brian turns around. Whispering, he says to the police chief, "I'll be in touch about Richard's body later." He knows Richard's older brother and sister-in-law are the ones who will handle that detail.

Greta decides this encounter is nothing like what she's seen on TV, but she tucks away the experience to use for a later book. She could never make up this kind of stuff herself.

As Greta and Brian make their way toward Brian's SUV in the visitor's parking lot, Greta thinks she spies Precious across the street, standing idly as if waiting for them.

"Hold on, Brian." Greta veers toward Precious. "What are you doing here?" she asks the woman.

"Did they tell you anything? About Mr. Richard? I can't sleep. . . . I need to know who done it. Who killed him?" The woman is wringing her hands.

"No, nothing yet." Greta finds it strange that she keeps running into the woman. *I guess Atlantic City isn't that big.*

Part Two

Assets

14

Greta cannot find words. She sits across from Brian at a chain restaurant, sipping on a lemonade, letting the emotional ride of the last few hours simmer down. She feels pummeled by the unexpected police visit to her room followed by her scheduled visit to the station. *Too many police for one day.* She is also keenly aware she must trek on to finish her great-uncle's list before she can go home. Go home and forget everything she's been through. Forget the AC forever.

Brian watches her as he pushes a forkful of grilled chicken salad into his mouth. "You okay?" he asks after he chews and swallows the bite.

"Sure," Greta answers without emotion.

"The next stop may be an interesting one. You'll be staying with Bill and Jean." Greta jerks her head up. "They are in their early eighties and live on St. Charles Place . . . by the beach. Maybe it'll be good for you. Did you ever meet Richard's brother and his wife?"

Greta shakes her head. "Not that I remember." Her breath becomes strained. She didn't know the couple still lived in the AC. With her grandfather's premature death—and having never met him—she hadn't kept up with extended family, people she barely heard about. "Weird they weren't the named heirs, isn't it? Did Uncle Richard say why he picked me?"

"As you know, they're older. And while Bill and Jean are quite nice and very low-key, Richard wanted to focus on the next generation—you. As you know, without their having kids, there is no family line there. Oh . . . and just to be clear, they are who would receive Richard's body and handle his funeral."

"Sounds good." Greta blows some relief out through her pursed lips.

What she doesn't know is that Brian feels somewhat responsible for Greta's mood. When Richard had first presented this idea of his great-niece visiting the places he influenced and meeting the people he loved months ago, Brian thought it would be fun, never guessing it would happen so soon or under these circumstances. He couldn't have known Richard would be targeted and murdered because of his wealth. Brian figured it'd be years before he'd be playing tour guide for Greta Goldman.

"I'm sorry, Greta. I'm sorry for your loss, for this trip, for the roller coaster ride this has been. I know you have a life to get back to. For what it's worth, I'm glad you're here." Brian's cheeks flush with the last sentence.

Greta glances at Brian and sighs. "Thanks. I know you're just doing your job."

"It's more than that. Richard was like a dad to me. Well, like I've said before, a grandfather, I guess. That's probably a better way to put it. But I've also gotten to know you a bit. And while you have some rough edges . . ." Brian pauses to see if Greta will smile at his attempt at humor, but there's nothing there. "You're fun to be around."

Greta acknowledges Brian's kindness. She gives him a thumbs up and then picks up her fork to dig into her salad.

At four-thirty, Brian and Greta are standing on the sidewalk in front of a beautiful, three-story yellow beach house. It has two wrap-around porches, one on each of the first two levels. The third story has three walls of windows overlooking the postage-stamp-sized backyard with the alley, the front street, and the ocean. The beach lies a couple of hundred feet to the left of the house. St. Charles Place, the street on her list, is the alley that leads to these beach houses' garages.

Greta spies only a handful of people on the sand as the sun sits low in the sky. It's still the off-season. Easter and Spring Break arrive soon, and Atlantic City will fill up quickly. But right now, most people are finishing up with their workday and thinking of dinner.

"It's gorgeous," Greta says as she looks at the house. "What is Richard's brother's name again? And his wife?"

Brian looks at her sideways. "William and Jean Goldman. He goes by Bill." Brian eyes Greta.

She sees Brian's confusion. "I've never remembered their names, okay? Our family wasn't close. . . . Right, Bill and Jean . . . as in, Billie Jean." Greta chuckles, humoring herself.

"Funny," Brian says with a laugh of his own. "I'd never thought of that. Now, I'll never forget it!"

The front door to the yellow house opens, and an elderly lady with short, straight white hair pokes her head out.

"That's our cue!" Brian says as he grabs Greta's hand and moves toward the porch. Greta's instinct is to pull her hand away, but something stops her: a feeling of security the likes she's never known.

"Mrs. Goldman. It's nice to see you again. Thank you for your hospitality. This . . ." Brian gently lets go of Greta's hand and steps to the side as he points to her, "is Greta."

"Hi, Greta. It's so nice to see you. I'm Jean. I can't believe we've never met! Please, both of you, come inside." Jean Goldman opens the door wider and gives them room to enter.

As soon as Greta steps into the foyer, she's met with the most wonderful aroma. "Is that apple pie I smell?" she asks as she places her duffle bag in the corner by the silver coat tree.

"Yes, it is! It's Bill's favorite." Jean looks up at Greta and grins.

The house is decorated in mid-century modern with hints of life at the beach sprinkled throughout. Greta spies a chair in the living room, the wide and open space directly ahead of where she stands.

"And is that an Eames' lounge chair?" Greta is a fan of the streamlined, warm tones and materials of the mid-century modern style. Her own house in North Carolina is characterized by the look and feel of it. Standing there, glancing around, a warmth flows through her, like she is, in fact, *home.*

"You know him?" Jean asks.

"Greta studied architecture." Brian jumps in before Greta, feeling uncharacteristically proud to offer some input.

"Yes. I adore everything mid-century modern. Charles Eames is famous for saying—"

"We don't do art, we solve problems," Jean says at the same time as Greta. Jean claps her hands together with glee.

Greta looks at Brian, her eyes large and her mouth forming an *O.*

"Can I just stay here for the next couple of weeks, Brian?" Greta half-jokes. Brian winks at her but shakes his head no.

"Oh, let me go get Bill. He's getting the grill fired up to make bar-b-que chicken. Then, after you meet him, I'll give you a tour!" Jean scurries away, much faster than any other octogenarian Greta has ever known.

A minute later, Jean approaches with Bill in tow. He seems just as spunky as Jean, a huge smile plastered on his round face, a face that gives away his relation to Richard; although, Bill is fitter and much taller than his younger brother. Bill's neatly trimmed mustache is silver, like his hair. Aside from height, the major difference is that instead of a signature top hat, Bill wears glasses fit for a twenty-something: a funky royal blue pair that Greta finds herself coveting.

"Greta, this is Bill," Jean introduces. The two shake hands.

"We're so glad you're here." Bill's voice is soft and friendly. "Brian, good to see you again." Bill gives Brian a quick side hug while shaking his hand. Greta catches Bill looking at her with curiosity.

"You all know each other well?" Greta asks to deflect Bill's attention.

"Brian is our estate attorney too," Bill answers as he looks back at Brian. "And a friend."

"Well, I have some things I need to do. Greta? See you tomorrow, say around four fifteen?"

Greta nods and waves goodbye to Brian as he leaves the foyer and descends the porch steps on his way to meet Antonio, who's standing beside the Cadillac outside.

"Well, darling," Jean says, "let's give you that tour and get you settled before dinner."

Jean leads Greta further into the house as Bill heads back to the patio and the grill.

15

Tuesday

Minutes before three o'clock in the morning, a figure stands in the shadows across from the yellow house on St. Charles Place. The black hoodie will soon become conspicuous as the air warms with mid-spring. The woman knows this, but tonight, it's hiding her bald head, which is even more conspicuous. She's dressed in black clothes and lightweight tactical boots —not exactly beachwear. The knife glistens in the moonlight as she turns it in her hand. Her thoughts are centered on her grand plan—moving on to her next destination as soon as possible.

The only person the killer has seen in the last thirty minutes is a middle-aged lady walking her fru-fru dog. The walk, the hooded woman surmises, was likely the byproduct of the woman's premenopausal hormones preventing sleep.

Standing there in the darkness, for the first time in years, the murderess is hesitant about this next kill. The soon-to-be-dead individual is female. The murderess knows it's not her *modus operandi*—to target women. *But sometimes, the best laid plans . . .*

GRETA WAKES up to complete silence. The sun's rays are hitting her eyes through the opening between the curtains, announcing a hot spring day, and she can feel the humidity index climbing, even though she's only stretching her long limbs. The king-sized bed with the down comforter and silk sheets feels heavenly. She slept like a toddler after a king-sized meltdown.

As Greta looks around the room, she notices the ceiling fan is off, as well as the digital clock on the bedside table. She grabs her phone from its charger. *Only half a charge. The electricity is out.*

Downstairs, she hears the muffled voice of Bill and someone else.

She sits up in bed and gathers from Bill's words that he's on the phone with the electric company. *I bet Jean is standing next to him, telling him what to ask and say,* Greta thinks. *Though, last night was really nice.* Her insides twist with the admission.

After dinner, the three had walked on the beach in the glow of dusk, listening to the rolling waves and not discussing anything of importance. Low-key, just like Brian had promised.

There's a soft knock on the door, and Jean speaks through the wood, interrupting Greta's thoughts. "Greta? You up? Sorry about the power. The power company says there was an outage overnight. Some accident on the road down by the pier. It'll come back on soon."

"I'll be down in a sec!" Greta calls out.

As Greta dresses in black leggings and a Pink Floyd T-shirt, the smells of waffles and warm maple syrup hit her nostrils. *More food.* The leggings were the best purchase she's ever made, allowing for her expanding waistline. She wonders what's on tap for today. Brian won't arrive until late afternoon.

She doesn't have to wait long for an answer. After breakfast, Greta, Bill, and Jean sit in the third-floor sunroom where walls of windows reach from floor to ceiling. A ceiling fan whirs above, the electricity having been restored an hour ago. They watch the ocean's heartbeat roll in and recede, leaving the sand it touches a dark brown color. The mesmerizing repetition has a calming effect on Greta. *So this is what retirement is like. Maybe I will live by the ocean.*

"Greta," Jean starts, "tell us about the last time you saw Richard."

Greta winces but collects herself. "I only met him twice. Once was at my parents' funeral . . ." She hesitates, waiting for a comment about the funeral, which never comes. "And the last time was at my college graduation, many years ago. I have no other family, so Uncle Richard came down to celebrate my graduation with me." *They know that already, stupid.*

"How thoughtful," Jean answers.

Bill is gazing out the window toward the horizon, lost in his own thoughts.

"What about you, Bill," Greta ventures. "I learned from Ms. Moore that you had left your childhood home before both Richard and my grandfather did. You're several years older than Richard was, right?" Greta thinks nothing of asking about his age, but suddenly her flushed cheeks tell her she's gone too far.

Bill snaps back to the conversation. "Yes. It was not a great home life for children. Our father was verbally abusive. He never laid a hand on us, but he might as well have. Later, we learned he had a mental illness. As soon as I turned eighteen, I left for good. Richard was always the more resilient of the three of us, which may be why our father kicked him out. He had met his match in Richard. Henry, your grandfather, had gone off to boarding school when he was twelve. He said he wanted a top-notch education, but I figured it was to get away from our father too. We were never close with Henry, and sadly, I only saw him one more time before he died in his forties from cancer. I'm sorry I missed your parents' funeral. And I'm sorry for your loss. I just never knew my younger brother's family. I'm happy we finally met, though." Bill smiles at the dark-haired beauty in front of him.

Greta nods, wanting to change direction as soon as possible. "How did you two reconnect, you and Richard?" She surprises herself with her probing questions and interest. Then it hits her; she likes Bill and Jean, and it's showing through her curiosity.

"When Richard was living with Ms. Moore, a few weeks before his high school graduation, he contacted me. We reunited, and I even made it to his graduation, knowing our parents probably didn't even know about it. After that, we met up monthly to grab a bite to eat and talk about 'brotherly things,' I guess we'll call it. Once I retired, *many decades later* . . ." Bill points to his silver hair. ". . . he came by the house, and we'd sit up here and watch the ocean together."

"We also spent every New Year's Day with Richard," adds Jean. "We were proud of his success."

"Yes, Jean is right. We were, but we were proud of the man he'd become. He used to say he wanted to start every year with family," Bill says with a frown.

"Sounds nice." Greta doesn't know what else to say but wishes she did. With no immediate family of her own, and very few friends for that matter, she can't relate to anything the Goldmans are sharing. And she's the one who had intentionally put off reconnecting with Richard. She had cut him out of her life.

Suddenly, Greta feels sadness overtake her previously cheerful mindset. The hole in her heart, left by numerous instances of abandonment and rejection, moves with the off-beat rhythm of a lonely child who grew up to become a lonely adult. And even Bill and Jean can't fix that.

AT LUNCHTIME, Bill turns on the TV in the living room while they eat. The local news is airing a breaking report. A perfectly coiffed, dark-haired anchorwoman with a serious face is speaking into the camera: "The power outage lasted until around nine-thirty this morning for residents on the north side of Atlantic City. Crews were able to remove the female driver, identified as a tourist. The woman, who was in her mid-fifties, was pulled from the wreckage but declared dead at the scene. No name has been released as officials attempt to notify next of kin through the partnering embassy. Police detectives are saying this was not an accident but not providing further information at this time. We'll be back after the break with more information."

The screen cuts to a commercial for Tide laundry detergent.

Greta's phone buzzes. Brian's name pops up on the display, and she excuses herself from the kitchen table to take the call.

"Hey," she says into the phone.

"Greta." Greta's grip tightens on her phone upon hearing the tension in Brian's voice.

"A woman died in a car accident overnight," Brian tells her.

"Yeah, I just heard." Greta enters the upstairs guest bedroom where she slept and closes the door.

"She was murdered the same way as Richard and the others."

"How do you know?" Greta sucks in a nose-full of air and holds it while waiting for Brian's answer, dozens of thoughts cascading through her mind. One of those thoughts is to run.

"The police won't say. Just that the manner of death is similar. She was visiting the States on vacation."

"You talked to the police? Already?"

Silence.

"Well, okay. Thanks for letting me know. I don't know what to do, though." Greta has never felt so many diverging emotions in her life.

"Me neither. But they say the murders are happening faster and now . . . and now, the victim profile has changed. Not a good sign. Let me think about it, and I'll see you at four fifteen. Sound okay?"

"Sure." Greta taps the disconnect key and sighs. She looks over at her sling bag, and her shoulders relax with the knowledge of what's inside.

Several members of the FBI criminal investigation unit sit in a square conference room in Camden, New Jersey, swiveling in chairs as they wait. The screen in front of them lights up with the recorded footage taken from the hotel hallway at the Ocean Resort & Casino.

"Well, dang," exclaims one special agent.

"Didn't see that coming," says another. One of the female special agents grunts in response.

"That changes the profile, Cal."

They watch as an individual dressed in black with long dark hair shuffles toward Room 2220. She uses an app on her phone to gain access, then slides her fingers through black gloves after pocketing the phone, enters the hotel room, and shuts the door. Her face is turned in such a way that every camera misses any identifiable features.

One of the special agents fast-forwards the video. An hour later, according to the timestamp, the special agents watch as Leon Swindler, a frequent-flying gambler from Maine who changed his name to suit his hobby, returns to his room after a successful run at the craps table.

A short three minutes after he enters, according to the timestamp, the woman with the long dark hair exits while staring at the floor, saunters down the hallway, and disappears through the door leading to the stairwell. The maid would find Swindler's body nine hours later.

"This is helpful," the special agent in charge, or SAC, an older woman whose accent gives away her Caribbean roots, blurts out. "What does this change about our profile?" She knows the answer, but she's testing her team.

"Female serial killers are motivated by a twisted sense of love or risk-taking, or even altruism."

"Bingo, Kat. Mickey, analyze her height. It's the only other thing we've got."

"You got it." The only noise in the conference room is the tapping of keys on a keyboard as the team watches lines and numbers zig zag across the screen. "About six feet. That's tall for a female."

"It sure is," says Special Agent Kat Turner. "Are we sure she's a *she*?"

"Good point, Kat. Did the forensics team find any synthetic fibers, like from a wig?" the special agent in charge asks the team.

16

It's late afternoon, and Greta is sitting on the bed in the Goldman's guest bedroom, not wanting to leave, reading another email from her publisher about her approaching deadline, when she hears Brian's Cadillac pull up outside. The beach house's open windows are entryways for the squawks of the seagulls and the low hum of the moving waves, and now the voices of Antonio and Brian. The yellow house on St. Charles Place has been blissful. Greta has never felt so accepted in her life, so *valued.* Bill and Jean made her feel like instant family, though she had never met them.

With a twinge of regret, she grabs her duffle bag and sling and makes her way downstairs, hearing the knock on the front door as she reaches the bottom of the steps.

Jean beats Greta to the door and is letting Brian inside as Greta steps into the foyer.

"Good afternoon, Mrs. Goldman."

"You know it's Jean, Brian." She hugs him and offers him some iced tea.

"Oh, I'm fine. Thank you," he replies as he looks at Greta. When his eyes take in her face, he again notices the scar on her lip, made clearer with no lipstick. In an instant, he realizes he's missed her these past twenty-four hours, and the revelation sobers him.

"Greta, hi. How are you?" he asks.

Greta sulks. "I love this place, and I'm not leaving."

Jean chuckles. "You're welcome anytime!"

Bill walks into the foyer and hugs Greta. "You're family. You better come back and say goodbye before you head back to North Carolina," he remarks.

"I will."

After nodding at Bill, Brian takes Greta's duffle bag and opens the front door for her.

As they walk down the front porch steps to the waiting car, Brian notices Greta's downcast eyes. "I have a surprise for you."

"Oh?" Greta asks, her voice barely audible.

Once they get settled in the back of the Cadillac, Brian shares the good news. "You're not spending the night at the next location. We're just going to stop by. I know you're getting tired of—"

"*Getting*?" Greta interrupts.

"I know you *are* tired of moving along Richard's list. I made an executive decision. We're not completely skipping States Avenue, but you don't have to stay there for twenty-four hours. And I'll see what else I can do with some of the stops."

"Where was *there*?"

"I'm not sure I want to say," Brian answers as one eyebrow arches skyward.

"Come on. What—was it a casino or something?"

"Actually, yes," he laughs, while bracing for retaliation.

"Seriously?"

"States Avenue is a dead-end street that separates the Hard Rock Hotel and the Showboat Casino and Hotel."

"Good grief." Greta rolls her eyes. She feels the car move forward as Antonio shifts it into gear. "Did Richard own them both?"

"No. Only one. But you'll see the real reason the location was so important to him in just a few minutes. You were going to stay at the Hard Rock. Don't worry; I canceled the reservation."

The two settle into their seats, and Greta pulls some gum out of her sling bag. She holds the package out to Brian to offer him a piece, but he shakes his head.

"No, thank you."

Greta pops a piece into her mouth and enjoys the savory taste of cinnamon. It reminds her of the apple pie from last night. *That was so good,* she thinks as she reminisces about the two pieces she had helped herself to without remorse.

Ten minutes later, the car makes a turn onto States Avenue. Greta reads the street sign and then looks up at the towering building outside the car's window, spying "Hard Rock Hotel" in longitudinal letters on the side of the high-rise. She also sees parking spaces and loading docks for the buildings and realizes States Avenue is truly a dead end. "Employee only" signs litter her periphery.

"This looks ominous," she says out loud.

Brian displays a sly grin but says nothing.

In no time, the car is parked, and Antonio is opening the back door. Greta peels her bare legs off the seat and steps out. With the temperature hovering around seventy-eight degrees, she's wearing a denim skirt and a long-sleeve blouse.

Brian leads her to a group of a dozen men sitting in a circle by a loading dock. They appear to range in age from their thirties to sixties, and they're all dressed in coveralls, jeans, or carpenter pants and T-shirts or flannels. A few are smoking. Greta tenses up as she and Brian approach. She expects to hear a few catcalls or inappropriate remarks, and she's glad Brian is here.

"Hey, guys!" Brian says with more enthusiasm than Greta thinks is necessary.

"Brian!" An average-looking older man stands, though not to a full height. His crooked posture is evidence of the years he's spent lifting heavy pallets and driving a forklift. The two shake hands, and Greta hears a greeting from nearly every man there.

"Guys, this is Richard's great-niece, Greta," Brian introduces her.

"It's nice to meet you, Ms. Greta," they seem to offer in unison.

A quick "hi" is all she can say.

"Greta, Richard and these guys spent an hour and a half together every week, right here in this circle." Brian seems at ease, so Greta loosens her grip on her sling bag. "Hey, guys, who wants to tell Greta what you're doing here and how you know Richard?"

"I will," a fortyish man raises his hand. He has light brown hair graying at the temples and wears a pair of olive chinos with a flannel work shirt. Greta notices a name stitched on the shirt that reads *Ben*. "We talked."

The man seems finished with his answer, and everyone chuckles except for Greta. Her heart races again. Finally, he continues: "Richard started comin' here about three years ago. He'd gather a group out here and said he wanted to get to know us better. After about a year of just comin' out and talkin', he started offerin' to pray for some of us. He prayed for our families, our jobs, even our health." Ben stops and looks around. "Am I missin' anything?" he asks.

"He was a good man, that Mr. Richard. He never pushed anything. The guy was just friendly, ya know? He mentored us," one man chimes in. He seems to be the youngest in the crowd, with greasy brown hair and a goatee. "He'd share some helpful hints about money and stuff. But we all felt better while he was here, looked forward to the next time he'd come."

"Yeah, I was one of the first ones he approached. Our group started with about three guys, and now . . . well, you see." A bearded man with navy coveralls and the name *Mitch* stenciled on them says, waving his arm around the circle of seven men. Then he adds, "We usually have about twelve or thirteen. We sure hate he's gone. Wish we knew why anyone would kill him."

"Yeah," one man pipes in. Dressed in dark clothes and sweatshirt, he stands apart from the crowd. "I want to know who killed him too." His eyes are red-rimmed and shiny, alight with the liquid of fresh tears. The man appears angrier than the others.

"Wow." Greta is at a loss for more words, feeling uncomfortable. *What kind of person just starts weird friendships with random guys at loading docks? And then prays for them?*

"We felt seen, you know what I mean?" Ben says as if reading her mind. "Most people ignore guys like us. We're just worker bees. Richard saw us as real people."

"He was a wonderful man," Brian concludes. Everyone nods.

"Greta, it's nice to meet ya," Mitch says. "How long are ya in town?"

"Oh, not long," Greta says vaguely. She stares at the concrete ground and toes it with her shoe.

"Hey, guys, it was great to see you." Brian senses Greta's unease and calls the conversation to an end. "Let me know if you ever need anything. You all have my number, right?"

Heads nod. "Thanks, Brian," says the older gentleman who had first stood up. "Stop by anytime!"

"They call you Brian? Aren't you a high-priced attorney or something? And they call Richard by his first name too." Greta tries to whisper, but a few of the men standing closest to them hear her.

Brian answers for them all to hear. "When I first met him, Richard taught me about humility. He hated when people bowed to him, so he always asked people to use his first name. I guess I learned that from him. Though that guy over there doesn't always listen." Brian nods toward Antonio and everyone laughs, except Greta.

"It's true," says Mitch. "Richard remembered where he came from . . . how he used to be homeless himself."

Greta's eyes grow wide. *Richard told these guys he was homeless?* She can't imagine admitting that to anyone, especially when you're worth billions.

Ben chimes in: "Remember who you are. Remember why

you're here. Remember what your goals are. Remember where you came from. That's what he told me. I'll never forget it."

Greta shakes her head, a nerve now triggered, sending shockwaves through her whole body.

"I gotta go." Greta turns and nearly sprints back toward the Cadillac where Antonio is waiting with the door open. She feels conspicuous, exposed somehow. Her only thought is *Richard had friends at every level of society. How does someone do that?* With shame, she thinks, *And I don't have any friends.*

"What's wrong?" Brian asks when they are inside the car, concern etching his face.

"Nothing. I just don't understand why my great-uncle wanted me to traipse around this city, meeting all of these people. Couldn't we just meet everyone in one big conference room or something? Get it over with in one day?" As this idea envelopes her, she feels anger surging just beneath the surface. "*Can* we just do that instead?"

"I think Richard wanted you to walk in his shoes for a while, learn who he was and what was important to him—namely people. No matter who they are or what they do."

Out of nowhere, Greta screams. "I just want to stop! I want to go home!" The car is already moving or Greta would jump out and walk, though she doesn't know where. She feels trapped in the car, on this journey, and even by Richard's benevolence.

Tears erupt from her lower lids, and she blinks them away. Brian reaches for her hand, and she pulls it away. "Just take me to the place I'm sleeping. I'm done for today," she says through pursed lips. Her cheeks are flushed.

Brian isn't sure what's happening, so he gives Antonio the next address as he slides toward the opposite window to offer Greta some space.

Fifty minutes later, the Cadillac pulls up in front of a run-down brick-façade building. Greta misses the sign that says "Virginia Arms Apartments" because she's staring at her lap, lost in thought. She and Brian haven't spoken a word, even after Antonio had hopped out of the car for a few minutes and then returned and offered them both a to-go meal from a local Vietnamese restaurant. Greta had eaten hers in silence in the back of the SUV with the window down as Brian and Antonio chatted about some golf tournament called The Masters while sitting on a bench outside the car. She had noticed Brian looking at her every few minutes, likely assessing if she needed space or companionship. She was grateful he had chosen the former and left her to brood alone.

Now, Greta opens her own door for the second time on this journey and exits the car to look up at the apartment building. It is a four-story, two-tone brick monstrosity at least two football fields deep. On the right side, there is a black iron fence with ample parking space behind it, presumably for the residents. Greta notes the old window panes, off-white trim, and two blooming cherry trees out front. The place looks old and neglected yet holds promise for something better.

"I'm staying here, at this hole-in-the-wall?" she asks.

"Yes. There aren't any residents in it right now. You'll have the place to yourself. We chose a second-floor apartment for you, and the fridge is stocked with things for snacks tonight and various drinks, including coffee. Richard owns it and was working to renovate it. So there's still heat—or AC—if you need it tonight."

"I'll be totally alone?" Greta feels the familiar comfort of isolation sweep over her. It's what she's used to.

Brian nods. "Unless you want company? I can stay if you'd like. There are furnished apartments throughout." Brian hopes his offer isn't too much. But he can tell Greta is not doing well. He's not sure she should be alone.

Greta looks up at the building again and nods slowly, figuring having Brian there would be better since the place is so old. She's afraid some drug addict might try to enter.

"Okay. I'll have Antonio take me home to grab a few items, and I'll be back in an hour or two. Sound good? Do you need anything while I'm gone?"

"I don't think so."

"Actually, let's get you situated first." Brian reconsiders and leads the way, unlocking the front doors. The hallways and staircases are narrow and well-lit with 60W bulbs, but the old white-turned-gray paint on the walls is peeling. The place smells clean and airy, though. This surprises Greta.

They walk up one flight and head to the first door on the right. Brian unlocks it with a key and leads the way in as he turns on the lights with a flick of his hand. The place lights up.

Greta sucks in a gulp of air. Tan paint colors the walls—at least that's what she hopes, that it's not just age and dirt. The wood floors have seen better days, many places chipping. As she looks into the kitchen, just to the left of the entry, she sees an off-white 1970s refrigerator, much shorter than she, and other appliances that have seen better days.

As they move further inside, Greta notices the plastic accordion-style blinds are half-closed. She walks over and closes them completely. The sun is going down, and she doesn't want anyone spying on her. The idea causes her to shiver.

"The bedroom has a queen-sized bed, and the sheets are clean. I put some toiletries in the bathroom for you. Why don't you go see if I missed anything before I go, and I can grab it for you while I'm gone."

Greta discovers Brian has done well. She has everything she needs.

He hands her the key, and as he closes the door to the apartment, she waves goodbye.

"Don't be long," she whispers to the air. Then she remembers her plan to move through her great-uncle's list as quickly as possible—her plan *not to get involved* with Brian. Having him stay in the building tonight would spell trouble. *What are you doing?* she admonishes herself.

"Brian, wait!" she runs after him into the hallway. "I'm fine. You don't have to return," she breathes.

"Are you sure?" He looks disappointed.

"Yes, I'm sure. I'll see you in the morning. Is there a plan?"

"I'll be here around nine o'clock. I'll bring us some breakfast sandwiches. Okay?"

"Sounds good." Greta gives him a half-smile to convince him she's fine.

Brian looks at Greta longingly, like she's a dream fading from memory, then turns and heads down the stairs and out into the evening.

Okay, bye.

THE MURDERESS TUCKS her body deeper into the brush across from the Virginia Arms Apartments as traffic zips by and street lights pop on with the approaching sunset.

An hour later, the killer takes off a copper-colored wig and places it gently in her bag. She pulls out her long dark-haired wig and sets it on her head, adjusting it so that it rests perfectly on her skull. Using her fingers, she pulls the long bangs around her face. Once satisfied, she walks out of the women's restroom and into the waiting area of the Amtrak train station in Atlantic City, holding a round-trip ticket to Paoli, Pennsylvania, a mainline suburb of Philadelphia. She plans to be back early the next morning, but she has something to take care of in the keystone state that just can't wait.

17

The Second Wednesday

Greta stares at her watch, waiting for Brian to arrive. *8:50. Come on, Brian.* She's famished, her stomach rumbling beneath her Pink Floyd T-shirt. She didn't sleep last night and threw her clothes into the washing machine at six o'clock in the morning—an old contraption, which she had noticed the night before tucked behind the hallway's double closet doors. This time, Brian had thought of her clothes situation and left laundry detergent on top of the washing machine. Her T-shirt, still warm from the dryer, is her favorite. She wants to feel comforted right now.

Greta hears a knock and opens the door. The sight of Brian makes her heart flutter. He is dressed casually in jeans and a maroon crew-neck T-shirt. He's even wearing a baseball hat.

"No meetings today?" she asks.

"Good morning. Nope. I took the day off. Had a late night working and thought I'd take a break." He smiles and hands her a warm bag, the breakfast sandwiches he had promised.

As Greta and Brian sit at the kitchen table, she probes him for more information. "You mentioned you have a brother. Where is he?"

"He lives in central New York with his wife and kids. Though, I'm hoping they're moving back to New Jersey soon. We'll see."

"Is he older? Younger? Sorry, I can't remember if you've told me."

"Younger. I was the oldest of the three kids."

"That's right. Makes sense."

Brian's eyebrows arch with Greta's comment. "Why do you say that?"

"Your perfectionism and success. Classic first-born syndrome," Greta says with a wicked grin.

Brian's exaggerated frown mimics hurt. "My turn. Tell me about you. How's your book coming along?"

"Fairly well. I have less than four weeks left, but I'm nearly finished. The last scene is in my head. I just have to move it to the manuscript."

"Isn't that the hard part, though?" Brian asks, his smile soft.

Her answer is a playful smirk. She knew the ending long before she wrote the book.

"What do you do for fun?" Brian continues. He's enjoying the back-and-forth, happy to see some of Greta's walls have come down.

"Fun?"

"Yeah, you know, hobbies or whatever."

"I enjoy hiking. And paddle boarding—"

"Is that how you got the scar on your lip?" Brian teases. Greta reaches for her mouth and rubs her scar while tensing up. "I'm sorry. That was cruel. I should have just asked how you got it." Brian's face scrunches up, making his chin dimple appear deeper. "Maybe I shouldn't have said anything. It's not my business."

Greta smiles, but it's forced. "I got this when I was a kid. I fell off some playground equipment. Needed ten stitches."

Brian doesn't believe her, but he lets it go. "Yikes," Brian replies. "I didn't mean to interrupt. What else do you do for fun?"

"I collect art. Not much else," Greta answers while pulling melted cheese from her breakfast sandwich and sticking it in her mouth. Just like that, she is relaxed again. "This is so good. Thank you for bringing it." Greta doesn't even realize she's changing the subject from her to something else. It's become such a habit. "So tell me about this place. What's so important for me to know?"

"Ah, yes, the Virginia Arms Apartments." Brian leans back and wipes his mouth with a napkin. "When Richard started getting involved in commercial real estate and development, this was his second purchase. The original owner had died, and his children didn't want to worry about it, so it went on the market. When Richard first walked through it, he fell in love with it—loved the two-tone brick and the trees out front. It was in perfect shape. Over the last forty years, it's aged, and over time, Richard got so busy that he never realized the true condition of the inside or the foundation. It had cracked. Then, about two years ago, the city told him it was no longer safe for occupants."

Greta's eyebrows fly upward. "Wait, I just stayed here!"

"Oh, don't worry. Richard already fixed the foundation. He was going to renovate the inside next, but . . ." Brian's eyes look down. "Anyway, the structure is sound. It's just needing some updates on the inside and new windows. He wanted it to be modernized before he invited people back in, wanting to give it an industrial-loft feel to go with the brick—new appliances, sleek cabinets, flooring, tile, you name it. He just hadn't gotten around to it yet."

"I see." Greta looks at the old GE stove and laminate counters and flooring.

"I guess he wanted you to stay at an early place that first launched him into the industry he loved being a part of—one of his first 'babies,' if you will," Brian finishes.

"So what happens to this place is up to me?" Greta asks. Her voice sounds weak, timid.

"Yes, this is one of the many things you will have to decide about," Brian says. He hopes she isn't feeling too overwhelmed. There are still a lot of people, real estate, and holdings to visit.

In Pennsylvania, Detective Moody from the Paoli Police Department arrives at the scene a few minutes after 9:00 a.m. Earlier that morning, a nurse had discovered a patient at Paoli Memorial Hospital had been brutally murdered overnight. The patient was Roland Warren, a thirty-eight-year-old motorcycle enthusiast who had taken a turn too fast on his bike three days earlier. He had suffered multiple rib fractures and sustained a concussion but was making a quick recovery.

Until now.

Unfortunately, Roland had been doing so well that he had been removed from the heart monitor the day before, in anticipation of his upcoming discharge. Because of that, his death went undetected for hours.

The nurse had gone into his room to give him his 8:00 a.m. dose of oxymorphone when she found Roland's pillow stained with brownish-red blood. After a pulse check revealed no life and a code blue was initiated, she rolled him over, discovering rigor mortis and a puncture wound at the base of his skull.

Detective Moody stares at the deceased man. Shaking his head, he pulls out his phone and punches in a number. He recognizes the manner of death from an alert that came across the national wire weeks ago.

"Pauley. Call the FBI. They're gonna want to come over here."

Roland was the founder and CEO of GlimmerOptics, a new mega tech company that had just released Retiva, a way for familial matches to happen through scanning people's irises. Roland had recently been listed as the newest member of the Billionaires Under 50 Club.

His wife now inherits his billion.

18

"It's time to head to the next place on the list," Brian says to Greta. It's mid-afternoon. They've spent the day relaxing, enjoying an early lunch al fresco at a charming café and walking on the beach—generally engaging in a self-care kind of day. Greta needed it, and she's enjoyed Brian's company. They laughed at the same things, and she can't remember the last time she felt so free to be who she is. Probably not since she was a young child.

Despite the carefree day, there is still a gnawing feeling in her gut, begging her to hurry through the list. Though, for right now, she ignores it.

"Do we have to?" Greta says with more energy than Brian has heard in her voice since the day he met her in the Extra Egg Café.

"St. James Place awaits."

"So what's there? Where will I be staying?" Greta asks.

"Brunswick Billiards is the main point of attraction. It's owned by a family who graduated from The Hope Floor. It used to be a house-turned-hotel, but it was permanently closed a few years ago. The Rodriguez family bought it with the help of Richard, and they renovated the space. They live on the upper floors and run the pool hall and alcohol-free bar on the first floor and have a small restaurant on the second floor."

"Wow! That's incredible," Greta exclaims. "What about sleeping arrangements? Am I staying there?"

"There's a Best Western down the street." Brian shrugs his shoulders, and Greta playfully punches him in the arm.

"Real highfalutin," she says. Then the realization hits her: she willingly touched him first.

"No synthetic fibers at Paoli Hospital, either, Boss. And no camera caught her—or him—this time. This is so weird." Special Agent Mickey sits with the members of the criminal investigations unit around the same table as before at the FBI offices in Camden, New Jersey, having left the Philadelphia office yesterday. "And nothing ever goes missing, which is odd. No trophy-collecting."

"Let's move forward with what we've got then—a tall female, at least until we can confirm something different," barks the SAC.

Special Agent Kat Turner nods toward their boss in agreement.

Inside Brunswick Billiards Greta looks around. Six pool tables take up more than half of the downstairs space. The other side of the rectangular room hosts a long, lacquered bar top with fifteen barstools and a half dozen tall round-top tables for people to congregate with their drinks and chat. Mr. and Mrs. Rodriguez stand behind the bar while Greta and Brian sit in front of them, sipping on Arnold Palmers.

They arrived fifteen minutes ago, and Greta is in awe of the couple's kindness but also their business-savvy minds. Mrs. Rodriguez has just finished telling them about their business mentorship experience through The Hope Floor program and how Richard co-signed their lease for this building. Then, once the place was renovated to suit their needs, he sold his share to them in exchange for free lifetime drinks and billiards. It all happened in just fifteen months.

"Incredible," Brian says after hearing the story. He had only known parts of it before today.

"Richard was an angel. We went from living in our car to staying at The Hope Floor to living above our brand-new dream business, which has been doing really well the past six months." Mrs. Rodriguez is beaming, and Greta thinks she looks like a celebrity. She becomes distracted by trying to figure out which one. *Penélope something?*

Mr. Rodriguez finishes the story, his thick accent making everything seem interesting, and Greta snaps back to the conversation. "When we open in an hour, people will be lined up outside to get in. Though, we can't take much credit. We couldn't have done it without Richard and The Hope Floor staff. Oh, and the Community Chest also helped us with the gift of these pool tables." Mr. Rodriguez points to the blue felt-top tables, each with a wooden triangle filled with pool balls placed in the center, waiting for the next customers to claim the table for an hour.

Greta nods but doesn't say anything. She can't believe this family's luck. *Or is it more than that?* she wonders.

"Greta, the Community Chest was the forerunner of United Way, but there is still a small LLC that kept the name to bless people in the community with monetary or material gifts when needed," Brian explains.

"That's right. As a thank you, we give back ten percent of what we make each month to the Community Chest so they can help others," Mrs. Rodriguez adds. She smiles at her husband.

"That's great." Greta feels like it's the same story at each location. Someone fell into hard times or had a need. Richard was there to pick them up. *Just one more.* Dawn's voice invades her private thoughts, and she feels a strange sensation. Her stomach dives toward the floor, and she fights an invasive thought. *What's the word Dawn used that night in her office? . . . Oh yeah, conviction.*

The Rodriguez's teenage son, Manny, arrives out of nowhere with plates of food, including grilled pineapple, black bean empanadas, and authentic street tacos with shredded chicken. As the smell of cilantro and fresh onion hits Greta's nose, she realizes how hungry she is.

"Oh, goodness. Lunch was a long time ago! Thank you!" Brian says as if he is inside her brain. She looks at him and shakes her head.

"What?" he asks. She doesn't answer.

"Mr. Rodriguez, tell us about the bar. You only serve non-alcohol drinks . . . why is that?" Brian asks as he picks up a taco.

"Ah, yes. That was a non-negotiable with Mr. Richard. You see, part of my history and why my family was in such a tight spot all those years ago was because I was an alcoholic. I guess you don't say 'was.' I'm a recovering alcoholic now. Both my parents too. As part of the deal with Richard, we couldn't open a regular bar. He didn't want me to fall into the temptations that would come with that type of business. But I didn't mind. I don't want to fall off the wagon either. I don't want to lose all this," he says as he sweeps his hand across the room and then moves to hug his wife. "I don't want to lose my family. And the community seems to love it. There's no pressure, no bar fights, no sobriety checks or worries of DUIs. But there's still loads of fun." Mr. Rodriguez grins.

"That's amazing and such a noble choice," Brian says. Greta is grateful that Brian is so relatable with others—able to talk while she can sit and listen. Ideas are rolling around in her head. She doesn't like them. An internal battle that started after her visit with Dawn and grew after visiting The Hope Floor is now a full-blown, raging war inside her.

After their early dinner, Greta and Brian say farewell to the Rodriguez family and thank them for their kindness.

As they walk out through the double doors to the covered

front porch, sure enough, there is a line of people waiting to enter Brunswick Billiards, even though all the drinks are non-alcoholic. *It's nearly five o'clock. Time to belly up for those BrewDogs and mocktails.* Greta laughs to herself in relief. It seems her normal, cynical self has won today's battle.

Once outside and away from the line of people filing into the pool hall, Greta and Brian stand on the sidewalk looking for Antonio and the Cadillac. "That's odd," says Brian. Just then, his cell phone buzzes in his pocket. He retrieves it, seeing "unknown caller" on the screen. He looks at Greta. She shrugs, and he taps the answer button.

"Hello, this is Brian Gogh."

Greta watches Brian's face move from curious to horrified. Her heart rate skyrockets. Fear envelops her as she considers the possibilities.

"We'll be right there," Brian says. He ends the call and quickly starts maneuvering through the apps on his phone. Greta sees him open the Uber app.

"What's going on? Where's Antonio?"

"He's been in an accident, over on Tennessee Avenue. They're taking him to the hospital. I'm getting a car to take us there," Brian says quickly. Then he pauses and looks up at her. "Unless you don't want to go." He cocks his head. "You can head toward the Best Western. It's a block that way." His head bounces the other direction to indicate a location over his right shoulder. "If you check-in and wait, I can call you when I know more. It's up to you." Brian looks back down to finish ordering an Uber to the hospital.

And Greta's heart enters a crossroads.

THAT EVENING, Greta is sitting in her hotel room at the Best Western, thinking about the day. It was unlike any day she's ever experienced before. "Self-care," Brian had called it. *The ludicrous-*

ness. What was stranger was the connection she had felt with another human—Brian again—and those alien thoughts and feelings flowing through her while at Brunswick Billiards. Then, the difficulty she had choosing whether to go to the hospital with Brian. Never would she have imagined considering entering a hospital voluntarily. The whole day has left her reeling.

She sips on a root beer and tosses another salted peanut in her mouth from the tiny package, both products courtesy of the hotel lobby vending machine. Part of her wants to run. To grab her duffle, order up a car to the bus station, and make her way home to North Carolina. She misses her routines and the solitude of her life. Certainly, Brian could maneuver the legal gymnastics required to exit this ridiculous plan since she has made it through half the locations on Richard's list. *What would Richard care? He's dead,* she justifies. She's ready to be back in her house, in the comfort and seclusion of her private space. Part of her is ready to sell everything her great-uncle owned, pocket the money—just like she had first planned—and disappear.

Then there's this other part of her. A new and surprising part, one that has been playing tug-of-war with her mind and heart. She can't stop thinking about her journey over this past week. The Hope Floor. The fire station. Dawn. Even Ms. Moore. Everyone has been kind to her. Last night, she had dreamed about donating some of Great-Uncle Richard's money back to the community college.

Absurd! Greta shakes her head. She owes no one. But her heart won't follow her head's advice, and it's scaring her. *No, it's making me angry!* Her phone rings and she jumps. She sees Brian's name across the screen.

"Hello," she answers abruptly.

"Hey. It's Brian. I'm going to be here awhile. Antonio is okay, but he has a concussion. They will probably release him in the morning, but they are running more tests right now, so I'm going to wait with his wife. You okay?"

"I'm fine." Greta's mood is sour.

"You sure?" Brian detects it too.

"Yup. I'm just going to do some writing," Greta says to pacify his concern and avoid any confrontation.

"Okay. I'll call you in the morning," Brian says.

Greta hangs up after a quick, "Okay, bye." As soon as she disconnects, she realizes she didn't wish Antonio a speedy recovery. *Oh well.*

As she watches Brian leave the hospital, she grins. The moonlight bounces off of the top of her bald head. The murderess wraps herself in her long gray sweater and, wearing pajama pants underneath, walks through the sliding doors of the hospital lobby. Her feet are dressed in the all-white sneakers she purchased at the Target store in Mays Landing hours earlier. As she passes the reception desk, vacant now that it's after hours, she slows her pace to a loping shuffle. With no make-up, she appears feeble. The third-shift hospital staff who pass her assume she is roaming the halls as a patient of the oncology unit, and they nod or smile in polite greetings. She reciprocates.

The killer steps into an elevator and presses the button for the third floor. When the elevator doors reopen a few seconds later, the woman steps onto a medical floor and limps toward Room 328. Once she reaches the doorway, she stops. There, asleep in the bed, sporting a few extra scrapes on his face, is Antonio Rossi. She steps into the room and closes the door behind her.

"I'm sorry, Antonio," she whispers.

19

The Second Thursday

Greta was awake until the wee hours of the morning, finishing her novel. Her publisher, located not terribly far from where she is in New Jersey—on New York Avenue in Brooklyn—can now stop breathing down her neck. The only thing left for her to do is read through it and make any last-minute self-edits before the publisher's editors take it and put their red ink all over it. She hates that part but realizes it's part of the publishing journey. Plus, her goal is to make the prestigious best-seller lists: *New York Times, Wall Street Journal*, and others. So if it takes editors changing things to make it better, she'll play nice.

Greta steps out of the shower and after toweling off, blow-dries her hair in the bathroom. She hears her phone chime from its position on the charger in the other room, signaling a text message. She flips off the hair dryer and investigates. It's from Brian.

I'll be there in an hour. Antonio doing great and is home. Driving us in my personal car until he's healed and Cadillac fixed.

Greta texts back.

hope you're a good driver

After she hits send, she realizes that may have been a poorly timed joke, given Antonio's situation and injuries. *Oh well, again.* Her whole life has been a series of social missteps. *What's one more?*

Greta finishes drying her hair, all the while hoping Brian has breakfast in mind because she's famished. Her stomach has been stretched during this AC fiasco, and she knows she'll have a hard time paring down her portions once she's home.

An hour later, there is a knock on her hotel door. Greta opens it to find Brian holding multi-colored flowers—a bouquet of gerberas.

"What in the world?" she says. "Are those for Antonio?"

"No, they're for you," Brian says. A blush creeps into his cheeks. She kinda loves it.

"What for?"

"I'm sorry I bailed on you yesterday. I hope you'll forgive me."

"I understood." Greta waves him inside and takes the flowers, which she realizes are already in a tiny green vase. *That was thoughtful.*

"Did you bring breakfast too?" she asks. Brian knows Greta well enough to let her apparently self-absorbed and seemingly ungrateful question slide.

"No, but I'm taking you out for breakfast, so are you ready?" He looks around the room.

"Yup." Greta grabs her duffle and sling and slides her feet into her blue running shoes, still her footwear of choice for the never-ending Atlantic City tour. "Ready. By the way, how is Antonio?"

"Doing better. Mild concussion and some cuts and bruises, but he'll be free to return to work next week, about the same time the Cadillac is repaired." Greta nods. "I parked in the only free parking garage in Atlantic City. It's down the street, so we'll walk to the restaurant and then return to the garage later today if that's okay with you?" After a pause, Brian looks at Greta's hand and adds, "I guess I didn't think through the flowers. I can carry them."

"Aren't you a millionaire or something? With the job you have? What's up with needing free parking?" Greta asks as she hands him the vase.

"Well, if you're not wise with the money you have, you won't keep it," Brian says matter-of-factly.

The two leave the hotel room, leaving the keycards on the dresser.

"Let me take that duffle bag for you too," Brian offers as they cross the street. Greta tightens her grip.

"No, thanks," she replies.

Logan's Café and Deli sits caddy-corner to the Best Western. When Greta sees the awning, she feels grateful it's so close. Her stomach is rumbling, and she's craving an extra-strong black coffee after her late night of writing.

"I finished my book," she says to Brian as they approach the breakfast and lunch-only restaurant.

"That's great! Did you turn it in yet?"

"No, I'm going to take one more pass with it to make sure it's everything I want and doesn't have holes in the plot or anything stupid."

Brian opens the door to the deli, and they enter. The low murmur of the patrons mixes with the sound of silverware and dishes moving around in the back kitchen. It reminds Greta of the first time she met Brian at the Extra Egg Café. There is a sign that says "Seat Yourself" at the host's stand, so the two make their way to a black upholstered booth in the corner of the restaurant.

As soon as they sit, a server appears.

"Drinks?" she asks abruptly. Her blonde ponytail sits high on her head, and she looks to be in her late teens or early twenties. A name tag on her white shirt reads "Olive."

"Black coffee and a water," says Greta.

"Same for me," Brian follows.

Olive turns and scurries off without a word. "Sorry," says Brian. "I've never been here, but the reviews say the service is excellent." He shakes his head, unrolls his silverware, and puts his napkin on his lap.

The two offer each other small talk and wait for their coffee to arrive. Greta notices that Brian, usually chipper, is mellow.

"Something wrong?" she asks him.

"Just tired, what with Antonio and everything. And I have to meet with the mayor after breakfast. A work thing. I don't suppose you want to come with me? It's at City Hall, just three blocks away."

Greta nods at Brian's navy suit and striped tie. "That explains that," she says and then shrugs her shoulders to answer his question. "Why not?" she says as an afterthought. In truth, she had gotten lonely after Brian had raced off to the hospital and she was left to check herself into the Best Western.

"Great!" Brian says, relieved that she accepted. "I'll make it up to you. How about dinner tonight?"

"Is this a date kind of dinner?" Greta asks before she can process her words. If she had, she would have held them in. Her upper chest and neck burn as the scarlet color appears.

"I'd love for it to be . . . but only if you want it to be." Brian eyes her, fully expecting her to jump up and run out of the restaurant.

They stare at each other for a long while. Olive approaches the table and places two mugs of coffee, two glasses of ice water, and a basket of jellies down. "Ready to order?"

Brian shakes his head no.

"Just holler when you are," she says as she turns away.

Greta and Brian don't break eye contact. It's as if a staring contest between two children has ensued, neither willing to look away first.

Finally, Greta clears her throat and looks down at her coffee. "Sure, we can talk about us and what the heck we're doing on this *date* tonight." She emphasizes the word *date* as if she wants to spit, but Brian is too thrilled to notice.

"Perfect! I'll make reservations at Landry and Sons Steakhouse."

Greta picks up her mug and sips the steaming caffeine. Her nerves settle almost immediately as the caffeinated liquid courses toward her bloodstream.

As they leave the restaurant with full stomachs, Precious appears in front of them, stopping them on the sidewalk.

"Ms. Greta. I think I have a clue about who killed poor Mr. Richard."

Brian and Greta stare at the woman. Brian speaks first. "What do you mean? Who?"

"Well, I guess I don't know *who*, but I don't think Mr. Richard was the only one. I think maybe he was one of those that the "Millionaire Club Killer" got to. Did you see that on the news?"

Greta tries not to laugh, clearing her throat with a snort and a fake cough. Brian gives Greta a sideways glance, reminding her without words that the police told them to keep quiet. He answers the older woman. "Yes, Ms. Precious. That makes sense."

"Well, I just wanted you to know. I just want who done it to be caught, you know?" Precious's pupils are wide behind her lenses.

"Thank you. Us too."

The three bid their goodbyes. Greta thinks this likely won't be the last time she encounters Precious. *I kinda like her.*

After walking two more blocks in the beautiful sunshine—a

cloudless day that has Greta's spirits rising—they arrive at City Hall on Tennessee Avenue, *the same road where Antonio had his accident*. She says nothing.

They get in line to pass through security. The guard charged with viewing the x-ray machine stares at Greta seductively as she and Brian wait. Greta is ahead of Brian, and when they reach the front of the line, she pushes her two bags onto the belt that will take them through the machine. Then she winks at the guard while Brian isn't looking. The guard sucks in some air and smiles back, his eyes narrowing and remaining transfixed on Greta, thus allowing her bags to slide through without so much as a glance, even when the red light above the machine blinks a warning. Greta shakes her head, both nauseated and entertained by how easy it is to distract some men.

Brian leads her to the second floor via the grand staircase in the center of the building. He approaches double wooden doors marked with a gold sign that reads, "Office of the Mayor." As always, Brian opens the door and lets Greta enter first, though she isn't sure why. She isn't the one here to meet with the mayor.

The waiting area they've entered is luxurious and modern, almost as if they've entered the lobby of a corporation rather than a government building. There is a curly-haired woman in her early thirties sitting behind a desk in front of them. *The gatekeeper,* Greta muses.

"Hi, Ms. Leah. I'm here for my appointment with Mayor Sampson," Brian says.

"Hi, Mr. Gogh. Good to see you again. I'll tell the mayor you're here," the woman says with a broad smile.

"Remember, Leah, it's Brian," he replies, kindness oozing.

Greta decides Brian must know everyone in the whole doggone city. She moves toward a caramel-colored leather side chair and sits, trying to make herself as inconspicuous as possible. She pulls a *People* magazine—something she stole from the Best Western's lobby last night—out of her sling and begins reading.

Brian places the vase of flowers next to her, and her attempt to disappear vanishes.

A booming voice causes Greta to look up.

"Bri. An. Gogh!" a large man enunciates as he comes through a side door into the waiting area. "Good to see you!" He slaps Brian on the back and shakes his hand.

"You, too, Mayor. Hey, I'd like to introduce you to someone special," Brian says. Greta's heart sinks. She looks up.

"This is Greta Goldman, Richard's great-niece," Brian says while waving toward her. Greta stands and puts her hand out to the six-foot-three man with dark hair and dark eyes who could be an offensive lineman for a pro football team rather than the leader of a gambling city. *Maybe those careers are not entirely different.*

"What! Related to Richard? I didn't know he had any relatives aside from his brother Bill and Ms. Edith Moore." Mayor Sampson lifts Greta's hand and shakes it. She slaps a closed smile on her face. "We're all going to miss him," the mayor adds.

"You ready, Mayor?" Brian says to rescue Greta from the mayor's attention.

"Yes, yes, of course. Right this way. Nice to meet you, Ms. Greta!"

The two walk through the same door the mayor had entered, and Greta sits back down with a sigh.

"*Men . . .*"

Greta looks up at the lady named Ms. Leah sitting at the desk.

"He means no harm. He's just loud," Leah continues. "Of course, I don't mean Mr. Gogh—I mean, Brian," Leah says. "He's always a gentleman." Leah gets a faraway look on her face, and Greta peers at her, her mouth opening as she understands what that look means. Her chest tightens.

"Yes, absolutely. Brian and I are going out to dinner tonight, a date," Greta says, her voice laced with a competitive edge that surprises her. *Why did I just tell her that? Stupid impulsivity!*

"Oh, wow. Nice," Leah says as she nods her approval. Though

she looks disappointed. "He's one of Atlantic City's most eligible bachelors. Maybe not any longer?" Leah is hunting for more information—information Greta fails to provide. Instead, Greta re-opens her magazine.

She tries to read but keeps glancing at Leah and having trouble concentrating, confused by her immature reaction to the young woman. She isn't dating Brian. She doesn't even know what they're doing. *I'm leaving town as soon as I'm done with this stupid list.* Her knee bounces.

An hour later, Brian walks back into the waiting area.

"Thanks for waiting, Greta," he says as he nears her chair. She stands up and hears Leah clear her throat.

"Nice to see you again, Mr. Gogh—Brian!—and nice to meet you, Greta," Leah coos.

"You, too, Leah. Until next time!" Brian turns to open the door for Greta.

Leah winks at Greta, who looks down at her feet in embarrassment and walks through the door, leaving the vase of flowers behind.

"So what was your meeting about?" Greta asks Brian as they walk toward the parking garage.

"The mayor has been trying to recruit me for years to work for him. I've turned him down countless times—I just don't want to be part of any political sway—but he seems to think repetition will win me over."

"Ah. I see."

"Um, Greta?" Brian looks uncomfortable, a frown forming across his face. "I received a message while in with the mayor. It seems the Cadillac's brakes failed. . . . And it wasn't an accident."

Greta stops walking. Brian also stops, faces her, and brings his hands to her shoulders to comfort her.

"It could have just been a coincidence—that it's *our* car. The police are investigating. They see no connection. The MO is different. Everything is different. They say there's been a slew of these over the last few years—kids tampering with breaks. Some sort of gang initiation."

A pause. "What do you think?"

"I don't know what to think." The two start walking again.

They enter the garage, and Brian pushes the button for the elevator. His angel wing bracelet jangles, and Greta's heart flutters. *Is this nerves or what?*

"My car is on the third level."

The elevator doors open on Level Three, and Brian approaches a line of four cars parked to their left. Greta trails behind.

"Where are we going next? My list says Kentucky Avenue. What's there?"

"Brown Park. You'll see in just a few minutes . . . Here we are." Brian steps up to a two-tone—black and silver—new-model Mercedes Maybach, and the doors automatically unlock.

"This is yours? It must be worth nearly two hundred thousand dollars!" Greta clenches her fists. She cannot believe she is falling for one of the wealthiest men in Atlantic City. She despises how rich people live. *He is so entitled! Look at this car!* "You're taking me all around this city in a fancy *Cadillac*, carrying your expensive bag, wearing your name-brand clothes, showing me how I should spend my great-uncle's money, trying to get me to help everyone I meet, and you drive *this* on the side? What have *you* done for the city, Brian?"

Greta backs up. Her cheeks are flushed, her face now twisted in rage. The stress of the entire trip to New Jersey erupts in one blow.

"Greta." Brian puts his hand up, trying to convince her to pause, to take a breath.

"And you're worried about *free* parking? You make no sense!" Greta turns on her heels and races back to the bank of elevators. When she's about to hit the down button, she spies a set of stairs to her left and course-corrects, racing down the steps as fast as she can, grateful she's wearing her running shoes. Her duffle bounces against her back. She can barely hear Brian running after her, calling her name.

"Greta! Wait! I can explain!"

But she's gone.

Part Three

Truth

20

Second Friday

Brian stares at the clock. He had spent the previous evening searching for Greta, checking the bus station, train station, and hotels where she had already stayed, including those closest to the parking garage. He checked the nearby bars, too, and called her countless times but without success. He stayed up late, sipping on whiskey, wondering how he had developed such intense feelings for someone like Greta—not only someone who doesn't live in Atlantic City but an individual who is as quirky as they come. She's attractive; everyone can see that. She's also frustrating and lacks some of the social etiquettes he's forever assumed he needs in a partner. One thing he knows for sure: He has to find her and explain—*everything*.

As Brian sips on the coffee meant to quell his slight hangover, an idea pops into his head.

He wonders if she'll continue trekking through Richard's list so she can go home with no further obligations or ties to Atlantic City . . . or him. He pulls out his copy of the list, then dresses in a pair of jeans and a T-shirt, calls his assistant to reschedule all of his appointments for the day, and races toward Kentucky Avenue.

GRETA ROLLS over and checks the time: 8:12 a.m. She sighs and slides out of the king-sized bed, throws on a pair of jeans and a shirt, and pulls her hair into a ponytail. After washing and moisturizing her face and brushing her teeth, she grabs her things and leaves the Madison Hotel where she had crashed for the night. Unknowingly, it was a hotel Brian had considered visiting the night before, but didn't, opting instead to head home after a lengthy search for her.

Greta had ignored Brian's calls all evening. She is still too angry to think about him but can't help it. "What a hypocrite," she says out loud as she checks the map on her phone. Brown Park is straight up Dr. Martin Luther King Jr. Boulevard from where she is standing. Her goal is to finish the list today by visiting each street, capturing a photo of something there, and sending them all to Brian with a nasty email that includes wiring information for deposits. She assumes electronic signatures will do the trick.

Then Greta plans to hop on the first bus to North Carolina tomorrow. She vows not to live like the wealthy but to sit on Great-Uncle Richard's money, living a comfortable life but not being showy about it. She wants his billions so others can't get to it. Her reasoning runs flawed, aided by her twisting emotions. She's always wanted to be financially secure—from the time she was a little girl. Perhaps some of her motivation is envy. But most of all, she tells herself, she wants the billions so others who already have enough in their bank accounts *can't* have it to flounder on lavish materialism or buy their way out of things. *Like Brian.*

She takes off for the park, walking faster than normal, her long legs flexing. But the humid air causes her to break a sweat, so she slows, not wanting to be forced to find another place to shower before heading home. The hazy sun spreads warmth across her face, and she pulls her sunglasses from her sling.

When she arrives at Brown Park, it's as if the world has transformed. Greta feels the change as she walks deeper into the park, witnessing the kaleidoscope of color around her shift from grays to greens, pinks, and whites. Gone are the cracked, concrete sidewalks, the trash on the street, and the lack of nature. The park hosts acres of lush grass, blooming cherry trees, vibrant flower beds, and mothers with toddlers sliding and crawling on playground equipment that appears to be in tip-top shape. An open bench several steps north of the playground calls her name. Greta sits to cool off and think.

Meanwhile, Brian has entered the park. He spies Greta on the bench sipping on bottled water, and his heart leaps as he lets out the breath he had been holding all morning. Now, he has to figure out what to say to her. He doesn't want to spook her for a second time and risk never seeing her again.

He treads softly. When he's within earshot range, he says a quick prayer and begins. "The car was a bribe from my parents."

Greta jumps. Her duffle bag falls to the ground. Brian closes the gap, picks it up, and places it on the bench beside her.

"What are you doing here?" she asks, her eyes narrowing.

"Can I sit?" he asks. "I want to explain something. I think, I hope, you'll want to hear it."

Greta turns away, blowing air through her nose. "Fine," she manages. "How'd you find me? . . . Never mind. *The list*."

"Thanks and yes." Brian moves the teal-colored bag and sits, placing it on his lap.

Greta snatches her bag from Brian and glares at him as she drops it on the bench on the other side of her. "What could you possibly have to say to me? What do you mean it was *a bribe*?" There's a bite to her words.

Brian takes a deep breath, not entirely convinced he wants to lay bare his family baggage to Greta, a client for lack of a better word right now. He decides it's worth it. "Growing up, my parents were never home. Their work and travel schedules left us, my brother and sister and me, being raised, for all intents and purposes, by our nanny."

"Intents and purposes? Is that lawyer speak?" Brian blinks in confusion, and Greta chews on her lower lip. Then, she whispers, "Go on."

"Even after I grew up, left for college—then law school after that—and started my career, they were absent for much of my life. They even missed my graduation ceremonies. This is why, after my uncle's death, Richard kinda became my grandfather-figure. He understood the pain of family abandonment. He knew what I was going through on some level.

"Three years ago, my brother and his family had a big falling out with my parents and moved away. Having already lost their daughter forever and then a son when he wrote them out of his life, my parents, well . . ." Brian takes a deep breath. "Last Christmas, they bought me this car. And, yes, I know it's extravagant. That's how they operate. They think they can buy people." Greta's body stiffens. Brian looks down at his lap where his hands are clasped and rubs his bracelet. "It was a bribe to keep up our relationship, even though they don't understand there isn't a *relationship* to keep up." Brian's fingers curl into air quotes as he says the word *relationship*. "A car won't salvage our dysfunctional family. I didn't want to cause more strife, so I kep—"

"*Of course* you did," Greta interrupts. Her anger flares, triggered by childhood hurts buried deep in her soul. She knows what it's like to be on the receiving end of those who believe they can buy themselves out of poor behavior. It's one reason she detests those who are wealthy.

"Can I finish?" Brian is now impatient.

Rather than apologizing, Greta nods her permission for him to continue.

"Richard suggested I take the Maybach and serve the community with it. During the week, while Antonio and I use the Cadillac, I loan it to people who either need transportation—like people who are going on job interviews, including those from The Hope Floor who need something to drive to get there—or who would enjoy a day or two with a nice car . . . for fancy events, like weddings or proms. Even funerals." Greta finally looks at

Brian. "I charge a nominal fee, enough to provide people with motivation to respect the car and avoid having them think they need charity." After a pause, Brian adds, "I barely use the car. I hate it, actually. You're right; it is a pompous piece of metal."

Greta looks toward the ground. "I see," she says. "And the Cadillac?"

"Well, that's mine too." A shrug. "I have money, Greta. I've earned most of it. Sounds like too easy of an explanation, but I give back where I can. My parents may have been MIA, but they taught me certain values. Richard too. He was an enormous influence on me."

Greta contemplates Brian's story. *What a goody-two-cars. And I'd like to punch his parents.* But part of her can't help but be impressed—though she thinks a little too much of Great-Uncle Richard has rubbed off on him.

After a minute of silence, in which Brian runs various scenarios through his head, Greta speaks again. "I guess I overreacted . . ."

"Well, I wish you would've let me tell you this yesterday." He smiles and hopes his attempt to lighten the air doesn't fall flat. This time, it doesn't.

"Yeah, you know how I can get. I just hate how rich people live." Greta and Brian look at each other and chuckle at the irony of Greta's statement.

"I'm sorry. But you know that you're about to be crazy-wealthy yourself, right?"

"Yeah. I know." Greta doesn't elaborate.

"So how come? Why the disdain?"

It's Greta's turn to shrug. "It's not important. I've always been leery of rich people. So what do we do now?" she asks while standing up to stretch her long legs.

Brian thinks for a moment. "I tell you about Brown Park while we walk around and enjoy the rest of the morning. Then tonight, you take a chance and have dinner with me during our rescheduled date at Landry and Sons." Brian's eyebrows go up in anticipation of Greta's reaction. He prays he didn't move too fast with that last line. She scares easily.

"Fine," Greta answers.

"Okay!" Brian stands up next to her and begins his tour. "Brown Park used to be just that: brown. No grass. It was a concrete playground, having no beauty whatsoever. As part of Richard's revitalization efforts, he paid to renovate the park. Now, it's a place where, as you can see," Brian says as he nods toward the playground, "parents and kids spend a lot of time. Richard pays for the landscaping service that comes a couple of times a week, and they have community Tai Chi and yoga classes in the spring and summer. Since his death, I've taken over scheduling the landscaping and payments, but that will be part of what you must decide." Brian abruptly stops. "I'm sorry. We don't need to talk about that now."

"It looks fabulous," Greta says as she does a 180-degree scan of her surroundings, noting the beautiful flower gardens once again and ignoring the responsibility Brian just placed on her.

"This was part of what prompted the city to honor him with Richard M. Goldman Day in May. On the Saturday closest to May Fifth each year, the city hosts a special farmer's market in the park, and food and health service vendors come and set up their spaces. There's even free face painting for kids."

"Yet another happy ending, care of Richard M. Goldman," Greta says, but this time, there is far less sarcasm in her comment than what Brian has detected in the past nine days.

21

Brian drives Greta to his home, an understated Tudor-style house just outside the Atlantic City limits. When Brian had offered his home as a place of respite for the afternoon—and a place to get ready for their date—Greta had balked, wondering if his house would betray his opulent wealth as much as his cars do. When they pull up, she is pleasantly surprised.

"Brian, this is beautiful," exclaims Greta. The 2,600-square-foot home is not too large, though the lawn is perfectly manicured, with modern stones and straight lines. "You like modern too!"

"Yes, I wasn't sure if Tudor-meets-modern would work, but I like it."

The white exterior is highlighted with gray Tudor finishes and accents, including a humongous gray-trimmed bay window centered on the second floor. Three sharply pitched gables make the house seem tall, and there is a white brick chimney on the right-hand side. An inviting cherry wood front door greets them.

Brian pushes a button on a remote strapped to the visor above the driver's seat, and the garage door lifts open. Brian pulls the car in, and Greta notes the organized shelves and clean garage floor.

"Do you clean your own garage and house, or do you hire

someone to do it?" She wishes she didn't ask. His answer might set her off again.

"Honestly, the garage is my space, and I clean it. I'm a bit obsessive that way. The house, though? Sorry to say I hire someone. With my work schedule, I just can't—or don't—find the time." Brian turns off the car and looks at Greta, waiting for a snide comment. None comes.

When they enter the house through the garage, Greta stands in a mudroom with laundry facilities, coat hooks, and a closet for more coats and shoes. However, what strikes her first is the smell. *Brian's cologne.* The fir balsam and coriander smell is stronger in his house than in his car. Her shoulders immediately drop into a relaxed position. She looks at Brian and smiles.

"I'll make us some lunch if you're hungry."

"You cook too?" Greta teases.

"My nanny taught me," Brian answers sheepishly. Greta snorts.

The two make their way to a beautiful kitchen, designed to impress, with an industrial-sized stove and other sleek appliances. The white glass backsplash gives Greta a sense of cleanliness, something she values.

"How long have you lived here?" she asks as Brian opens the refrigerator.

"Three years." He pulls out some store-bought chicken salad and sunflower seed bread. "Do you want to check the pantry for chips or something?" he directs Greta, giving her something to do other than assess his space. He knows she's trying to balance her disdain for the expense with the beauty of the modern touches. He smiles to himself.

Once their lunch is prepared, they sit in the breakfast nook that overlooks the backyard, with its spring flowers in full bloom. Greta spies a hummingbird whiz by the window.

"I love those things," she says of the winged rocket.

"So what do you think of all the places you've been and all the people you've met so far?"

"Well, that's a lot to talk about. I will say this: Ms. Leah at the mayor's office has a little bit of a crush on you." Greta laughs when Brian's face belies his surprise. "She says you're the most eligible bachelor in town." Greta is relishing the awkwardness the conversation creates for Brian. *For once, someone else feels out of place*, she thinks.

"Interesting." He shakes his head as if the movement will brush off the direction the discussion has taken. He tries to assist with a change in topic.

"Tell me more about you. What's it like in North Carolina?"

Greta shares about her life as an author and how she enjoys North Carolina, how the four seasons are fairly equal, and how living between the mountains and the beach is ideal.

An hour flies by as the two sit and chat, neither wanting the moment to end. But soon, Greta's rear end feels tingly, much like it did on the bus ride to the AC. Brian notices her shifting around in her seat.

"Want to go for a walk?" he offers. "It's a beautiful day."

"Sure."

Already in her running shoes, she waits for Brian to change clothes, and they step outside through the front door, both grinning and feeling the most comfortable they've ever felt with someone of the opposite gender.

BRIAN AND GRETA make their way to the steakhouse, care of the Maybach.

Once seated and after the order their drinks, Brian leans back. He's wary of her response, but he's dying to know about her family.

"It must have been hard to lose your parents so young. I'm so sorry that happened to you," he begins, and genuine compassion laces his face. Greta looks at the table and prepares her answer in her head. She wants to make sure it's right . . . for the moment and the person across from her.

"Yeah, thanks. It was hard. I'm just grateful I was almost finished with college. I was nearly a grown-up . . . already independent, you know?" She takes a sip of her red wine, just delivered by their tactful server.

"I just can't imagine. And no brothers or sisters . . ."

"Nope. Just me." She laughs. "Probably better that way!"

Brian joins her with a chuckle of his own. He studies her. She had curled her black hair at his house when she'd gone to the powder room to get ready for the date. It's now hanging down in neat rolls, making her look heaven sent. Her scar is barely discernable under her red lipstick. A new color that has him feeling crazy things inside.

"What were your parents like?" he probes further and reaches for her hand. She doesn't move it, but caution drapes her eyes. Before Greta can answer, their server is back to take their dinner order.

After the server leaves their table, Greta asks Brian about his work, and the topic of her parents falls by the wayside. He tells her about a new client and she listens without interrupting once, which he finds remarkable, given her propensity to do so.

The rest of the evening is an easy back and forth, made smoother by a couple more glasses of wine between the two of them. It's a night filled with building closeness through conversation about everything from future dreams and favorite flavors of ice cream to first concerts and holiday traditions.

Greta grows sad, realizing this burgeoning relationship will soon end. Eventually, she'll complete the list and head back home.

"Are you definitely returning to North Carolina?" Brian asks toward the end of the evening.

I swear it's as if he can read my mind!

"Why wouldn't I?" she asks abruptly, feeling forced to play defense.

"I don't know. Have you ever thought of living somewhere

else? You're going to be quite wealthy soon, no matter what you decide to do with Richard's projects and real estate holdings. And you write for a living. Couldn't you write from anywhere?"

Greta almost misses the point—that this is Brian's way of telling her he'd like her to consider him and their new relationship.

"Hmmm," she says, thinking about her cozy home in North Carolina. Then she rests her eyes on Brian's dimple. "Maybe."

In the next beat, her face turns serious. She doesn't play games. "Brian, I like you—I admit it. This has been fun. I just don't know what to think. I don't want to move too fast, and moving here would be a fast decision. I'm not a person who does well in relationships. They never work."

Brian nods. "I'm just thinking out loud." He reaches toward her face and brushes a hair from her cheek. "I like you too," he says with a grin.

Then, the tender moment is over as quickly as it started. Greta looks at her watch, and it's back to business when she says, "Where's the next stop? Don't you have to drop me off soon?"

"Oh, okay. Yes," Brian replies. Greta is unaware of the hurt her rejection just caused, doesn't realize Brian was half-expecting—hoping even—she might want to stay at his house tonight.

"We're up to Indiana Avenue, right?" The evening has Greta almost forgetting about her main purpose in the AC. *The stupid list.*

"Yeah. A bookstore," he laughs lightly, "that's also a family home—with kids." He blinks at her playfully. Greta kicks him under the table.

"Then you owe me dessert."

AFTER THEY LEAVE THE RESTAURANT, stomachs full, Brian drives Greta to 1230 Indiana Avenue in the inky darkness. It's just before nine o'clock. On the residential street sits a small ranch-style home with gray siding and red brick. A ramp leads into a door positioned on the left side of the home. Brian tells her it's owned by Allison and Scott O'Leary, who, as Brian promised, are the proud parents of three young and rambunctious children.

Greta spies a tricycle in the driveway and inwardly groans. Brian parks on the street and turns the car off. But he makes no move to leave the Maybach and open her door for her. Greta turns to face him, heart pounding. She inhales his intoxicating scent and closes her eyes, willing herself not to talk or move.

"Tomorrow, when I pick you up, I'm going to take you to the Ocean Casino Resort to stay for two nights. Consider it some good old-fashioned R&R. I have some work things and life things I have to handle."

"Oh, Brian. I don't want to slow down my progress," Greta complains.

"I know. I know. I could send you to the next street alone. But Antonio and the Cadillac won't be back until Monday. You could use Uber—"

"No," Greta interrupts. "I'll wait for you . . . *and Antonio,*" she says with emphasis.

"I had a great time tonight," Brian tells her. Without preamble, he leans over and kisses Greta. His lips are warm on hers, his clean-shaven face smooth. Greta doesn't back up. She doesn't lean in. She accepts the intimate moment right where she sits and enjoys the idea that someone actually likes her. It's never happened before. And she tries not to hate herself for liking him back.

22

The Second Saturday

Greta wakes, forgetting where she is for a moment. *Oh yeah, the pull-out couch in the family bookstore.* She swings her legs to the bare tiled floor and throws on a hoodie, which she pulled from her duffle. The air is wet, and the damp chill invades her body right to her bones. She checks her phone. 7:16 a.m. She notices a text from Brian, which came in twenty minutes ago.

Had fun last night. Thanks for going. Hope you slept well.

She's hesitant to reply. She had fun last night, and that realization both excites her and scares her. She's been fighting her feelings for Brian for so long; she's just not sure what to do now. One thing is indisputable: it's all a big, complicated mess.

Greta throws on her jeans and running shoes and opens the door leading to the main part of the house, trying not to wake anyone. She hopes she can find some coffee. The three kids who live in the house were up late last night, running and jumping around on the floor above the couch where she had been trying to sleep. At ages five, seven, and eight, she had wondered why they weren't sleeping, especially as the clock ticked past eleven. Their parents didn't seem to mind.

Finding no coffee, nor even a coffeemaker, in the kitchen, she considers searching for a nearby coffee shop. She pulls out her phone to open Google Maps. Allison shuffles into the kitchen and startles her.

"I'm so sorry, Greta!" she exclaims. "I didn't expect you up so early."

"Me either," says Greta.

"Can I get you some hot tea?"

Greta nods. *Any warm beverage will do, I guess.*

ALLISON SITS with Greta in the cozy bookstore reading chairs, both sipping from warm mugs. Allison and Scott are not coffee drinkers, so Greta acquiesced to oolong tea, hoping the small amount of caffeine would put a dent in the fogginess stored up in her brain.

"Richard used to come here and read for story hour every Tuesday afternoon from three to four. He used to do these funny voices for each character." Allison smiles at the fond memory. "The kids adored him." Allison explains that mid-to-late afternoon is the hardest part of the day for most mothers. "We used to call it the 'witching hour' in our home," she says. "The days are long when you have young kids at home. You forget there is a whole world of adults out there. All young mothers know is the chaos inside their home—the crying, the diapers . . . and as the babies grow into toddlers, the need to entertain them, or they'll get into trouble. It's exhausting."

Greta nods though she doesn't have a clue what being a mother entails.

"Story hour and having this bookstore to visit helps moms keep the walls from caving in as they wait for dinnertime, when relief arrives in the form of husbands or, for some, their own parents."

"How did Richard know about this place? It's so small and inconspicuous. I'd never have guessed there was a public bookstore in here." Greta asks.

"There's a park across the street. So we would hand out flyers to families who visited the park. Then, somehow, the local news media discovered us. They ran a story, and Richard saw it. He was here the next day, asking how he could help."

"That doesn't surprise me," Greta says with a lopsided smile.

"Well, we wouldn't let him help without first spending the afternoon here, seeing what we did and who came to visit. We didn't think of ourselves as a charity case—still don't. And then I realized he didn't either. He was genuinely in love with the kids and so good with them. When I saw how easily he interacted with them and how animated he got, I knew how he could help . . . being our resident storyteller for weekly story time." Allison takes a sip of her tea. "He agreed right away."

Greta looks around the library. Children's picture books and beginner-level chapter books neatly line the shelves, and she remembers The Hope Floor's library, where the books were haphazardly thrown on the shelves. Her insides swirl at the thought of The Hope Floor. She looks forward to staying at the Ocean Resort & Casino again. Maybe she'll visit a family there. The thought terrifies her, but she decides that's her plan. Maybe a visit will stop the churning conflict in her gut.

"Greta?" Allison interrupts her thoughts.

"Oh, sorry. I'm daydreaming."

"I asked if you'd like to shower. The bookstore opens in an hour. Then, maybe you'd like to read a book to the kids?"

"What? Oh, no, no." Greta's face bunches up. "I'm not good with kids."

Allison chuckles. "I bet that's not true."

"Trust me," Greta argues, "I *shouldn't* read to them."

"Okay, suit yourself. I'll show you to the upstairs bathroom you can use. There are clean towels on the vanity."

"Thank you," Greta says, but her mind is already back to The Hope Floor.

When Greta has showered and redresses in leggings and her hoodie, her phone rings.

"Hey, Brian," she says as she sits in the bookstore chair once again. Looking around, she notices Allison had put the pull-out couch back together and stowed the bedding somewhere.

"Hey," he says. "You never replied to my text. Everything okay?"

"Oh, sorry. Yeah. Just fine. Allison tried to convince me to read to the kids at story time, but that's a hard no." Greta fills him in on the morning.

"I'll be there around three o'clock to take you to the Ocean Resort & Casino. I also booked a massage for you in their spa, but I can easily cancel that if you want." Greta isn't the type who likes physical touch, especially from strangers. As he says the words, she thinks, *You should have asked*. Instead of letting those words spill out, she makes a decision she doesn't normally make.

"It's okay. I'll try it." Greta pinches her nose with her thumb and forefinger. She's trying to play nice and seem easygoing, but she's not sure it's possible for the long-term.

They say goodbye just as Allison enters the bookstore and flips the *closed* sign to *open* on the door. She sits next to Greta.

"Now, we wait," she says.

Greta sighs.

Fifteen minutes later, a car pulls up and parks on the street outside the library. A mother and her three children slide out, each one bouncing around as if they must have had sugar cereal for breakfast. As they move up the ramp leading to the door, a minivan pulls up and parks behind their car. Another mother and two more kids jump out. They yell to the first kids to "wait up!"

"They know each other?" Greta asks.

"Yes, the moms are friends. They bring their kids here a few times per week."

As the children tumble into the bookstore, Greta panics. The noise level escalates, and she's sure her brain won't be able to handle the stimulation. Just as she's about to walk through the door leading into Allison's house to escape the chaos, a kid tugs on her sweatshirt.

"Miss? Can you read me this book?" Greta looks down and into the eyes of a brown girl with natural hair rising in all directions from her head. Her round eyes plead with Greta as she lifts a chapter book and shakes it at Greta. "Pa-leassssse?"

"Sure," Greta relents after noticing all of the eyes in the room turn to her. She's grateful that at least the noise level has subsided.

The kids whoop and holler and take their places on the rug in front of the main reading chair. Allison smiles at Greta. "Kids, this is Ms. Greta," she says as she makes the introduction. "Her great-uncle was Mr. Richard."

"Whoa," says a boy with reddish-orange hair. He wears a Paw Patrol T-shirt that hangs loosely on his skinny frame. "Richard was sooooo cool!"

"*Mr.* Richard," his mom admonishes. Then she looks at Greta. "We were so saddened to hear of his passing."

A fat tear rolls down one girl's cheek.

"Honey, I know it's sad. But Mr. Richard is in heaven now, remember?" The same mother reaches down to comfort her daughter. The little girl nods and then looks at Greta. "Can you do the voices like he did?" she asks.

Greta's eyes go wide. She looks at Allison who simply shrugs.

"Okay. I'll try." Greta can't believe her ears. *What? Why did I just agree to that?*

Greta opens the chapter book and begins to read. She begins in her normal voice, but when the character changes to a talking dog, she uses a deeper voice: "Ruff! Let's play in the snow!" she says. The kids on the rug giggle. Greta feels her cheeks and neck flush. For a moment, she pauses and considers escaping to the house, but after taking a deep breath, she finds the will to continue.

When she finishes the book, Greta says, "Okay! That's all for now." The kids look at her with disappointment, but then they start to clap. "Thank you, Ms. Greta!" they yell in unison. She smiles at them, feeling a tiny bit of adoration.

That wasn't so bad, she thinks.

AFTER DINNER with the O'Leary family, Brian picks up Greta and takes her to the resort. Once she's checked in, he gives her a peck on the cheek and tells her he'll see her on Monday. She waves to him as the hotel door closes.

Greta is exhausted from the long day with the family of five. She eyes the TV and then the bed and decides to be lazy and fall asleep while watching a show. After washing her face and brushing her teeth, she slips into a T-shirt and slips under the covers. She finds a *Friends* marathon. Before Joey can say, "How you doing?" she's out cold.

GRETA IS RUNNING down a dark alley, her heart booming in her chest. She's dressed in all black, and a shadow chases her, but she can't see who it is—the person's face is obscured. She senses she must move as fast as she can. She stumbles over a curb, and as she falls, she sprawls not onto the sidewalk, but onto the living room floor of her North Carolina home.

Her house feels hot, and she somehow understands the warmth is coming from the dancing flames alight in her gas log fireplace, not some nefarious source. It's still nighttime, and her home is tucked into darkness but for the glow of the popping fire. She turns toward the light, and relief floods her as the familiar safety of her home flows over her.

With her next breath, she spies a figure in the corner of the room. Startled, Greta jumps. The black-clothed individual who was chasing her in the alley emerges from the shadows and holds up a mirror. Greta sees her reflection, but she also spies the metallic glint of an unidentified object hanging from the intruder's belt.

"Finally," the figure says.

Greta tries to scream, but her lips are immobile from fear.

"Yes, it's time." The words crawl from the intruder's mouth and slither to her ears.

Greta wants to yell out the response floating in her mind, but a distant horn, like that from a train, interrupts the exchange. It doesn't matter. She can't find any of her words in the jumbled mess of her distraught brain.

The figure dashes through her front door, and Greta falls back to the floor, the numbness creeping from her lips to her entire body. She lies on the living room rug, paralyzed and weeping. A dog barks in the distance . . .

Greta awakens in a dark room and feels a mass pinning her to the bed. She kicks and thrashes until she discovers it's the weight of the bedspread and blanket holding her down. She sits up, panting, her heart beating wildly in her chest. Perspiration has seeped through her shirt. Spying the hotel-standard alarm clock on the side table, she realizes where she is. *The Ocean Resort & Casino.* The clock's red numbers cut through the darkness.

3:11 a.m.

Greta squeezes her eyes shut and stifles a sob by biting her fist. Her attempts at ridding herself of the nightmare's aftereffects are futile. She pushes the small knob at the base of the bedside lamp, piercing the darkness with the yellow glow of the light. Breathing slower now, she gets up and moves toward the bathroom. She hasn't had a nightmare like that in a long time.

23

The Second Sunday

Greta sleeps until noon and showers to mitigate the continued effects of the nightmare. She throws on the same leggings and sweatshirt. She has an hour-long massage scheduled for two o'clock. She knows she'll just shower again afterward. The thought of someone else's hands moving across her skin makes it crawl already, but she's determined to try it. Everyone she's ever known has claimed how wonderful massages are, and she hopes it eases the pounding headache she is now experiencing.

After the massage, she has a thirty-minute slot reserved in a salt room—*whatever that is.* A real self-care kind of day. *Brian would be proud.* Then she wonders why that matters. She doesn't like the answer she comes up with.

Before her pampering, though, she wants to go back to The Hope Floor, now five floors above her. She hopes the passkey is the same code as before: 9141. She has always been good at remembering numbers.

Greta grabs her sling bag and walks to the elevator bank, then hits the up arrow.

When the doors close, she presses the *H* and punches in the code. It works, and the elevator starts its accent. Excitement builds with each passing floor; her heart rate ticks higher and warmth floods her cheeks. She wonders if what she's feeling is not excitement but anxiety, realizing she's not sure how much different the two emotions are from each other. She visualizes the next few minutes to help her calm her nerves.

The doors open, and Greta spies the hardwood floors. This time, the hallways are dead quiet.

Brian leaves church and heads home to call his brother. They've been playing phone tag for a few days, and he's wondering what Brent and his family have decided about moving to New Jersey.

"Hey, man. How are you?" Brian says when Brent answers his phone.

"Good, Brian. How are you?"

"Hey, sorry I've missed your calls. I've been swamped."

"The law business that crazy, huh?" Brent asks, a twinge of jealousy sneaking through and making Brian wince on the other end of the line. The two have always wrestled with competition; first for their parents' attention, then for measures of success.

"Sorta. But not really. It's—"

"A girl then?" Brent laughs, fully aware his relentless jabs about his big brother's love life don't always land well. "I'm just joking."

"Actually, yes. Sorta."

"Lots of 'sortas' in there. What's going on?" Brent presses Brian.

"Richard Goldman's great-niece was his named heir, and he left a lot for her to accomplish before she can do anything with his estate. He had only met her in person one or two times, about eight years ago. I'm helping her navigate the hoops—or list, I should say."

"Aah. Yeah, I'm sorry, again, to hear about his passing." Brent had met Richard Goldman several times after he had set up the scholarship at ABCC in Bethany's name. But he had never grown as close to the man as Brian had. *Those two,* Brent often thought, *were like father and son.*

"Thanks, man. So anyway, Greta Goldman . . . Brent, she's every bit odd and fantastic. I think I like her, but I'm not sure it's a good idea."

Brent pauses before replying, gauging his older brother's tone and determining it's not the time for more jokes. "Look, if you like her, you like her. What's the problem?"

"She's a little different. She's direct and impulsive, doesn't really understand nuance . . . but she has a kind heart. She's a successful author too. She's just great. We laugh. Joke. We've really connected. But part of me wonders . . . I don't know. She lives in North Carolina and . . . Brent, she's gorgeous, but is a blunt woman who doesn't catch social cues right for me? I've always pictured someone in my head, and she's not the type. . . . I'm rambling." Brian sighs. "This is not why I called."

Brent laughs on the other end of the line. "It's okay, man. So what if she's odd or whatever? Do you like her? Would she be good for you? And I don't mean for your career or image."

"Yeah, I know. I don't care about that. I'm not that superficial. She's just taken me by surprise. I wasn't expecting to have these feelings. . . . Look, we can talk about this later. What's the news with you and your family? Are you moving back? Did the job transfer work out?"

"Yeah, bro! It did! You're talking to the new assistant director of tourism for Atlantic City!" Brent's voice is animated, and Brian smiles, feeling his brother's exhilaration about his career track and his own joy about having his brother and family move back home again.

"That's fantastic! I'm so happy for you. You deserve it. When are you coming back?"

"I'll be there in a week or so to look for a house. So if you know of any leads, let me know. We can talk about . . . what's her name? Gina Goldman?"

"Greta." Brian closes his eyes in silent frustration. He knows his brother's strengths, and active listening is not one of them—nor is a penchant for remembering names. He wonders how Brent will fare in the tourism industry.

"Right, Greta . . . when I get there, can I crash with you while I'm house-hunting?"

"Of course. You're always welcome here. I can't wait."

"Cool. I'll let you know the exact dates in a few days. So much to work out on our end here."

"Sounds good. Talk to you later, Brent," Brian says as he runs his hand through his hair.

"*Ciao*, bro."

"*Ciao*," Brian mimics as he pulls the phone away from his ear and taps the end button.

GRETA TIP-TOES down the hallway on the right, nervous about getting caught. She looks for cameras and spies two in corners where the ceiling meets the wall. With no invitation, appointment, or official host on The Hope Floor, she's not sure how her arrival will be received. She stops in front of a resident's door. The plate reads "The Howards. Suite 11."

Sounds good to me. Greta squares her shoulders and knocks.

A peculiar girl opens the door. Greta guesses her age around six or seven. The girl's curls spring up and down with every movement of her head, and her brown skin glistens with sweat.

"Who are you?" the girl inquires as she cracks the door, appearing confused by the strange woman standing there.

"Hi. I'm Greta. Is your mom or dad home?" Greta asks, her hands clasped in front of her, hoping to project a trusting pose but realizing she probably looks awkward.

"Mom!" the girl yells. Then she turns and stares at Greta. "You're tall."

"I am." Greta likes this kid.

"Honey, who is it?" Greta hears the woman's voice before she sees her. She practices what she wants to say in her head to gain entry.

"Oh, hi. Can I help you?" A full-figured woman opens the door wider. Greta watches as her other hand shoos her daughter away, presumably to safety down the hall. The woman, whose mind is quickly processing the stranger in front of her asks, "How did you get on this floor? It's private."

"Yes, I know. I was here a few days ago, talking with Shu. My name is Greta Goldman . . . as in Richard Goldman. Do you mind if I come in?"

The woman's eyes go wide with the name recognition. "Oh, of course!" Her protective demeanor melts as she swings the door open and waves Greta inside. "We are devastated by Richard's death. What can we do for you? . . . Come, let's sit. My name is Crystal Howard, by the way. . . . Kira, you can go back to what you were doing." The precocious girl, who had been peeking around the corner of the hallway to spy on the exchange, flitters away.

Greta feels the power of the awkward encounter snake through her core, and she fights the urge to stifle her curiosity and run back into the hallway. A few seconds later, Greta hears the whooshing sound of a rowing machine.

"She is *exercising?*" she asks the woman. Crystal nods once but doesn't verbalize an answer, clearly wondering the reason for Greta's visit. "Do you have a husband? . . . I mean . . ." Greta's face twists as she admonishes herself for the way everything is coming out.

Crystal chuckles, detecting Greta's discomfort. She finds it somewhat endearing, albeit curious. "Yes, he's at the grocery store. He'll be home soon. What brings you by?"

She leads Greta further into the suite, and the two sit at a round glass table with metal legs in the kitchen. Greta sees fingerprints scattered across the surface and keeps her hands in her lap.

"I wanted to talk to you about your experience here. What brought you to The Hope Floor?" Greta looks around the kitchen, avoiding eye contact with Crystal for as long as possible. The dark mustard-colored kitchen is small, and there are dirty dishes piled in the sink.

Crystal stares at Greta, assessing how much to reveal. When Greta's eyes land back on Crystal, she doesn't discern the woman's hesitation, let alone the reason behind it, so she just sits there.

After several long seconds, Crystal answers. "We lost our home in a fire. Then, my husband lost his job. We knew about The Hope Floor through some friends, so we called." Crystal pauses. "Can you tell me again why you ask?" Greta never told her specifically.

"Oh, right. I'm sorry. I guess it's strange that I'm here, huh?" Greta shakes her head, and her long dark hair shimmers in the sunlight streaming through the nearby window. "I just want to know more about the families here. I want to understand Richard's need to help. . . . Um, I mean, I want to understand why this place is so important."

"I see," Crystal decides Greta is harmless. "The Hope Floor saved our lives. The staff here immediately got my husband, John, a job. He unloads deliveries for the restaurants and the casino. He also washes dishes from time to time at Villain and Sai—"

"I've eaten there," Greta says, interrupting Crystal.

The woman smiles and continues. "We've been here for about four months now, and we're already doing so much better. John has an interview for a full-time job next week." Crystal seems to decide further details aren't important—after all, Greta is a *stranger*—and ends her story.

"That's great. What did you make of Richard? Did you meet him personally?"

Chrystal's eyes narrow briefly, then soften. "That's actually a funny story." Greta catches a far-off look on Chrystal's face, but then Crystal quickly snaps back to the present.

"John and Richard were enemies for some time. They didn't like each other at all. It's amazing what God can do with two people with good hearts, even when they dislike one another."

"Enemies? What do you mean?" Greta leans forward, still avoiding the glass tabletop.

Crystal gazes at Greta, trying to determine her angle. Greta inches back to rest against the chair again. "I'm sorry. I guess I'm being nosy. You see, Richard left me in charge of determining a lot of things, and I didn't know him all that well."

Crystal nods, now understanding Greta's purpose here. "After the fire, my husband, John, started gambling. Became an addict. It's why he lost his first job. He worked for Richard as an accountant for Goldman Enterprises, and unfortunately, his addiction compelled him to steal some of Richard's money to pay off his gamb—"

The front door closes, cutting off Crystal's sentence, and a booming voice echoes through the apartment. "Hello? Crystal? Can you help me with the bags?" John's towering presence appears in the kitchen. "Oh, hello." He thrusts his hand out to Greta. "I'm John. We haven't met." Greta first notices his shaved head and then his dark eyebrows that seem to stretch as one long caterpillar above his eyes. Kind eyes. His full goatee is neatly trimmed.

"John, this is Greta Goldman, Richard's . . ." Crystal stops, unsure of the exact relationship.

"Great-niece," Greta finishes.

"Hi! Nice to meet you." John looks to Crystal for more information, but Crystal only shrugs. "What brings you by?" he asks Greta, unease in his tone.

"I wanted to know . . . why The Hope Floor? Why did Richard pour so much money into this place that caters to addicts and the homeless? Why not send people to a rehab center or a homeless shelter? It seems you can get what you need there." Greta's cheeks burn as her words spill out, but she can't stop them. Her hand reaches toward her mouth. She senses it's far too late. "I'm sorry. I'll just go." She lunges toward the foyer.

"No, wait." John blocks the exit.

Greta stares at the floor. "I just want to know why he'd help you. Any of you . . . but especially you. You stole from him?" There is no judgment in her question, only curiosity.

Crystal's eyes dart toward John with a silent apology.

He shakes his head as if to say, *it's okay.* In his twelve-step program, the first thing John learned was humility. When he turns to Greta, compassion cascades from his eyes. "I understand your questions. If you'll help us with the groceries, I'd be happy to explain." John splays his hands in front of him as a peace offering. His voice is gentle, as if he's speaking to a child.

Greta nods, her body shaking. She hates people, strangers in particular, and she can't believe she opened herself up to this fiasco.

GRETA LIES PRONE, the skin on her cheeks and forehead pressed outward by the hole at the head of the massage table. The lights are dim, and the soothing smoke of the lavender incense permeates the room. The temperature in the massage suite is perfect, neither too warm nor too chilly. Her body melts into the sheets spread across the table as she waits for the masseuse to enter. While she isn't looking forward to the touch of a stranger, her body covets relaxation.

"Are you ready, Ms. Goldman?" the young woman calls as she knocks lightly, then opens the door.

"Mm hmmm. Yes," Greta sighs. Then her ears find the soft jazz music bubbling through the speakers. She doesn't hear anything else the woman says.

As the woman's strong hands collide with Greta's knotted

muscles, Greta can't stop thinking about the Howards and Richard.

John Howard had deserved nothing Richard had done for him. John had stolen money from Richard, and in return, Richard had paved the way for him to find a home and a *new job.* The irony leaves Greta confused. John was an addict—*a gambling addict of all things*—and Richard had put him up in a charity that sits within a casino. None of it makes any sense to her.

Greta knows that addiction can be tricky. She knows most people fall "off of the wagon" at least once. Why did Richard give him the second chance? Why risk it? And yet, John and Crystal seem to be doing well. Their daughter is happy and healthy, and John now has an opportunity for work that will move them out of The Hope Floor and let them start over.

And what does all of this mean for her decision about The Hope Floor? For her life?

The most confusing aspect is that Richard and John had been at odds when John was fired. Enemies. Why give an enemy a leg up? None of it makes sense to her.

"You seem to be getting tighter!" the woman reports as she digs her knuckles into Greta's shoulder blade.

As she continues to think through it, Greta finds some hope in the idea that maybe mistakes aren't permanent. Maybe redemption *is* real.

"Okay. All finished."

Greta tries to lift her head and realizes the sheet is now stuck to her forehead. *So much for relaxation,* she complains to her constant companion—the loneliness living within her.

24

The Second Monday

Just before noon, Antonio pulls up to Brian's house in the Cadillac, which looks spotless after the repairs, and parks in his driveway. A second later, Brian appears by the driver's side window, an open-mouth smile spreading across his face.

"Antonio! Hey, man! I'm so glad to see you back in action!" Brian reaches for the car door and after opening it—before Antonio can even unbuckle his seatbelt—reaches in with both arms to hug him.

"Well, hello to you too, sir."

"Sir? Did you hit your head harder than the doctors said? Please, Antonio. We've been friends for ages."

"I know. I'm just messing with you. . . . Any word on the investigation about the faulty brakes?"

"None. I think they're chalking it up to hoodlums."

Antonio takes a breath. "Hope so. Hey, something weird happened at the hospital." Antonio's face loses some of its color.

"What happened?"

"I was asleep, and maybe I was just delirious on the medications, but I thought Greta visited my room. And apologized. It was very weird."

Brian cocks his head.

"I was probably dreaming. But I thought she came in and said she was sorry."

"Sorry? For what?"

"No idea. Again, when I finally opened my eyes, there was nobody there."

"I don't think she would've been there. I didn't drive her. Plus, why would she do that?"

"I don't know. It was late one night. Again, probably just my concussion. Hallucination or something. I was on narcotics, you know. Are you ready to go . . . MLK Boulevard, right?"

"You bet. Let me grab my bag. I'll be right back." Brian jogs up his front porch stairs, taking two at a time, and enters his house.

Antonio shakes his head, clearing his mind, and grins. *It's good to be back,* he thinks. He loves his job nearly as much as the man he works for.

TWENTY MINUTES LATER, Antonio parks the Cadillac in front of the Ocean Resort & Casino, and Greta emerges from the lobby. The sunshine hits her face, and as it does, she tries to hide the smile that forms when she sees Antonio behind the wheel.

"Antonio," she says with a forced, yet subdued, nod. Antonio, who is holding the door open for her as always, grins and nods back.

"Ms. Greta," he says. Greta now enjoys Antonio's formal, albeit simple, behaviors and conversation. She knows where she stands with him, and she appreciates that. She leaves her duffle bag at his feet as a show of her relief and gratitude for his return. It's easier than a hug. Then she bends into the backseat.

Once inside the car, Antonio takes a chance. "Did you come see me in the hospital, Ms. Greta? I can't remember much."

"What? No. I'm not a hospital kind of person. I'm glad you're feeling better, though."

Antonio nods in reply.

"Hi, Brian," Greta offers. He grabs her arm and gives it a squeeze. She involuntarily pulls back a little but then relents, allowing herself to be touched.

"So before we go to Dr. Martin Luther King Jr. Boulevard . . ." Brian says, finally removing his hand. "How was your stay?" He looks at Greta with a mischievous grin and waits.

"You know?" Greta wrings her hands and looks at the floorboards.

"I know. It seems you met a Hope Floor family?" Brian's tone is light, not accusatory, as Greta had feared.

"We're not going to discuss it so . . . so just move on," she says. "And Richard's list doesn't say Dr. Martin Luther King Jr. Boulevard. The next stop is Illinois Avenue."

Brian's nonchalance about her visit with the Howards unnerves Greta. She assumes he'd rather not let her trip to the family's suite go undiscussed, but he's not showing that with his tone, and that confuses her. She probably crossed a line. Though she has no idea what that line would be. She has decisions to make, after all.

"Okay." Brian opens a notebook that's sitting on his lap. "Richard petitioned the City Council seven months ago to change the name of Illinois Avenue to Dr. Martin Luther King Jr. Boulevard. The council members voted, and it passed five months ago. He never had the chance to update his list. The change was made at a ceremony in the Civil Rights Garden, which is where we're heading now."

Greta doesn't speak, deciding to let things play out regarding the Howards. She doesn't have an opinion about the street name change. She wonders why any of this matters at all. Any beneficial effects from the massage, if there were any, are long gone, so she stares out of the SUV's window.

After a few awkward minutes, Antonio comes to the rescue. "Mr. Brian, we're here," he calls from the driver's seat.

"Thank you, *sir*. Just park wherever you can. We'll get out and walk since it's such a beautiful day." Greta watches Brian and Antonio share a look and a chuckle through the rearview mirror.

"What?" she asks. "What's going on?"

Brian is quick to dispel her paranoia. "I'm teasing Antonio about something he said to me earlier. We're just having some fun."

Brian and Greta step out of the Cadillac and meander the fifty yards to the garden's entrance. They walk under a metal arch that reads "Civil Rights Garden." Greta spies a few things around her: a black iron fence marking the border of the garden, colorful flowers, a bronze liberty bell, and what appears to be miniature smoke stacks rising about seven feet into the air with engravings. Greta counts eleven of the black statues and asks Brian about them.

"They are African granite columns, each one etched with quotes from great Americans, including former slaves, students, presidents, and religious leaders, all referencing the struggle of Black Americans for equal treatment. The central column, over there," Brian says as he points to the unique feature with the raised hand, "symbolizes the passion of the human spirit."

The two circle the reflecting pool, following the brick path, as they read the inscriptions on the columns. "This is really cool," Greta says. "I'm glad—"

Pop! Pop! Brian and Greta duck into crouched positions as the sound of gunfire erupts around them. Brian scurries closer to Greta and puts his arm around her in a protective hold. A few more shots are fired.

Then the sound of screeching tires on the pavement comes from just outside the fence of the garden. Greta sees a red pickup truck fleeing down the street. It crosses the center line and zooms past the car in front of it as it heads away from them.

Antonio comes running into the garden, his dress shoes slapping on the bricks beneath him. "Brian, Ms. Greta, are you two okay?"

"Yes, why? What just happened?" Brian huffs. He stands up and straightens his pant legs with his hands. Greta brushes off her knees and fixes her hair, moving a few strands that had flown into her eyes.

"I don't know. Someone in a red truck shot at someone who was walking down the street near the entrance to the garden. They missed, and the person who was targeted took off in the other direction, also holding a gun. Maybe rival gangs? I'm just glad you two are okay!"

"Yeah, me too." Brian looks at Greta.

Greta feels her heart rate slowing. She pulls her sling off her shoulder and opens it. In one fluid movement, she pulls out a knife, wrapped in a pink towel a moment ago. Both Brian and Antonio take a step back.

"Whoa! What's that for?" Brian says, holding his hands up in semi-mock self-defense.

"Protection. You don't think I'd travel all the way to New Jersey alone on a bus and *not* carry something to defend myself with, do you?"

"I think we're okay now," Antonio says. "Plus, guns beat knives." Greta shrugs and puts the knife away.

The three head back to the Cadillac. On the way to the next hotel, Greta feels Brian's eyes on her. She turns her head, smiles at him with an exaggerated look of innocence, and bats her eyes for good measure. His gaze involuntarily darts to her sling bag.

The Cadillac bounces as it crosses a pair of railroad tracks. As it does, the passengers are jostled, breaking the spell of Brian's curiosity and concern. Greta slides her hands between her pinched knees and hopes her showing them the knife doesn't become a problem.

A THIRTY-YEAR-OLD WOMAN with boot-cut jeans and a white lace blouse sits in first class, sipping the last of her pinot grigio and staring out of the window at the approaching white clouds below. Her tan arms reflect the years she's spent in the sun.

The flight will land at ACY—Atlantic City International Airport—in about fifteen minutes, according to the co-pilot. The woman slips her feet back into her black ankle boots stowed underneath the seat in front of her.

When the airline attendant walks by, the passenger hands her the now-empty wineglass. Then she maneuvers the food tray into its case in the seat's armrest and closes her eyes. She absent-mindedly combs her straight, chestnut-brown hair behind her ears with her fingers.

For the past eight years, she's made her home in Chios, Greece. With a population of fewer than 27,000 people, Chios—a seaside town filled with beautiful beaches—is a tranquil place to go, especially to repurpose oneself. And that is exactly what she's been doing. Until now.

The flight attendant brings the woman a payment slip for the alcohol. "Here you go, miss." The passenger opens her eyes and hands the crew member her credit card. The flight attendant scurries off to run it through the machine behind the partition toward the front of the plane.

I hope I'm welcomed here, the passenger thinks as she watches the plane's wing pass through the white poofs of cumulus clouds.

There's movement to her right, and she looks over toward the aisle. "Thank you, Ms. Goldman. We hope you enjoy your stay in Atlantic City." The crew member hands the passenger her card.

"Oh, I hope so too," Greta says. "Thank you."

Greta pulls out her iPhone and scrolls until she finds Bill Goldman's number.

The plane lands, taxis, and comes to a stop at Gate A2.

Greta taps the green phone icon on the screen. It rings two times before someone answers.

"Bill? It's Greta Goldman. We've never met, but I am your and Richard's great-niece. I haven't seen him in nearly eight years, but I heard what happened. I'm so sorry. I've just arrived in town —from Greece. Can we meet?"

25

The Second Tuesday

Mid-morning the following day, the globe-trotter calling herself Greta sits across from Bill and Jean at the Vita Café on Ventnor Avenue. It's a family-owned boutique breakfast and lunch establishment with exposed brick walls and upscale food. Though they'd arrived fifteen minutes ago, none of the three patrons in the mint-green upholstered booth has ordered any of the fine cuisines. They are all assessing one another, clearly confused by this turn of events.

"What do you mean you've already met Greta, and I'm not her?" The young woman with the face full of freckles who, when standing, reaches five feet, eight inches, stares at Bill's eyes behind his blue glasses.

"We mean, you're not Greta. Greta has been in town for over two weeks, invited by Brian Gogh, Richard's attorney. They've been tying up Richard's estate. So who are you?" Normally-kind Bill is losing his patience with this emerald-eyed woman who claims to be Richard's heir. After she had called yesterday, he planned to contact the police to meet him and Jean at the café. "She must be an imposter, trying to claim Richard's billions," he had told his wife over and over. Jean, always more inquisitive than her husband, first wanted to meet this new Greta before causing a scene or accusing someone of such a dastardly thing.

Jean's cooler head had prevailed. And Bill finally agreed to wait and meet the young woman first. He still hopes she doesn't run for the hills when her scam is exposed.

"I can assure you; I am Greta Goldman. I've spent the last eight years in Greece. After graduating from college—"

"And where was that? What school?" Bill asks, not meaning to cut her off but wanting to protect his brother's estate from someone's obvious fraud. The woman stops talking and stares at Bill. He takes a breath. "I'm sorry to interrupt," he says. "You can imagine my concern." *She has the same color eyes as Richard,* he thinks as he returns her gaze. *And as me . . .*

But the taller woman, the first Greta, fit right in, and that is who Richard told Brian to contact. Richard certainly knew who our great-niece was! He'd met her!

"The University of North Carolina at Charlotte," the young woman calmly answers.

"Why Greece? Why go off the grid for so long and suddenly come back . . . and not tell anyone?"

Jean looks from Bill to the young woman after this last question, eyebrows raised.

"I needed a fresh start." The freckled woman sighs. "As you know, my parents died when I was twenty." She looks between the two octogenarians. "I toughed it out to finish school, then just left. I thought I needed a little time away to grieve. And Richard, actually, is the one who suggested that idea when he came to my graduation. He could see I was lost and said something about us all needing a break from life sometimes. So I picked a beautiful location that I'd always been interested in learning more about and simply left. But one year turned into two, and well, two turned into eight. I've been working at a seaside shop I now own in Chios. It's on an island off the eastern coast . . ." The woman's voice trails off. She knows she's talking too fast. She slows herself down before she alarms the couple. "It's off the mainland of Greece," she says carefully. "I can pull up my website. You can see my photo on there—"

"You could have built that website yesterday," Bill points out, though his accusatory tone is lessening.

"True," she says with another deep exhale. Her eyes narrow. They seem to have hit an impasse. Her nose twitches, and she spins the silver ring on her right hand. "Okay, how can we prove that I'm who I say I am?"

The three look at one another as they silently brainstorm. "We could do a DNA test. You and Bill would have some common DNA, right?" Jean offers. She sits on her hands to prevent them from shaking.

"What?" Greta asks.

"That's a good idea, Jean," Bill says to his wife.

"You want me to spit into a cup? I'm sorry . . . I imagine this is difficult for everyone. I'm a bit jet-lagged, and this is just all so . . . so crazy." The woman rolls her shoulders to calm her nerves.

Bill remains silent.

"Okay, if that's what I have to do," she relents.

Jean chimes back in. "Well, I think it's done with cheek swabs, not spitting into a cup."

"Of course. Okay."

"Maybe we can have it done at the police station?" Jean continues to strategize out loud, and Bill eyeballs Greta, gauging her reaction to Jean's idea about going to the police.

Great idea, Jean. Let's see how she reacts to that!

The young woman nods gently. "Sure," she replies. "I can do that."

The three stand and agree to meet at the police station in one hour. They leave the café, having ordered nothing. Their bony server, with her gray hair tied up in a tight bun, stares after them with a frown, her pen and paper primed for an order that will never happen.

Once outside, Bill and the young woman claiming to be

Greta nod goodbye to each other, then she turns to the right and walks away down the sidewalk. Bill turns to Jean. "Before we go to the police station, I need to run by Edith Moore's house, Jean."

"What for, Bill?" Jean touches Bill on the upper arm, and a look of concern plasters her face.

"She may have the proof we need. And I'm not sure this woman will ever meet up with us again."

BRIAN AND GRETA sit in the back of the Cadillac, on the way to the next stop on Richard's list. Brian contemplates holding Greta's hand as they both look out of their respective windows, lost in thought. Instinctively, he knows it's too soon, and she'd probably pull away. Brian's not ready for the rejection, so he keeps his hands where they rest, deciding to avoid an awkward encounter, opting for a more organic approach to maximize intimacy with Greta.

What he doesn't know is that Greta is thinking about him too. *I can't believe I like him. I can't believe this is happening.* She admonishes herself. Then, *Should I just surrender? No, I should forget him. Just go back to my life in North Carolina.* A sense of defeat snakes through her. She's never been good at handling emotions, hers or others'. She's never understood the point of falling in love, only to be hurt later. In her experience, love equals pain. Forever doesn't exist, and everything is hard when it comes to relationships.

"So this next street with the restaurants dotting it up and down . . . What did he do, give out free meals or something? Did he restock the restaurants' fridges? Deliver their babies?"

In the front seat, Antonio laughs at Greta's last line. Her upper lip curls, grateful someone appreciates her wicked humor.

"Atlantic Avenue," Brian begins, "doesn't hold another sweet story about Richard. This is a place that caused him a lot of grief and sleepless nights. It's a street that holds many regrets. We call it 'Restaurant Row'."

Greta's interest is piqued. "How so?"

"He failed here. Big time. Restaurant real estate decisions are complex and require substantial research. Since certain types of restaurants have specific space requirements, you need to balance the restaurant concept you think will be successful with the available real estate. His vision outweighed his skill at the time . . . or his co-owner's skills or the building's capacity—I don't know exactly. In one joint venture, early in his career, his mistakes were the driving force that caused the new business to shutter. And when that happened, he hurt someone else—his partner in this endeavor. After the business went bankrupt, his partner, who had lost everything, including their home. He and his family, suddenly homeless. Richard tried to step in and help, but the relationship was too strained. The individual wouldn't accept support from Richard, and the guy hit rock bottom. He died of an overdose a year later."

Greta shakes her head. When Uncle Richard succeeded, he really succeeded; and when he failed, he truly failed. The story leaves a stain of sadness on her heart.

She looks out of the window and notes the Greyhound bus station on her right. Still, a part of her longs to jump on another stinky bus and escape. She reminds herself she's well past the halfway point. She can manage this new information, her crazy-town emotions, and her attraction to Brian for one more week—and then run for the hills of the Piedmont.

Bill and Jean pull up to Ms. Moore's townhome on Mediterranean Avenue. They are oblivious to the fact they have just passed Brian Gogh's Cadillac going the other direction, with Brian and Greta seated in the back.

They park their white Chrysler sedan on the street and Bill

moves to the passenger door and opens it to let Jean step out onto the curb. He locks the doors, knowing this neighborhood is not the safest in town.

On the drive to Edith's place, Bill had filled his wife in on his idea. When Richard had traveled to North Carolina to visit Greta for her graduation, Richard had asked a waitress to snap their photo with his phone one night at a restaurant, a phone he assumes Edith now has with all of his other belongings.

Bill knows this because his brother had shared the story with him during one of their third-floor get-togethers in Bill and Jean's house shortly after Richard's trip to Charlotte. Bill remembers Richard's pride and compassion as he spoke about having a great-niece who had graduated from college—and about his sadness that all he had to remember her was the photo. Richard had seemed to know then that he wouldn't see Greta again, though Bill knows he had tried to reconnect with her for years afterward. Richard had shown Bill the photo on his phone, but Bill cannot remember the photo, or the young woman in it. It was too long ago, and both women have dark hair.

Bill explains to Jean that not once during their conversations did Richard ever mention how tall Greta is, and it seems to Bill, that's something his short and portly brother would have talked about. Though, to be fair, their brother, Henry, was the tallest one in their family at five-foot-ten. He seems to remember hearing Greta's parents were on the taller side too. So that may be where she got her height. And this new woman stands above average too. It is the only detail that leaves Bill curious. Otherwise, it's obvious to him: this new Greta is a fraud, attempting to take advantage of the Goldman family.

"Let's hope Edith still has the photo," Bill says as they walk past the bicycle rack and reach her front door.

As Bill knocks, a clap of thunder sounds in the distance.

"Oh no," Jean says. "I forgot my umbrella."

"I think we have bigger problems right now, honey," Bill says.

He knocks again in case Edith didn't hear the first one with the impending storm.

As Edith opens the door, the dark clouds open up and rain pummels their car and the sidewalk behind them, creating an instant river of water heading toward the ocean.

26

"Wow, that's heavy rain!" Greta exclaims as the large drops batter the windshield.

"I have a big umbrella," Brian offers as a solution. "Antonio?"

"Yes, sir? I mean . . . Brian."

"Can you drop us in front of Sofia's Luncheonette—as close to the door as possible?"

"Of course. Then I'll wait down the street until you're finished to take you to the next spot. You definitely don't want to walk in this storm!"

"Great," Greta mumbles.

"Oh, it'll be fun. Didn't you ever go puddle jumping as a kid?" Brian asks. "My brother and I loved doing that. My sister—not so much."

"No, I never went puddle jumping. What is that?"

Brian looks at her in disbelief. "When you put on rain boots and run around in the rain, jumping in puddles and splashing water everywhere, like the term suggests?" Brian shakes his head, then says, "It was a lot of fun."

"Maybe for kids," Greta mumbles.

Antonio pulls up to Sofia's Luncheonette, and Greta reads the cling letters on the front window advertising

"Breakfast All Day." She notices the hours. They close at 2:00 p.m. *All day! Right!* Through the rain-streaked window, she sees a blue- and yellow-striped awning covering a small corner restaurant that looks like it's seen better days. A couple of wooden tables and chairs sit on the sidewalk, just beyond the cover of the awning. The rain drenches the worn wood.

"Don't let the outside deceive you." Brian reads her mind, and she wonders how he keeps doing that. Then he's gone, out through the door on his side of the car.

"We better eat fast," Greta says when Brian opens her door while shielding her from the downpour with his umbrella. "It's almost eleven-thirty."

Brian isn't sure what Greta is talking about, having no ability to truly read her mind. They enter the glass door, and a bell jingles, signaling to the staff there are customers.

"It seems all we do is eat," Greta whines. "I just want a hot tea, if you don't mind."

"Sure thing," Brian says. "We'll make our day a progressive meal. How's that sound?"

"Whatever," Greta replies. Greta's gloom-and-doom mood matches the weather.

There are a few patrons scattered throughout the restaurant, and she and Brian opt for a four-top table toward the back.

Once seated, Brian orders their drinks and then asks the server if they can speak with Sofia, the owner. "Tell her Brian Gogh is here. Thanks!" He winks at Greta.

"Why do you do that?"

"Do what?"

"Wink all the time."

"I didn't realize I did. I guess it's like subtle communication with someone. Like with you, for instance—when we have an inside joke or some connection . . . I don't know . . . sorry. I'll try not to wink if it makes you uncomfortable," he finishes.

"I don't mind. Just curious," Greta says, suddenly hoping he doesn't stop. As she thinks about it, she realizes it does make her feel more connected to him—like she matters.

"Brian Gogh!" A middle-aged Latina woman with rosy cheeks and a loud voice enters through a door from the kitchen. "*Hola*!" Her face falls when she sees Brian with Greta.

Sofia turns to Greta and stretches out her hand. "Hi! I'm Sofia. You must be Greta Goldman," she says. "Your great-uncle and my family have a lot of history." Her *i* sounds like an *e*, and she annunciates the *s* in history.

"So I hear." Greta doesn't know what else to say, and the two stare at each other for a beat.

"Sofia, why don't you join us?"

The woman reluctantly sits down at their table and eyes Greta. Greta inwardly deflates. *More small talk. More people to interact with.* This time, though, the other person doesn't seem happy to meet her. She hears a boom of thunder overhead and wishes the lights would go out.

"EDITH, it's good to see you again. It's been too long," Jean says as they make their way to the flowered living room.

"Well, it's good to see you, too, dear. You two don't look a day over sixty!"

Bill chuckles. "Neither do you, Edith. Neither do you."

"Oh, hogwash!" Edith shakes her head, but her eyes betray her gratitude. "So I'm afraid I have some bad news. I searched the two boxes I got from Dawn and the police with Richard's personal effects while you were heading this way. I didn't see his phone."

"Oh," Jean says and looks toward Bill. "That's too bad. I wonder where it is?"

"Well, dear, that's my question too," Edith replies. "I called Dawn to see if she knows. I hope to hear soon. Why do you need it?" Bill had been vague on the phone before they arrived.

"Unfortunately, we don't have a lot of time. We were hoping

there was a photo on it from many years ago. But now that I think about it . . ." Bill shakes his head in embarrassment. "Richard probably upgraded his phone at least once during the past eight years. How foolish of me not to think of that!" Bill's face falls. The surprise visit from this second Greta and his hope of solving the mystery had clouded his common sense.

"He may have moved the photos to somewhere else, a computer or another drive or something," Jean adds, trying to comfort her husband.

"I'm sorry to waste your time, Edith." Bill shrugs and then bends his hands into a prayer position in front of him. "I feel silly for having made you look for his phone."

"Oh, any time spent with you two is no waste of time. Care for something to drink?"

"We'd love to, but we have somewhere to be. Raincheck?" Bill asks. "No pun intended," he says as he nods toward the windows where the rain has turned sideways and pelts the glass with the ferocity of a carpenter hammering a stubborn nail.

Edith laughs from her belly and has to adjust her nasal cannula. "Raincheck! I love it!"

Jean laughs alongside Ms. Moore. "Yes, Edith, what about next weekend? We can bring something to eat if you supply the tea—Saturday or Sunday afternoon," Jean adds.

"Sounds like a great plan. I'm going to hold you to it!"

Bill answers, "You bet. Sorry to run off like this. But we'll firm up our plans for next weekend with you soon. Don't get up. We can let ourselves out."

Jean stands up from the couch and walks toward Edith, bends down to hug her, and straightens up again. Bill does the same and adds a peck on her cheek. "Bye, Edith."

"Goodbye, dears!"

Jean and Bill leave through the kitchen and speed-walk through the rain to their car, where Bill opens the door so his wife can get inside quickly. After he sits in the driver's seat, Jean notices his shirt has been drenched. "What a day!" she exclaims.

When they reach the police station twenty minutes later, a male lab technician in a white coat and the freckled woman are waiting. Bill is surprised to see her. The lab tech escorts them to a room with a sink and a couple of chairs. The young woman remains standing while offering the two seats to the older couple.

"This will be a quick mouth swab for you, Mr. Goldman . . . and you, um, Ms. Goldman," the tech announces. They both nod. Greta goes first. Then Bill opens his mouth. The whole thing is over in a matter of minutes.

"We'll get you the results as soon as possible."

Jean frowns. Bill groans, saying, "Nothing concrete yet, huh?"

"Nope. But given the circumstances, we'll try to jump you ahead. Most times, it can take several weeks."

"Well, thank you," Greta adds. Her voice carries the same notes of discouragement as Bill, but it's difficult to discern how she truly feels.

The three march back outside, where the damp air carries the musky, earthy scent of the worms that wiggled to the surface during the deluge. The rain has eased up but still falls as tiny droplets, so they stand under the cover of the entryway and vow to get in touch with each other the minute the results are back.

Bill studies the confident woman in front of him. He's torn. After Greta stayed with him and Jean, and now remembering her quiet, yet direct and brutally honest personality—much like Richard—he still suspects this woman in front of them must be lying. But she doesn't seem all that nervous. Either way, they now have to wait. His heart aches with impatience.

On the sidewalk, the woman takes Jean's hands in hers. "This is all so strange. I'm sorry. I hate I made everyone's lives hard by showing up. But I'm also glad I did. I hope the truth comes out soon, and we can all move on—as family." It's a beautiful gesture. Maybe a bit dramatic. Bill's heart drops a little lower in his chest as he prepares himself for whatever news might come in the next two weeks.

As Sofia explains the dark history of losing her father to an overdose and how she felt the burden to start a restaurant business herself, to honor her family, Greta is ready to bolt. While Sofia acknowledges the fact her father made his choices and Richard didn't force him into drugs, she explains that Richard's negligence in the business deal started the downfall.

"Richard was so gung-ho," Sofia recalls from her childhood. "He didn't do his due diligence, and my father trusted him. I think Richard's ego got in the way, and my father—our family—was the wreckage left behind." Sofia's cheeks redden and her lips push together into a straight line and then relax. "I wish he'd just been honest about his restaurant experience upfront. And when things got bad, I wish he'd let my father know sooner. Richard was too controlling." Sofia sniffles. "Our family was never the same after my father died."

Brian clears his throat. Greta imagines this isn't easy for him to hear, either. But she's had enough. *Everyone makes mistakes. It's not like Richard killed him. . . .* Greta's heart bounces in her chest. That thought and her newfound defense of Richard ushers in a slew of feelings, which Greta is not used to experiencing. That thought also triggers another, making her anxious.

"I have to use the restroom." Greta jumps up and heads toward the corner of the deli. She hears Brian and Sofia exchange a few words, and when she returns, Sofia is gone, presumably in the back kitchen again.

"You ready?"

Greta moves her chin up and down with a force that makes Brian chuckle.

They hop back into the Cadillac, dodging light raindrops. Their next stop is a restaurant and bar for a much-needed meal.

"Why did Richard want me to meet her?"

"I think he wanted you to know that he wasn't perfect. That

he had failures. He was human. Also, he still carried regret for what happened."

"Am I supposed to do something with this restaurant? Did Richard?"

"No. Sofia wouldn't take his money or any kind of help. Called it charity she didn't want or need. I think Richard wanted you to see that life can be hard sometimes. That you might make enemies along the way. Might even hurt others. But you keep going, doing the best you can, no matter what. And when you mess up, you make things right where you can. It's a lesson I learned from him that I'll be grateful for until I die."

Greta looks away. Then, she says, "That family hated him."

Brian remains silent, and she thinks maybe he's also realizing the extent of how much that statement is true. Greta is reminded of Precious and her relentless pursuit to find out what happened to Richard. *Maybe I should see if Precious wants to do some digging.*

Harry's on Atlantic is an all-American sports pub with a dozen or more TVs streaming five different sports high above the tables and the central bar area. There is a low murmur emanating from a few patrons. It's the lunch hour, but Atlantic City isn't a metropolis filled with professionals who typically head out to eat every day, opting instead to work through lunch so they can get to the beach sooner. The smell of fried food floats through the space and tickles Greta's nose.

There is a hostess who shows them to a table on the left wall of the restaurant. Once seated, Brian looks at Greta, and she knows immediately; he has something he wants to say. Perhaps it's the way his eyes throw out caution or the way he folds his hands into a ball as if to protect himself. Either way, it's obvious to Greta. She won't like whatever it is.

"Don't treat me with kid gloves," she warns. "What is it?"

"Detective Reed called me today." Greta briefly closes her eyes. "Richard's murder remains unsolved. He expects the FBI will call to interview us next." Brian tries to gauge Greta's reaction, but deep down, he knows it's useless. Her poker face wins again. "What are you thinking?"

"I don't know. It's weird. Are we suspects?"

"What? Us? No. Of course not," he says, reaching for her hands, hoping what he says is true. "It is unnerving, I know. They just want to learn more about what we're doing, his last will and testament, and things like that. I hope they find the person soon." He pauses for a beat. "Another thing . . ."

"'Cause that wasn't enough?" Greta asks. Her left knee bounces under the table. Brian can feel the vibrations through the floor since his foot is nearly touching hers.

"I have to go out of town unexpectedly for a couple of days on business. I asked Dawn Marshall if you could stay with her for two nights. I'll be back late Friday night. Since you enjoyed your stay with Bill and Jean on the beach, I thought you'd like her house too. She has a bungalow right on the ocean, and I know you and Dawn hit it off that first time you met her." Brian is rambling, hoping to convince Greta it's a good idea even before she reacts. "Or . . ." he offers, "you can keep going through the list without me. I can call ahead to the places you'll be staying and ensure it's all set up. Antonio can drive you." Brian waits for her answer. He didn't know he'd have to wait so long.

Greta sips on her Diet Pepsi and stares at Brian's shirt, his words tumbling around in her brain. When Greta had stayed with Dawn in her office, she had felt a kinship of sorts. Dawn's soothing voice and gentle spirit had impressed her. Greta almost thought of her as a mother figure. *My "fairy mommother,"* she thinks. *And a few nights in a beach house sounds nice.* But she knows that means another two days' delay, and she's ready to go home. *Needs* to go home. As her mind ticks through the pros and cons of each option, her breath catches. *I wouldn't mind more time with Brian,* she realizes. Her heart wins.

A last clap of thunder, farther away than when the core of the storm pulsed over the AC, brings her words back. "Okay. I'll wait at Dawn's. But no more delays."

"Great! I was hoping you'd say that. I'll see you Friday. I know you'll enjoy your time there—just you, Dawn, and the ocean."

Greta lets herself breathe. *It sounds nice,* she thinks.

"One catch," Brian adds, erasing the smile from Greta's face. "Dawn asked that I drop you off tomorrow morning. That's why it's just for two nights. She already has plans for tonight. So . . ." Brian peers at Greta. "You can stay at my house tonight if that's all right with you." Brian holds his breath. He wonders if he should add, "Or I can get you a hotel," but this time, he presses his tongue against the roof of his mouth, preventing any further words from escaping. He can feel the muscles in his shoulders tense. Greta almost laughs as she sees him waiting, but somehow, she catches herself before teasing him.

Both try to navigate the awkward encounter, to control their electrifying relationship.

"Sure." Her stomach cuts a few flips, and inside her running shoes, her toes curl with anticipation. They hadn't kissed—nor even discussed it—since the night in front of Allison's bookstore house.

27

Early that same evening, Brian unlocks his front door, with Greta and her teal duffle bag in tow. He waves to Antonio as the Cadillac backs out of the driveway.

The two adults, feeling more like nervous teenagers sneaking around behind their parents' backs, enter Brian's house, and he flips on a few lights. The sudden glow warms Greta as her body and brain remember and respond to how pleasant his home was the last time she was here.

"Can I get you anything? A soda? Glass of wine? Snack?" Brian throws his keys into a basket on the kitchen counter and opens the refrigerator. He thinks twice and shuts it. "First, let me show you where you are sleeping so you can drop your bags. And I bet you want to do some laundry." A faint hue of pink creeps into his cheeks.

"Okay," Greta says with an edgy laugh. Her stomach is clenching as she wonders what the night will hold. She follows Brian down the hall and up a flight of stairs.

When Brian opens the door to the second room on the right-hand side of the hall, Greta gasps. Walnut beams stretch across the ceiling, interrupted only by a tiny modern chandelier that hangs over the bed.

The bed!

The stunning black platform bed is wrapped in a luxurious white comforter, with a chunky hand-knit throw draped over the foot; silvery blue and dark gray pillows are scattered across the top half of the mattress. The bed sits against a charcoal-colored modern accent wall, which contrasts with the three concrete-patterned wallpapered walls. On the far side, a large, striking print rests on the floor, framed in simple black metal. It reveals the silhouette of a woman sitting with her legs bent and her head on her knees, back-dropped in all-white. I tiny red line cuts diagonally through the picture. The raw emotion of the piece nearly moves Greta to tears.

"Brian, this is gorgeous," Greta breathes as she walks toward the artwork. She stands rooted to the floor, staring at it in silence. But in her head is anything but silence. The piece calls to her, reaching out to envelope her in an abstract hug, leaving her feeling an ache of delight.

Brian clears his throat. "So do you want something to drink?" he asks, his awkward question almost an intrusion into Greta's deep emotional ride. "Greta?" he says with some more force.

"Oh, sorry. I'm entranced!"

Brian points to the ensuite bathroom at the other end of the bedroom and offers Greta a few minutes to get settled. He closes the door behind him and strolls back down the stairs to the kitchen, his pulse quickened by Greta's approval of his house and its artwork—*his home.*

AFTER DINNER, Greta and Brian find themselves in the family room, seated on the leather couch. The windows sit open to let in the mild springtime air, and Greta hears crickets chirping with insect desire as they seek mates for the new season.

With flushed cheeks, they unwrap themselves from their first passionate embrace since the kiss they had shared in the car. To

Greta, it feels as if that initial kiss was ages ago. Her blue eyes are hooded with barely controlled longing as she looks into Brian's steel-colored irises. Lifting her hands away from their perch on his stubbled cheeks, she leans back against the arm of the couch and breathes in deeply. The scent of the sandalwood incense burning on the kitchen counter is carried up through her nose, and she sighs. Right now, her world is perfect. And she's not sure she's ever believed that could be the case in all her life. It's intoxicating. Brian is intoxicating.

"You're one of the few people I can look in the eye," she admits. Her eyes dart toward her lap as if she's jinxed it. She moves into a cross-legged position two cushions away from Brian. This new level of vulnerability squashes her, leaving her wondering if she'll ever find normal.

"Why is that?" He drapes his arm over the back of the couch as if he's reaching for her, willing her to come back toward him. But she refuses the invitation for now.

"Why is what? That you're the only one or that I can't look people in the eye at all?"

"Both," Brian says with a guilty grin.

"Brian, I don't play games. I can't play games. What you see is, well, what I am. I don't understand nuance. I don't get social cues. And I don't like feeling exposed. Theretofore, to use lawyer-speak, I don't like eye contact."

Brian laughs out loud. "Do I talk like that?"

"No." She looks toward the gas-log fireplace, wishing it was cool enough to ask him to turn it on. But then the thought of a fire, no matter how cozy, reminds her of her nightmare, the one where she was being chased, and Greta shivers.

"You okay?"

"Yeah. And to answer your other question: I like you. No games, okay? What do we do with this? With *us*?" Greta's words tumble out.

"I like you too, Greta Goldman. A lot. I have wondered the same thing. Where is this leading?"

"And what have you come up with?"

"Honestly, I don't know. I was not expecting to feel this way about you . . . about anyone right now. I don't want to assume we're far enough along for me to ask you to stay in Atlantic City, to possibly even move here, but the idea of living states apart isn't sitting well with me either." Brian runs his hand through his hair, causing his cowlick to stick up. Greta reaches over and smooths it down.

"Yeah." It's all she can say as the weight of her past, her family drama and loss, her and Brian's current responsibilities, and so many unknowns force any of the words she wants to say down into her throat. "We barely know each other."

"I want to get to know you. For example," Brian's heart-fingers cross as he treads forward, "tell me about your knee. It bounces when you're uncomfortable. Is that something you've always done?"

Greta frowns. "Yes. It's like a tic. I can't control it. It happens all the time, but it's more pronounced when I'm tired or . . . or stressed." She puts her hands on her knees. "It hasn't been this bad since college."

"Richard's list? Is that the problem?" Brian internally prays he hasn't caused more anxiety.

"Probably. I also smile or laugh at inappropriate times." Her shoulders move up, then down in surrender.

His head drops. "Why didn't you tell me about your anxiety?"

"You said there was no work-around to Richard's list!" Greta's voice rises and echoes off of the walls. "I didn't think there was a point, and I barely knew you."

"I'm so sorry, Greta."

"We're almost finished with it—the list. There's no point in turning . . ." Greta realizes she is yelling. "There's no point in turning back now," she finishes in a quieter voice.

"Have you always struggled with anxiety?"

Greta blinks and looks to her right, unsure of what to say.

Then, "Ever since I was a kid. It worsened with my parents' . . . you know."

Brian knows.

"Well, what do you want to know about me?" he asks, ready to dive in and unravel the feelings he has for the woman sitting in front of him—the awkward, direct, big-hearted woman with the cobalt-colored eyes, leg tic, and sometimes loud voice who captured his attention the moment he watched her duck to enter the Extra Egg Café.

"All of it. But not now," Greta says as she leans toward him. "I just want to forget about everything." She giggles as he wraps his arms around her and draws her in.

So much for no games, she thinks.

28

The Third Wednesday

After a night of flirting, cuddling, and talking, followed by a few hours of rest in their respective bedrooms, Brian reluctantly drops Greta off at Dawn's home, an oceanfront one-story bungalow that sits on pylons ten yards from the beach. Its baby-blue siding and bright white trim indicate a house well cared for by its owner. The front door hosts a full-length pane of glass, which allows Greta a sneak peek inside. Greta first spies light gray, almost white, hardwood floors, and when she lifts her eyes, she's able to see directly through the house, all the way to the alluring blue-gray waters of the vast ocean on the other side.

Then Dawn is at the door, a dazzling smile taking up most of her face as she opens it.

"Welcome to my abode on the beach!" Her throaty and rich voice reminds Greta of why she was excited to stay with Dawn.

"Hi," Greta replies. "Are you ready to host me?"

"Oh, I am *so* excited you're here. We're going to have a lot of fun." She hugs Greta.

"I'll see you on Friday?" Brian says as he turns to Greta after thanking Dawn with a nod.

"Yup."

He kisses her on the cheek and turns to leave. Dawn raises an eyebrow at Greta, who blushes. They watch Brian stride down the stairs and into the front passenger seat of the Cadillac. As Antonio drives off, the two women enter the house, neither mentioning the very comfortable and very physical goodbye Brian just offered Greta.

After dinner, Greta tells Dawn she needs to run an errand.

"Take my car."

"No, that's okay. I'll just call for an Uber."

Greta turns away and types the bus station into the app as the destination.

When Greta's car arrives, she tells Dawn she'll be back soon. Then she grabs both of her bags and walks out the front door.

When the Uber arrives at the Atlantic City bus station, Greta steps out of the car. Without a thank you or any words, she shuts the door and strides to the car rental booth.

Precious sits behind the plastic window, and Greta breathes out a sigh. She hadn't realized she was holding her breath. Precious's smile grows wide as Greta steps up to the window.

"What are you doing here? Need a rental car again?"

"No. But can you talk?"

Precious eyes Greta with interest. "I have a break in ten minutes."

"I'll wait." Greta steps to the side and pulls out her cell phone.

When Precious's break arrives, she meets Greta at a bench. The two sit. Greta doesn't know how to start so opts for a few more seconds of silence.

"So what can I do for you, Miss Greta?"

"You seem to have liked Uncle Richard. I want to tell you something."

Precious's eyes shine, and she shifts herself on the bench to face Greta fully.

Greta continues, "First, why were you leaving the casino early on a weekend?"

"I was investigatin', of course." Precious smiles. Greta stares at her.

"Well, I might know who wanted to hurt him. But I don't know why there would be other victims. Why there's a serial killer." Greta realizes she's done the very thing the police asked her not to do—tell others of the multiple relate deaths. Shrugging internally, she realizes it's been on the news. *Who cares?*

"Tell me what you know." Precious stares at Greta in anticipation.

"Uncle Richard made a certain family angry. Like very angry. They still hold a grudge."

Precious nods her head. "I know who you mean. Sofia DeMarco and her family, right?"

"I don't know her last name, but they own the lunch place."

Precious looks into the distance, then shakes her head. "Maybe. They didn't like Richard, but they ain't bad people. Worth a thought, though."

Greta shrugs. "Just wanted you to know." She pulls out her phone and taps the Uber app once again.

Precious peers at Greta, thinking she's quite a character. For her part, Greta is thinking the same thing about Precious.

When the Uber ride pulls up a few minutes later, the two women nod to each other. Then Greta stands and ambles toward the waiting car.

It's nearly midnight, and neither Bill nor Jean can sleep. They toss and turn on their respective sides of their queen-sized bed, eager for the results of the DNA test. Though they both know the other is wide awake, they don't speak to each other.

Finally, Bill gets up, puts on his glasses that are sitting on his bedside table, and climbs the stairs to the third-floor sunroom.

The moonlight on the ocean is breathtaking, bouncing off of the small white-tipped waves like a flashlight hitting a mirror. He sits in his usual chair. As he stares out at the beach, he notices a tall, dark figure strolling by the water, the moon's light is just enough to give the individual a shape but nothing more. The person is wearing a black sweatshirt, the hood up, and black pants. While it's not unusual to see people enjoying the peace found late at night on the vacant sand, this person makes the hair on Bill's neck rise—not because of anything they are doing. It's simply a feeling of unease, which he just can't shake. He blinks a few times, trying to decide if something about this night-walker warrants more action. Then the figure is gone.

29

The Third Thursday

Bill and Jean, after little sleep the night before, relax in their third-story sunroom. They are sipping on iced tea to fight the mugginess in the early afternoon May air, when Bill's cell phone rings, causing them both to jump.

"Hello, this is Bill Goldman."

"Mr. Goldman, it's Lacy Grubbs with the Atlantic City PD, calling about the DNA lab results." Bill sets down his mug on the coaster in front of him.

"Oh, hi. Thanks for calling, Ms. Grubbs. That was fast. We weren't expecting your call yet."

"We put a rush on it given . . . the circumstances of your brother's death."

"Well, what's the verdict?" Bill glances at Jean and nods. She reaches over the armrest of her chair to grab his other hand to squeeze it. Bill feels the coolness of Jean's hand from holding her iced drink.

"We can't say with one-hundred percent certainty, but the woman who was with you at the police station is *very likely* a family member. She had an 11.3 percent match to your DNA, indicating a family connection consistent with a great-uncle-great-niece relationship."

"So she *is*, in fact, Greta Goldman, as she says," Bill confirms what he's hearing. His heart skips a couple of beats, then pounds through his shirt as his eyes grow moist, realizing the implications. The sound of a thousand buzzing bees takes over his brain, and he barely hears the next words spoken through the phone.

"Again, we can't tell you that for sure, but yes, the odds are very good. Would you like us to notify the other party, um . . . Ms. Goldman, of the results?"

"Yes. Certainly. Thank you, Ms. Grubbs." He pauses as the woman relays a few more things, but his mind is gone from the conversation.

After a beat of silence, he says, "Okay, have a good day." Bill taps the end button and looks at Jean. He squeezes her hand.

"The new Greta is the real Greta?" Jean's eyes enlarge as she filters the information through her mind. "So the woman who stayed with us . . ." She can't bring herself to complete the sentence.

"*Isn't* Richard's great-niece," Bill finishes.

"Then who is she?" Jean asks, knowing full well Bill doesn't know but just cannot comprehend what's happening, causing the rhetorical question. "What now?"

Bill jiggles his head back and forth, unable to form more words until he can process his own bewilderment and betrayal.

Jean lets go of Bill's hand and puts both of hers to her face. She unleashes a waterworks of emotion, evidence of the fear, anxiety, confusion, sorrow, and suddenly . . . the anger she is feeling. "We have to let Brian know!" Jean suddenly blurts out.

"Yes, you're right. I'll call him right now." Bill is thankful for something to do.

"Wait!" Bill looks over at Jean and stops searching for Brian's number in his phone. "Should we call the police or something?" she asks.

"We just hung up with the police!" Bill laments. "But yes, maybe."

"Let's come up with a plan and get reinforcements before we notify Brian. The authorities will know what to do."

Bill agrees and the two stand up to leave their little sanctuary overlooking the ocean. It seems their peaceful retirement, their grief over losing Richard, and their life at large will be put on hold for a bit as they unravel this mystery.

As they make their way downstairs, Jean whispers, "But the first Greta was so nice. She *felt* like family! . . . *I loved her,* Bill." Her last words come through a fresh wave of tears.

"Me too, Jean. Me too."

THE AUTHOR STARES at her laptop's screen as she sits in Dawn's living room overlooking the immense ocean, realizing her churning emotions are swirling like an eddy. Sometimes crashing, sometimes receding, over and over. Before her is her final manuscript. She had crawled out of bed earlier in the morning to review it for a last time. She had trouble falling asleep last night after watching *The Proposal* with Dawn. Once she finally found deep sleep, around two o'clock in the morning and after a short walk on the beach, she didn't wake until ten-thirty. Now, mid-afternoon, she's ready to hit the send button on the email to her publisher.

As she stares at the words THE END on page 388 of the double-spaced Word document, she feels a fluttering in her gut. *Could this be the one?* Her previous books—two published in the past five years—had done well, selling around twenty to thirty thousand copies each, but neither had topped those big charts she is desperately after. Those first books helped her gain traction as an author to watch and follow, and that had been her plan. Her following had grown, especially with the benefit of being related to the most well-known commercial real estate mogul who ever lived in the Northeast, *or so people think*.

She sighs. Maintaining the false identity has been easier than she thought it would be. No one suspects a thing. But she never expected to be tangled up as Richard's named heir in the first place . . . or to fall in love. When Brian Gogh had called to say she needed to travel to the AC, she panicked, wondering what she should do. After going back and forth about whether to just come clean, she took her chances, figuring if she walked away as a billionaire, she'd simply sit on the wealth. She didn't want to become one of *those* wealthy people who use their money to get away with things. And the real Greta Goldman had disappeared, anyway.

The entire escapade was taxing her nerves. And she certainly never expected the FBI wanting to interview her. She wonders if she can escape New Jersey before that interview happens. Briefly, she thinks about Brian and his dimple. *Is he worth it?* Pushing Brian from her thoughts, she turns back to the computer screen.

The last few words in her manuscript blur as her eyes grow wet. It has been a long journey. She hopes for luck and the universe's mercy and whatever else one might wish upon as she moves the cursor over the send icon and taps the mouse pad on the keyboard. She hears the swoosh indicative of a sent email. Greta leans back in her chair and allows the tears to flow. The pent-up frustration of her unscheduled trip to the AC, the fear of being discovered, the stress of managing the billionaire's list, the relief of finishing her book, the confusion over her profound feelings for Brian, and several upcoming decisions warring inside her changing heart overflow and slide down her cheeks. It's as if sending her book off to her publisher releases every weight she's been carrying, even if only temporarily.

After a good, long cry, Greta stands up. She stretches her arms over her head, then pulls out her phone to call Brian. An impulsive move that rattles her once she remembers he's out of town.

She still wants to celebrate, so she walks outside to find Dawn who told her earlier she'd be lounging on the sundeck.

DAWN REJOICES with the woman she believes is Greta, saying they have to celebrate her book with something tangible. "Let's go out for a fancy dinner," Dawn offers.

"I'd rather just stay in. I'm exhausted from these last two weeks. I feel like I've been everywhere Atlantic City has to offer," Greta confides.

"All right then. Let's grill some steaks!"

"Perfect."

After a quick trip to the local market, Dawn returns with filets, red potatoes, asparagus, a bottle of Merlot, and non-alcoholic beer, and that last item is one Greta finds interesting. As Dawn fires up the grill and prepares the potatoes in the kitchen, she asks Greta about her childhood. As she's now accustomed to doing, Greta sidesteps the truth—that she was orphaned as an infant by a birth mother hooked on drugs. She spent the first twelve years of her life bouncing around the foster care system. The journey was a tumultuous one, including three years with one family where her foster "dad," a functional alcoholic, once pushed her so hard, she fell onto a glass table, splitting her upper lip. She had needed ten stitches, but she didn't get them until a full day later, once everyone in the family had the "story" down pat. The very scar, she thinks about now, that Brian believes came from a playground mishap during an otherwise happy childhood as part of the Goldman family.

That foster family with the abusive father had been wealthy. The father had hidden his alcoholism and abusive behavior behind his reputation as a wholesome family man—a church-going man to boot. He hid behind his fortune, too, creating a false narrative the entire community in North Carolina had believed. No one knew he frequently downed at least ten adult beverages nearly every day.

It wasn't just Greta he'd become abusive with, either. Over the years, her foster mother and another foster child had needed to cover up bruises along the way. It was a home filled with intimidation and lies. Ever since that season in her life, Greta had harbored resentment toward the uber rich who, she believes, tend to buy their way out of anything they want, including culpability. *Like Brian's parents.*

At age thirteen, she finally landed in an adoptive family's home as an *official* daughter. Against all odds, they had nurtured her, offering her everything she had needed, from security and grace to approval and love—and years of counseling—even when she rebelled to see if that love would be conditional. It wasn't. Over time, when her new parents' efforts to support and love her remained consistent and they didn't abandon her, her grades improved in high school, and she was accepted at the University of North Carolina at Charlotte, into their English and Creative Writing program—not architecture like the real Greta Goldman had studied. And she had flourished for the first time in her life.

Instead of that history—the truth—Greta tells Dawn about a happy childhood as an only child of the billionaire's younger brother's son. A life filled with opportunities, attention, and smooth sailing, which is what she assumes the real Greta experienced—at least until her parents died in that car accident.

"I grew up in North—northern Maryland," she begins, almost slipping up and trying to act natural while recounting all the facts she'd learned about Henry Goldman's side of the family. She gets it all out, but even she knows it sounds like a forced recollection, as if she has practiced it in front of a mirror for hours. Because she has.

"They died in a three-car accident on ice-slicked roads when I was a junior in college."

Dawn shakes her head. "Tragic. I can't imagine how hard that must have been."

Geta merely nods her head. The two women walk out onto the deck. The temperature of the salty air hovers near ideal, the ocean breeze minimal. And the rhythmic crash of the waves settles Greta's heart, which had ratcheted up while talking about her false childhood. She looks at the water and sighs. "What about you, Dawn? You're so successful and seem so happy. How did it all start for you?" Greta is genuinely interested in her *mommother's* life. She wonders why Dawn is single. She seems like the perfect human being. "And why aren't you married?"

When she sees Dawn's fleeting, albeit pained, expression, Greta puts her hand to her mouth. "Sorry. That was rude." She giggles to cope with the awkward moment. "I tend to do that, blurt things out without thinking."

Dawn smiles and rubs her hand along Greta's upper arm. "Oh, I don't mind sharing, but first let's get our meal ready," she says as she flips the steaks on the grill.

"Sure." She's grateful Dawn moved right past the embarrassment with an ease that buried her discomfort within seconds.

"Steaks are done. Let's get inside and put together the other parts of our meal while these rest a minute." They slip back inside, where the smell of the roasting potatoes is heavenly. Greta's stomach rumbles.

Once seated at Dawn's kitchen table, Dawn pours Greta some wine, opens a can of "virgin" beer for herself, and pours it into a wine glass. As she brushes her copper-colored bangs to the side, Dawn nods toward her beverage as she begins her story.

"My parents divorced when I was eight. They were both alcoholics. My dad played the disappearing act while my mom took on the role of the mean drunk. Only once did she hit me, thank goodness," Dawn says. She speaks with compassion for the little girl she describes, but also as someone who is no longer held down by the trauma of her yesteryears.

Greta's eyebrows rise as Dawn admits her family baggage. *No way,* she thinks.

"From a young age, I started comparing my life to other girls' lives, especially the ones with intact families. I wanted what they had: support, security . . . joy. I felt none of that but vowed I'd find it. I guess you could say I entered the proverbial fork in the road. Even though I felt chained to my family and all of its dysfunction, I realized I had choices. I could either become like them—join the chaos and learn from my terrible role models—or do a complete turn and run the other way. If I joined them, I'd be acting out my negative feelings, which I intuitively knew would lead me further away from where I wanted to be—which was someplace safe and content . . . no, not just content. Filled with joy."

Dawn puts a bite of food in her mouth and chews slowly, thinking, choosing her words carefully. Greta leans in, enthralled, trying to understand how the successful and wise woman in front of her came from that kind of background. *A background kinda like mine.*

"Generosity and gratitude paved the way for my choice to turn my back on the negativity and trauma. When I was sixteen and finally able to drive myself, I would leave the house as often as possible, then living with my dad. I did some volunteer work at the local hospital—brought magazines to patients or just sat and spoke with them in their rooms if they were lonely. I guess that's where I learned to love seniors. When I turned eighteen, I escaped to college, never looking back. This may be why Richard and I connected so deeply. We both came from troubled pasts. And we both still loved people. Enough to help in any way we could. I remember the first charity I supported with a few meager dollars here and there. I was only seventeen."

"Wow." Greta doesn't know what else to say.

Eventually, as the wine knocks down Greta's defenses, she asks, "I can't believe you started donating money that young. What did those places do that was so special?"

Dawn smiles but sidesteps answering directly. "Leaning into helping others, even while desperate myself, was the best decision I ever made. The satisfaction we get by helping others fills us up when we're feeling empty inside. It gives us meaning. When we're hurting or lonely, helping others reminds us that it's not all about us—even our most personal problems—I guess. There's something bigger at stake, and when we view the world that way, our horrific circumstances shrink in comparison to the bigger picture."

Greta's face contorts. "I don't get it."

"When we make life *not* about us but about others, all of our hard stuff seems to diminish, and we realize we have a larger purpose, more than just surviving in this world. It's a strange phenomenon, but it seems there is less responsibility on our shoulders. That's when we thrive—as we come to understand the *why* of our existence. *Why* we are here in the first place."

"The *why*?" Now, Greta shakes her head. "I'm sorry, but aren't we all just living on a spinning ball of rock for however long and then . . . that's it?"

"No, I don't think that's the case at all. I think that's a limited way of viewing ourselves. We were created for so much more than eating, sleeping, working, and even having fun."

Greta tilts her head.

"We were created to spread goodness. To make an impact that extends past our lives here, which, as you agree, is fleeting. I believe in eternity, in heaven. And while I don't think we have to *do good* to get there, I believe how we live here impacts our forevers. I don't believe any of us are insignificant. And I don't think lives are pointless or random."

"And donating to charities helps you feel significant?"

Dawn nods. "Yes. That's certainly part of it. When we help others, we indirectly help ourselves. It's a weird equation, but I've found it to be true hundreds of times over."

"How do you decide who to support?"

"Well, I think long and hard. But that's just using my brain. I also use my heart." Dawn pauses. "What makes you smile, Greta?"

"Huh?" Greta wrings her hands under the table.

"What makes you so thrilled that when you see it or do it, you could just get up and dance because you're so excited?"

"I'm not a very good dancer."

"No, I mean what makes your heart feel full, happy?"

It suddenly occurs to Greta that this woman sitting across from her is showing an unusual amount of gentleness and patience, pressing into Greta with more compassion than she's ever experienced. Where others in Greta's past would have given up or ridiculed her inability to grasp expressions of speech and make fun of the way she takes everything literally, Dawn is rephrasing and waiting, intent on driving home her point. She's not backing down but leaning in, giving Greta time.

Greta wonders if Dawn can sense her growing anxiety, and doubt creeps in. Greta tries to push it down. *It seems she still wants to connect, to show me she cares.* Greta considers what makes her happy.

"That's a weird question. I don't know what makes me that excited. Writing, maybe?"

"Yes," Dawn says with a smile of approval. "Outstanding. Your stories connect you to others and others to each other, soul to soul. Your words impact people. You can use that gift for even more good, more than just entertaining people. If you're up for it, we can figure out a way you could serve others with your writing in new ways, besides writing novels. What do you think?"

Greta, unsure about what Dawn is offering, but fully willing to trust her this once, nods.

Dawn clinks Greta's wine glass with hers. "Here's to finding your *why*."

30

The Third Friday

Bill and Jean sit in the lobby of the state police station on N. Rhode Island Avenue, having been directed by the city police to go there after Bill had called them late in the afternoon yesterday, explaining the gist of his and Jean's concerns.

They are expecting a state trooper, or even a state investigator, but an athletic, dark-haired woman in a gray pants suit arrives to greet them. Her face is narrow, much like the rest of her, and a dark mole sits near the corner of her mouth as if someone dotted her skin with a brown marker.

"Mr. and Mrs. Goldman?" she asks. Her caramel-colored eyes look serious even though she smiles gently at them.

"Yes?" Bill replies.

"I'm Special Agent Kat Turner with the FBI."

Jean sucks in her breath and grabs Bill's arm.

"We've taken over your late brother's apparent identity theft case as a federal fraud case. Can we talk?" she says in explanation.

"Of course," Jean says and looks at Bill. He seems lost in thought but nods his agreement.

The three make their way to a small conference room deep in

the belly of the police department. When they enter the brightly lit room, they are greeted with a nod from an Asian man in a midnight-blue suit and matching tie.

"This is my partner, Special Agent Cheng." Her partner barely looks at them, focusing instead on a tablet he holds in his hands. "Have a seat," SA Turner waves to a couple of tan fabric chairs.

Once they are settled, Bill asks, "What do you want to know? Or what do we need to know? I'm not sure where to begin." Nervous energy spills like a waterfall.

"Why don't you tell us what you know, and we'll go from there?" The special agent's words come out friendly through her smiling mouth, but there is something no-nonsense about her too. Bill wonders if she ever gets nervous and decides likely not.

"Well," Bill begins, "We discovered the woman who claimed to be me and my late brother's great-niece is not. I don't know how long she's been impersonating her. But our attorney—my brother's attorney—doesn't know about it yet, and he's still taking her around the city, showing her Richard's holdings. I guess she's doing this to claim his estate?" Bill is rambling, but SA Turner lets him. "My brother—Richard Goldman—he was killed a few weeks ago."

The FBI woman nods but keeps quiet. She looks at Jean to see if she wants to add anything. Jean, now misty-eyed, stays mute, glancing between Bill and the FBI agent. With her arms crossed, she rubs her forearms.

"Okay," Special Agent Turner says. "Is that all?"

"The real Greta is in town; she came in a few days ago, and that's when all this came to light. We had a DNA test done to confirm that the new Greta—the real Greta—is our family. We don't know who the old Greta is." Bill slumps in his chair. It seems he's finished.

"And Richard's murder remains unsolved," Jean adds. "Don't forget that, Bill!"

Special Agent Turner studies the couple. They seem genuinely concerned and certainly distraught.

"Mr. and Mrs. Goldman—"

"Please, call us Bill and Jean," Bill interrupts.

"Okay. Bill and Jean, your late brother was the victim of a serial killer targeting some of the wealthiest men around the country. I'm sorry the police hadn't told you that yet, but I think they were trying to keep the information quiet, especially since the FBI took the case almost immediately. They probably didn't want to create a panic while we're still making leeway in our investigation, and most people don't fit the killer's victim profile, anyway. That's also why your brother's body has not been released. But you should have been notified. There's no excuse for that." Special Agent Turner watches Bill's face turn pale. "Are you okay, sir?"

Bill only nods. Jean starts shaking. SA Turner hands Jean a tissue from the box sitting by her partner. SA Cheng had turned off his tablet and is now listening intently to the conversation.

"I'm sorry to bring you that news." Special Agent Turner pauses out of respect. "Second, we want to find this *old* Greta, as you call her, as soon as possible. . . . You've met her; what's she like?"

Choking on his words, Bill describes the tall woman as a charming but odd individual who spent the night with them in their home. "She told us she was twenty-nine. I don't know what she has, but she's kind of wired differently. Not in a bad way," he says with a shrug. "Sometimes, she says things that seem a little off or doesn't pick up on social cues. But she's so nice and . . . *understated*. We would have never guessed she wasn't who she said she was. She's quiet and introverted—respectful. We liked her!"

"And Richard thought she was our great-niece too," Jean adds. "He spoke to her on the phone a couple of times over the years—at least we think so. I'm so confused! She must have been doing this for a while!"

There is a single knock on the door.

"We'll be back. I'll have someone bring you something to drink. Waters? Soda?" SA Turner asks as Special Agent Cheng leaves the room first.

"Water would be nice," Jean answers meekly.

Then the agents are gone and Bill and Jean are left staring at the closed door, unsure what to make of everything they've just learned.

DURING BILL and Jean's meeting with SAs Turner and Cheng, Greta Goldman had been brought into a different conference room, the FBI having already contacted her using the number she provided for the DNA test. The two special agents enter. Greta stands to shake their hands.

"Greta Goldman, I presume," the female agent speaks as she shakes Greta's hand. "I'm Special Agent Kat Turner. How are you?"

"Doing okay, all things considered," Greta replies. She sits back down in her chair and leans forward on her elbows. Her green eyes sparkle with wetness. "Sorry. I just can't believe someone was pretending to be me. . . . I'm not that important!" She tries to lighten the mood with her joke but realizes it's not that funny. She *is* someone, or at least, will be soon with the money—that Bill confirmed yesterday—she'll now inherit from her great-uncle. It's just all too much for her right now.

"Mind if we ask you a few questions?" SA Turner dives right in. SA Cheng types on his tablet, which he had turned back on after they entered the room. Greta looks from one to the other.

"Sure. Of course," she says. "Anything to help."

"When did you move away from the States?"

"Almost eight years ago. I've been in Greece the whole time," Greta says. She plays with the silver band on her right ring finger, feeling the serious attitude of the agents wash over her. Suddenly, she misses Greece.

The questions continue rapid-fire. "And what have you been doing there?"

"I own a boutique shop in the coastal town of Chios. I sell gifts, cards, books . . . you know."

"When was the last time you saw your great-uncle, Richard Goldman?"

"At my college graduation—from UNCC, in Charlotte. He came down to visit; we had dinner, and then he left. I think I moved a week later."

"How did you find out about your great-uncle's death?"

"I saw the news online while skimming for updates from back home. I rarely do that, but I happened to see the headline in *The Press*, the city's newspaper, that he had been killed. I immediately booked a flight home. But I had to close up my shop and handle some things before I could come back."

Silence fills the space.

Greta shrugs her shoulders. "What now?" she asks.

"A few things. I'm sorry to tell you, but your great-uncle was the victim of an apparent serial killer's spree, one targeting wealthy men—billionaires and some multi-millionaires too."

Greta stares at the agent. "What? How? . . . I mean . . . what?" She blinks rapidly, her pupils constricting underneath her fine lashes. "Did the woman who stole my identity kill him?"

"It's still under investigation. I'm sorry for your loss and for the circumstances surrounding everything. Do you need a minute?" SA Turner asks, watching Greta the same way she watched Bill and Jean.

"Um . . . no. It's shocking, for sure. And scary. But I didn't know him very well. It's just really sad," Greta says, trying to process everything. The room seems dimmer to her now, as if the lights have been turned down.

"Okay. If you're sure. Are you planning to stay in the area? If not, at least stay in the States for a bit while we iron all this out, okay? We have your contact info."

Greta nods. The information pours over her like someone has

dumped ice-cold water on her head. "I'm staying for a few more days."

The agents stand, shake Greta's hand, and escort her out of the building, reminding her to keep her phone on at all times.

NEARLY AN HOUR after they had left them, the special agents return to Bill and Jean, who are still sitting in the first conference room. The water bottles they had received from an unknown office gopher are empty.

Special Agent Turner apologies for the delay. The two FBI special agents sit, and with Bill and Jean's information, work out a plan to grab the woman impersonating Greta. As they strategize, Bill and Jean can't believe it's happening at all. They're still in shock, their ordinary lives now something straight out of a TV show.

After everyone understands the strategy, SA Turner nods as step one begins. Bill pulls out his phone. He taps a name he finds in his contacts and puts the phone to his ear. Jean holds his knee under the table for support.

"Brian, it's Bill Goldman. Hey. . . . Listen, what are you up to?" There is a long pause. "Okay. Do you mind if we meet you guys there? We'd love to see Greta again. . . . and y-you too, of course." Bill does his best not to stumble over his words. His heart races. "Great. See you then!" He hits the end button and lays the phone in front of him.

"Marven Gardens. One hour." Bill puts his hands over his face and rubs up and down violently, causing his blue glasses to fall to the table. He wishes he could erase the last several weeks of their lives. He wishes Richard was here. He misses his brother, the one with the stovetop hat. And now, he hopes he can help ensure Richard's legacy is protected.

Next to him, Jean drops her head to her chest, unable to understand any of it.

31

Meanwhile . . .

Having been delayed until the mid-afternoon by an impromptu client meeting, Brian and Antonio are finally on their way to pick up Greta when Bill calls.

"Hello, this is Brian Gogh," Brian answers without looking at the caller ID.

"Brian, it's Bill Goldman. Hey . . . Listen, what are you up to?"

"We're on our way to get Greta and then heading to Marven Gardens, the next stop on Richard's list for Greta to visit. Why? Do you need something? Everything okay?"

"Okay. Do you mind if we meet you guys there? We'd love to see Greta again. . . . and y-you too, of course," Bill replies.

"Sure! I bet Greta would love that. She really enjoyed her time with you and Jean. We'll be there in about forty-five minutes. Want to meet in an hour in front of the mustard-yellow house? Everyone seems to know that one."

"Great. See you then!" says Bill before he abruptly hangs up.

Brian finds the brief exchange odd but shrugs his shoulders and quickly forgets about it.

Marven Gardens is a neighborhood, now also a historic district, in the heart of Atlantic City. Encompassing sixteen acres, most of the homes were built in the 1920s and 1930s. The National Register of Historic Places added it to their list in 1990 because of the noteworthy architecture of the homes and the way the city had preserved the community. Brian can't wait to tell Greta how Richard played a part in that designation process.

The car pulls up to Dawn's beach house, and Brian sees the two ladies already waiting outside—Greta's duffle and sling packed and ready to go. They're sitting in a couple of chairs on the street-side deck of the house, sipping on what looks like iced tea. Brian hopes the stay went well. When he emerges from the Cadillac, he yells up to them.

"Thought you two would be on the other deck, facing the ocean!"

"We were, but the winds shifted, and it was too chilly," Dawn explains.

"We almost slept out there last night, though. So peaceful," Greta adds. Her skin looks a little tanner than Brian remembers. His breath catches and happiness fills every space in his body when she smiles at him. He realizes both women are in good spirits, and he relaxes.

He and Antonio climb the stairs as Greta and Dawn say their goodbyes. Both women know this might be the last time they see each other, at least for some time.

"Let me know what you decide," Dawn tells Greta as they hug.

"I will," she replies. Brian's eyes go up. "None of your business," Greta answers his curiosity. Brian contorts his mouth into an exaggerated frown with his bottom lip jutting out, but inside, he's even more interested to know what they were talking about now. He hopes it involves Greta staying in Atlantic City. He can't help but dream of where that decision might lead.

Antonio picks up Greta's teal duffle and then looks to her for permission to carry it to the car. She nods, having become more trusting of these two men she's spent these last few weeks with. Antonio nods back and bounds down the stairs to the Cadillac to leave the three of them to continue their farewells.

"Time to go to Marven Gardens," Brian reports. "We're meeting Bill and Jean there. They wanted to see you again before you leave Atlantic City," Brian offers as an explanation.

"We still have another few days, don't we? Like five or six . . . actually almost a week!" Greta says as she pulls out the rolled-up list from her sling and looks at it. She has crossed out just over three-quarters of the line items.

"That's true," says Brian. "I guess they just want to see you. Period."

"Well, you two, thanks for giving me more time to hang out with Greta," Dawn interjects. "I had the best time. Please stay in touch, okay, Greta?" Dawn wraps her arms around Greta one more time.

"You know I will." Greta reciprocates Dawn's hug, basking in the warmth of her kindheartedness. *No one hugs like Dawn,* she thinks.

"ANTONIO, let's stop here, and we'll hoof it in," Brian directs his driver and friend.

Antonio parks the Cadillac on the outskirts of Marven Gardens. On the trip over, Brian had explained to Greta that Marven Gardens is the historic district of the city. "I think you'll love the architecture," he tells Greta. "We're meeting Bill and Jean in about fifteen minutes in front of the neighborhood's most famous home. It's a bright yellow color, and I can't wait to explain why!"

"Okay." Greta rolls her shoulders and closes her eyes. She has just said goodbye to Dawn, someone who had snuck in and lodged herself into Greta's once-cold and walled-up heart. Now, it seems she's going to have to say goodbye to Bill and Jean *again.*

Then, in another week . . . to Brian. Tears prick at her eyes. She never expected to come to the AC and learn how to love.

"Hey, are you okay?" Brian asks, noticing the glaze overtake her eyes.

"Yeah, I'm fine," Greta answers. "Let's do this." She stuffs her feelings deep down where she can manage them. That is something she's always been good at, and right now, it seems like the best thing to do. There is a historic district to cross off her list.

They exit the Cadillac and Brian gives her the rundown of a few homes in the area. "Richard was involved in this area for decades. He held a place in his heart for the history, and one of his goals was to preserve as much as he could as the homes aged. As you can see, the architecture is unique. The first female architect in the world designed these homes. She left her imprint—" Brian stops when he looks at Greta who is staring at him with a smirk. "What?"

"Brian, I don't care about the architecture. Art, yes. Architecture, no. Just tell me what Richard did here and let's go."

"Okay, but I thought you went to school for architecture."

"What? Oh, I—um—I did. But I realized I was more of a writer and art connoisseur." Greta's heart rate ticks up. *Don't blow it!*

"Really?" Brian presses, something needling his memory bank and not sitting well with him.

"I guess. Come on, let's keep walking," she encourages him. They had stopped on the sidewalk, and she wants him to skim over this topic as quickly as possible. *No more mistakes!* she silently admonishes herself.

"Brian!"

Greta looks over her right shoulder and spies Bill and Jean approaching them. They are holding hands and to Greta, look older than the last time she saw them. *Jean has dark circles under her eyes,* she thinks as the pair gets closer. Greta is happy to have them interrupt the awkward conversation between her and Brian.

"Bill and Jean!" Greta cheers. She moves to hug Jean, something she'd never have done in the past, but Jean backs away and puts her hand up. The sting of the rejection reaches deep into Greta's heart and slices it open, releasing old wounds and causing Greta to shift into a heightened state of alert. Every wall that's ever been built is re-erected. *What in the world?*

"We need to talk," Bill offers as a way of explanation. He looks at Brian with regret, then at Greta, and his eyes narrow. "We know you're not Greta Goldman." Bill waits to see how the tall woman will react.

Twenty minutes earlier, the FBI had planted a device on Bill. They had instructed him on what to say and when, all part of the strategic plan Special Agent Kat Turner had laid out. Part of him expects Greta to run. The other part still believes he's face to face with his great-niece, but he compresses that longing down. It is dead hope. He knows science has proven otherwise.

"What? What do you mean?" Greta says. Her eyes blink rapidly. Her hands become slick with moisture, and she glances at Jean in desperation.

"You know what we mean," Bill says.

"Bill, what is this about?" Brian says, confused by the tone and the words Bill is using. Brian's head swivels toward Greta for an explanation, but she is silent, suddenly unable to look at him, unwilling to see that dimple. Those pleading eyes.

"Brian, I'm sorry to say this isn't my great-niece. It's not Richard's great-niece. She's a fraud, right?" he says as his eyes seek Greta's for confirmation.

"Greta, what is he talking about?" Brian feels time slow down. The neighborhood around him turns fuzzy in his periphery as he focuses on the woman he thought he knew—thinks he loves.

A bird chirps in the tree nearest the group on the sidewalk. A car door slams on another block. No one moves.

Greta's shoulders slump, and she loses a full two inches of height as she seems to deflate before everyone's eyes. Tears well up above her lower lids and spill over in rivulets of sorrow and shame.

When Brian sees her reaction, his gut nose dives toward his shoes, and he takes in a quick, shallow breath to keep from passing out.

Greta finally looks toward Brian, her eyes still unable to reach his face but instead, gazing at his chest. A tear sheds down her cheek. "Brian, I'm so sorry. I never meant to hurt you—or anyone," she adds as she turns to Jean. Jean blinks at her in disbelief.

"You're not Greta Goldman?" Brian confirms what his ears hear but his brain cannot process, his voice barely a whisper.

"No. My name is Mallory Jones. And I wanted to tell—" A dark barks in the distance, and again, as when she and Brian were in the throes of affection on his couch, fragmented memories of her nightmare at the Ocean Resort & Casino flood her mind, cracking her composure. Her face crumples and her legs buckle, rendering her to a kneeling position on the pavement in front of Brian. He moves to grab her, but it's too late.

With Mallory's admission, there is a sudden swarm of activity as four FBI special agents emerge: two from around the corners of nearby houses, one from behind a parked van, and the last from behind a row of bushes across the street. Their weapons are drawn and pointed at Mallory. The bird in the nearby tree takes flight, startled by the change in the atmosphere and the flurry of action. The dog's barking recedes into nothingness.

"Miss, put your hands up!" shouts a female special agent as she points her gun at Mallory. The next thing Mallory realizes, someone, whom she'll soon learn is Special Agent Cheng, is behind her, grabbing her elbow and forcing her to a standing position. He guides her hands behind her back. Her sling bag, which was perched on her shoulder, falls to the ground, and the sound of handcuffs snapping into place fills Mallory's ears.

Brian stands dumbfounded. He hasn't moved from the place he's been rooted, still just inches from Mallory. He looks into her face, silently begging for an explanation. None comes. The woman in front of him focuses her glassy-blue eyes on the ground between them, too ashamed to do anything else.

"I'm Special Agent Kat Turner," a pony-tailed woman in an FBI vest explains. "We'll take that sling bag," she says as she scoops it off the ground. SA Turner pulls out the pink towel from the bag.

"Careful. There might be a knife in there," Brian says, still unable to comprehend the scene playing out in front of him. SA Turner's eyes don't betray any surprise.

"We'll take anything else you have," she says as she peers up at the tall, dark-haired woman. Mallory doesn't speak. The special agent pats her down and retrieves the smartphone tucked in the hip pocket of her white capris pants. Mallory's cheeks redden.

"There's another bag in my car," Brian offers, looking toward the Cadillac down the street. He spies Antonio handing a third special agent Mallory's teal-colored duffle.

The special agent begins the sentences everyone knows: "You have the right to remain silent . . ."

Jean, standing several feet away, weeps, causing her mascara to darken the circles beneath her eyes and stain her cheeks like raindrops sliding down a window. Mallory's heart explodes with regret, and then she simply shuts down, unable to tolerate the onslaught of emotions and activity.

After Special Agent Turner removes the device from inside his collar, Bill paces, his righteous anger settling deep into his chest as he watches the FBI escort Mallory away.

"Gret—Mallory, don't say anything," Brian yells after her in an impulsive attempt to help the woman who just broke his heart. "Not until you have an attorney!"

He walks over to Jean and hugs her hard. He's not sure who the hug is meant to console more: her or himself.

Bill lopes over to his wife and attorney-turned-friend. "Brian, we're sorry we had to spring this on you. The FBI had a plan, and well, we were stuck right in the middle of it. We wish we could have told you sooner."

Brian looks at Bill and nods. He's at a loss for words. Despite knowing all about the depths of society and what people are capable of by virtue of his career choice, Greta's lies—*Mallory's lies*—have left him gutted. His legs feel weak, but he's determined to show a measure of strength for Jean and Bill.

"I understand," he whispers as he releases Jean.

"Let's get you home, Jean," Bill says, taking his wife by the hand. "Brian, if you want to talk more, you're more than welcome to come with us."

"I think I'll take you up on that—just not right now," Brian replies, suddenly feeling nauseous. "I'm going to go home too." His lawyer-brain ramps up again. "And I guess I need to find the real Greta and figure out what to do from here."

"Oh, she's in town. That's how we knew—again, a long story," Bill says, momentarily forgetting Brian hasn't been privy to anything since Greta showed up from Greece a few days ago. "She's at the Hard Rock Hotel. Room 1317. She's aware of this *Mallory* woman and everything she's done."

"Thanks," Brian says, more confused than ever. He shakes his head. "Yeah, we'll catch up soon."

The three of them part ways, with Brian shuffling toward his Cadillac, which Antonio has pulled closer to the scene now that the FBI has left. Bill and Jean walk to their car, which is parked a block away. The bird that had been startled by the afternoon's events flies back to the tree and perches on the same branch on which it started, and a few minutes later, the dog down the road starts barking again.

32

The special agents usher Mallory to the Northfield Resident Agency in a nondescript blue sedan, a stop on their way to the Camden office. When they pull up, Mallory, who is seated in the back behind the passenger seat and next to Special Agent Cheng, notes the white stucco building the FBI shares with a Morgan Stanley office. *How ironic*, she thinks. The only indication from the road that this is also government property is the US flag, flapping on the pole out front. Special Agent Turner pulls past the fence and parks.

The special agent seated in the front passenger seat exits the vehicle followed by the other two. Mallory never caught his name. The three speak with each other just outside the car in hushed voices, their eyes darting toward Mallory every few seconds. Agent Cheng is animated, waving his hands around as he talks. Mallory stares straight ahead, the shock of her capture receding, leaving her feeling crushed by the consequences of her choices from so many years ago. She had never wanted to hurt anyone. It's the reason she had avoided most of the calls from Richard to the house in North Carolina. She figured if she ignored him, he'd go away, never imagining he'd leave his entire estate to her. Never imagining he'd be *killed*. And never imagining she'd have to face his friends and family.

Her shoulders ache, with her arms still positioned behind her back and handcuffed together. A minute goes by, and the doors of the car open. Special Agents Turner and Cheng slide back into their original positions. The third special agent is gone, leaving the front passenger seat empty.

"Get comfortable, Mallory," Special Agent Turner says over her shoulder. It's a bit of a ride to Camden.

Mallory doesn't respond. Numbness has taken over her body and muzzled her emotions.

IN CAMDEN, there is a rush of activity to get Mallory booked and in front of the magistrate, or judge, as soon as possible. No federal magistrate wants to come in late on a Friday night. Mallory waits in a holding room with dark gray cinder block on three sides, and a windowed wall with reflective glass on the other. She's already been fingerprinted and photographed. Special Agent Turner told her to wait, that she'd be back to take her statement. That was a half-hour ago. Mallory's bladder burns with fullness, so she hopes the special agent comes back soon.

The clock on the wall tells her it's 4:48 p.m. Mallory doesn't feel hungry even though it's been several hours since she scarfed down a quick lunch at Dawn's house before Brian arrived. *That was today?* she thinks. It feels so long ago. So much has changed. The room grows cold in more ways than one, and she shivers.

The door to the gray room flies open, the noise echoing off of the bleak walls, and Special Agent Turner walks in. She looks tired too. The starched white blouse under her blazer is wrinkled, and her hair is different, the band holding it back now slipping down toward her shoulders.

"Mallory, help me understand," she says without preamble.

She reaches back and tightens her ponytail after she slaps a folder on the table. Her light brown eyes peer at her prisoner.

"I'm happy to tell you everything, but I have to go to the bathroom," Mallory says, a pained look on her face.

Special Agent Turner sighs and nods. "Come on," she says as she stands and unlocks Mallory's handcuffs from the table.

When they return from the restroom, Mallory is locked back to the table.

SA Turner sits across from her. SA Cheng takes the seat next to his partner, a pen and paper poised for note-taking.

"Your rights were stated earlier. We'd like to talk, to understand . . ." Mallory can't focus on the words floating to her ears, and her thoughts take her to Dawn's beachfront house. She wonders what Dawn would think of her now, and she wishes she could put her head down on the table in defeat.

When SA Turner stops talking, Mallory weighs her words and sees nothing to lose. "I'm an unlucky nobody."

"Unlucky?" SA Turner's eyebrows go up.

"That's literally what my name means. *Mallory Jones. Unlucky nobody.*"

SA Turner closes her eyes and takes a deep breath. "We know you grew up in the foster care system. We also know you attended the University of North Carolina at Charlotte." Mallory nods, not surprised they've identified her, having spent most of her childhood traipsing through *the system.* Her prints would be everywhere, she assumes.

"It seems you were doing well. You have no criminal history, no juvenile records. So I wonder where it went so wrong. I asked myself, 'Why would someone like this pose as Greta Goldman?' Then it hit me. You're an author. And a fairly successful one at that. And, as Richard's heir, you have everything to gain by Richard being gone."

Brian's words echo in Mallory's mind: *Don't say anything without your attorney.*

Mallory shifts in her seat. "Do I get a lawyer? I'm only asking because I'm impulsive and tend to say things that come out wrong. . . . I don't want to say the wrong thing and—"

"An attorney has been called. He'll be here shortly," Special Agent Turner says. With her eyes, she begs Mallory to say something more. SA Kat Turner has always been good at assessing people, one of the many talents the Bureau has utilized her for, and her gut is telling her there's more here. But, like Mallory, her hands are tied. Mallory asked for an attorney.

"Thanks," Mallory replies in response to the pending legal representation. *Now,* she decides, *I will keep my mouth shut.*

Special Agent Turner shakes her head and follows Special Agent Cheng to the door but turns around before leaving. "You don't seem the type."

Mallory's shoulders sag, and a sob erupts from her throat.

TWENTY MINUTES LATER, a young, court-appointed defense attorney enters.

"I'm Pierce Johnson. Have you said anything to anyone?" he asks. His dirty-blond, wavy hair is longer than how most men who work in the justice system seem to wear their hair, and a computer bag is slung over his shoulder.

"No," Mallory says.

"It's time to go before the magistrate," he explains. "Do you know the charges?"

"I can guess, and I vaguely recall what the agents said when they arrested me in Atlantic City," Mallory replies tersely. "I was kind of in shock."

"Identity theft, or fraud . . . with financial institution fraud, a.k.a., bank fraud." Pierce looks at Mallory's face, his crystal-blue eyes highlighting the poignant choice his parents made when naming him. "And I heard through the United States Attorney's Office grapevine they have other suspicions."

"Like what?" Mallory asks, her eyes widening.

"As I believe you know, Richard Goldman was murdered, as were others. Know anything about that? You had a knife in your possession. I urge you to tell me now what we're up against."

Mallory's face drains of color. Her mouth opens, but nothing comes out. She looks toward the windowed wall, wondering if the special agents are behind there.

"They can't listen in when you're talking with an attorney."

"It doesn't matter," she says after a few long seconds. "I didn't kill anyone. Do I look like I could *kill* anyone?" She stares at the wall behind him with bloodshot eyes.

Pierce studies her. "Some might say you don't look like a thief either. We'll get back to that later. For now, just stand when I tell you to stand and sit when I tell you. Okay? Let's go." He moves to the door and raps on it twice with his knuckles.

Mallory doesn't like Pierce. She doesn't get the sense he's on her side. *They suspect that I'm the serial killer?* Her appetite may not return for a long time.

Forty minutes later, Mallory is standing before a salt-and-pepper bearded federal magistrate who, as expected, looks none too thrilled to be called back to work on a Friday evening. He had been a mere three miles from home when the request came in.

After some back and forth between the US Attorney, her defense attorney, and the magistrate, Mallory hears the words, "The defendant will be detained at . . ." and the gavel comes down. She doesn't hear the location of her pretrial detention and looks to Pierce for information. He ignores her. The realization settles into her chest wall and pushes hard, making breathing difficult.

She knows the truth. Her life is over.

At home, lying in bed—despite it being early in the evening—with his clothes still on, Brian hears a text come through on his phone. When he picks it up, he sees his brother's message.

Be there Sunday afternoon. Can't wait!!!!!

Brian sleeps his phone and puts it back on his nightstand. He curls onto his side, bringing his knees toward his chest, and squeezes his eyes shut.

Part Four

Bankrupt

33

The Third Sunday

After arriving home from church, Brian has been sitting on his backyard patio for the past two hours, thinking—ruminating. He hears a car in his driveway and walks around the house to meet his brother.

"Brian!" Brent shouts as he pulls his overnight bag from the trunk with his right hand. He's carrying a tray with sodas and a small white paper bag in his left. "I brought sandwiches. You hungry?"

Brian watches as Brent stands up to his full height, a height four inches taller than he. Brent's brown sideburns have traces of silver at the edges, making Brent appear to be the older brother, though he's three years Brian's junior.

Brian grabs the bag and opens it, realizing his stomach is rumbling, having forgotten to eat anything since breakfast. "Thanks, man," he says as he envelopes his brother in a tight hug. "Welcome to the AC." *Good grief,* he thinks. *She rubbed off on me.*

Brent doesn't notice Brian's new nickname for the city. He's complaining about the growing Spring Break traffic as the two head through the house to drop Brent's bags in the first-floor guest room—not the one Mallory stayed in. Brian may not open that door for some time. Then the brothers retreat to the back patio where Brian had been brooding earlier.

"How are ya?" Brent asks as they find their seats. He takes a big sip through the straw in his drink and peers at Brian, noticing for the first time that Brian's eyes look red-rimmed.

"I've been better. You're not going to believe what happened Friday."

"What happened?" Brent leans forward, his mouth forming a straight line.

"Greta Goldman, Richard's great-niece, who I've been shepherding across town, wasn't who she said she was. Her name is Mallory Jones. She was impersonating Greta, and the FBI arrested her right in front of me." Even as Brian says the words, they don't seem real. Nothing seems real.

"Are you serious?" Brent whistles.

"There's more," Brian says. "Went on a date and she spent the night here—" Brian sees his brother's eyebrows go up. "Not like that." Brian pauses to steady his emotions. "Brent, I liked her—a lot. I think I even asked her if she'd be willing to move here! I'm such an idiot."

Brent's mouth falls open. "Oh, man. . . . I don't know what to say." Brent sits back in his chair, suddenly not as hungry as he thought he was when he arrived. "What now?"

"I don't know. She's been transferred to Camden. I haven't seen or spoken to her. I don't want to. I may never want to." Brian shakes his head. His stomach growls, and he takes a small bite of his turkey sandwich, hoping to quell the hunger pains. They're not nearly as bothersome as his heart pains. After he finishes chewing, Brian adds, "The real Greta is here. I'm taking her to the next spot on Richard's list tomorrow. I've spoken with her, but I haven't met her yet."

Brent pauses again, unsure what to say. "Do you want company?"

"Nah. You have things to do. Speaking of which, what's on your schedule this week?" Brian is ready to change the subject.

"I have meetings with the Tourism Board tomorrow. Then, I'm on the hunt for a house. Are there any in your neighborhood?" He smiles half-heartedly at his brother as he looks around the backyard. "Seriously, I have scheduled a meeting with a realtor, so I'm all set. But if I find a house, I'd love for you to check it out, give me your opinion. I'm hoping the fam will like whatever I find, but I'm not sure I trust myself. I'll send Marie pictures, of course. Get her vote . . ." he says, referring to his wife. Brent falls easily into talking about himself, and Brian relents to the safe routine. It's what the two brothers have always done.

"I'd love to. Just let me know when and where." Brian takes another bite of his sandwich and a sip of his Sprite. It is the last bite of food he eats for another two days.

THE NEXT DAY, Brian and Greta Goldman are on their way to Pacific Avenue where they plan to visit Atlantic Care Regional Medical Center. When he had picked Greta up from the Hard Rock Hotel, he first noticed the slight difference in height between her and Mallory. The second thing he noticed was Greta's freckles, which pepper her nose and cheeks.

After their chat on Saturday, Greta had agreed to finish the list created by her great-uncle ahead of his passing, a way to hopefully understand him better and honor his wishes. Though, she requested they find her another hotel that wasn't so loud and touristy. "The Hard Rock is just not my style," she had explained. Brian promised to do just that.

As they travel in the back of the Cadillac, Brian explains the reason her great-uncle included this street name—Pacific Avenue. Greta leans toward the attorney to listen.

"This hospital meant a lot to your great-uncle. Every Christmas Eve, Richard brought a half dozen toys for *each* child who was staying in the hospital, the kids who would miss being home for Christmas."

"Wow. That was nice of him!" Greta exclaims. Her lips disappear in a half-frown. "I just hate that he's gone, Brian. I only spent time with him once. I should have contacted him at least a few times through all these years." Greta's voice grows quieter with each passing word as she tries to maintain emotional control. "Then none of this might have happened."

"I know. I can't imagine how hard it was to learn that he had passed away," Brian offers. His empathy is great, but he's also still reeling from the fact that Mallory wasn't Greta and the woman in front of him *is*. He's still processing the betrayal and the feelings he had for the tall, quirky woman who stole his heart . . . and then stomped on it when he learned she had stolen someone's identity. And not just someone's—she had deeply hurt the Goldman family, whom he loved, which means she had hurt him too. Brian clears his throat and pushes Mallory from his thoughts.

"I love that he was such a caring person," Greta replies after a moment. She gazes through the window of the car, deep in thought.

When they arrive, Antonio opens the door for Greta, and she exits. She breathes in the warm spring air and looks around. She used to volunteer at a hospital when she was a young teenager—back when her parents were alive. Hospitals don't make her nervous at all. She almost feels right at home in them and has always thought the human body to be a fascinating machine. She had even wanted to be a doctor, but then, in her mid-teens, she grew to appreciate design and changed her goal, opting to study architecture when she entered college at UNCC. Nothing came of it, though. In college, after her parents died, she felt lost and alone. She didn't know what to do, and her passion for the career she was working to achieve vanished. That's when Great-Uncle Richard visited and convinced her to take a break to find herself again.

Brian and Greta enter through the large sliding doors leading into the main lobby of the hospital. Brian approaches the information desk where an older Black woman sits, assisting visitors with directions.

"We're here to visit the fourth floor and were told to ask for Roman Silva when we arrived," Brian says to the woman. She picks up a phone to dial the appropriate person, and Greta notices the receptionist's extra-long, intricately manicured fingernails—painted a myriad of colors—and wonders how in the world she can maneuver any keyboard or buttons with them.

After she hangs up, the woman looks at Brian. "Mr. Silva will be down soon. You can wait over there," she says as she uses her pointer finger, with its long red nail, to indicate a corner of the lobby with ample seating. The two make their way to a sofa and sit in silence.

Roman Silva arrives five minutes later.

"Brian Gogh and Greta Goldman?" he asks. Roman is a thirty-five-year-old with a goatee and pale skin. His burgundy sweater vest and chinos shout *bureaucrat.* When Brian nods and stands up, Roman continues. "I'm Roman Silva, an administrator here. Nice to meet you." Everyone shakes hands.

Brian and Greta follow Roman toward the elevators as he continues chatting.

"We are so very sorry to hear about Richard's passing. He was such a positive force around here, particularly at Christmastime."

"That's what I've heard," Greta replies. "I'm glad I can see some of what he's done to support this city."

"He was so good with the kids. Really . . . so easy-going." The elevator doors open, and the three enter. Roman hits the button for the fourth floor.

When the doors open again, Greta sees a colorful mural indicative of any pediatric floor in a hospital, but this one stretches at least a hundred feet down the hall and includes an underwater scene. Greta gasps at the intricate details of the marine life.

The three of them turn right. On the drop ceiling draping the nursing station, Greta reads the words "The St. Nick Wing," painted in green lettering.

"This is his wing," Roman explains when he realizes Greta is reading the name. "We named it 'The St. Nick Wing' because, for the past seventeen years, Richard showed up in a Santa costume on Christmas Eve. He would fill six huge bags with gifts and hand them out to the children who were staying here on Christmas—came dressed in a complete Santa costume, with the white beard and everything. Some of the kids thought he was the real deal." Roman chuckles at the memory. "He *did* look like a short Santa."

Greta smiles. "That's awesome."

"Richard also brought a small gift and paid for a catered meal for every person on this wing who had to work on Christmas Day—facilities and nutrition staff included. He knew they were taking time from their families to care for others, so he wanted to care for them."

"Richard loved family," Brian adds with a nod. He looks at Greta and pats her on the upper back. "I'm glad you got to see this."

"Me too," she replies.

As Greta listens to the beeps of the monitors and the rumbling of the wheels of the medicine cart down the hall, she's thankful Richard could help children and families and the hospital staff for the time he did. *It's a real shame for the kids that he's gone,* she thinks.

Mallory is prepped for the attorney visitation room where she'll meet with Pierce again. When she enters, she immediately feels the coldness, not just from the sterile walls and floor but from her lawyer, his beady eyes staring at her with no hint of kindness.

Mallory sits, crosses her long legs, and waits.

"Tell me about the first time you saw Richard Goldman."

"I never met Richard. You know that." Mallory can't keep eye contact with her attorney. As she looks away, she wonders if she can fire him and ask for another one. "No games, okay? You're my lawyer."

"Okay. Tell me about the first time you saw Greta Goldman."

Mallory sighs, surrendering to the reality that she needs to get the story out. "I discovered who she was in college, at UNCC. She was a year ahead of me, but we had one class together. I ended up following her and learning about her for six months. She fascinated me. Her confidence. Her family, even her freckles . . . she has these freck—" Mallory shakes her head. "I was writing my first novel, and I lacked the confidence I saw in Greta. So I studied her, trying to emulate her. Then I met her again in person at a bar just before she graduated. We chatted briefly, and I learned she was heading out of the country for a while.

"After she left for Greece, she rented out the house she had bought. By the way, who buys a house while still in college? Never mind—another entitlement story. Anyway, she rented it to a few people I knew. I ended up subletting a room from one of those renters when they left town unexpectedly."

Mallory looks at Pierce who is jotting notes on a legal pad every once in a while. He nods for her to continue. "I'm sure someone will want names of the renters, but right now, I don't remember any."

Pierce snorts. Mallory ignores him.

"When Greta didn't return after the first year, she sold the house to one of the renters, who allowed me to stay, even though most of the others had moved on. I had just graduated and was making little money with few job prospects as a creative writer.

"Richard called the house once, early on, looking for Greta. I happened to answer. He thought I was her. I guess we sound alike. I don't know. But I didn't correct him. Then it happened a couple more times. That kinda sparked an idea." Mallory stops to pull on her hair, straightening it with her fingers. Finally, she drops her hand to her lap and sits in silence.

After several seconds pass, she hears, "Go on."

"My idea was that if Greta never came back, I could use her name as my pen name for my books. That would have been okay if I had stopped there. People use pen names all the time, and I could have played it off as coincidence. I took it too far, though. I researched the Goldman family, everything I could. Then I used Greta's short bio in my book, figuring I was such a new author, no one would even notice. The plan kind of snowballed after my first book was as successful as it was. I realized the Goldman name was powerful, so I took it on in full, along with everything that meant. I even found her social security number in some of the paperwork at her house. I knew it was wrong, that I was going too far, but . . ."

"So is that when you decided to kill Richard and the others? So that you'd never be caught? So you could inherit his billions?"

"No! Of course not!"

"And why not kill Greta to protect your scheme?"

"I'm not a killer!" Mallory cries, then clamps her mouth shut and stares at the door. A guard takes a step toward them. Pierce shakes his head, communicating they are okay. She wonders if she should ask the guard to take Pierce away. *But then what?* Her heart beats faster in her chest. She focuses on its rhythm as it echoes in her head, counting the beats and waiting for them to slow. It is a strategy one of her former counselors suggested years ago. "I've never killed anyone. If you don't believe that, then just leave."

Pierce scribbles something on his pad. "Okay, let's say I believe you. Keep going," he says. Then he adds, "This is what we're up against. You should get used to it."

If my attorney doesn't believe me, then . . . She chokes on her next words.

"I was . . . I was afraid Richard would eventually figure out I wasn't Greta, so I stopped taking his calls. I figured I'd keep using Greta's name as my pen name for my future books—no harm, no foul. But I would stay far away from the family. Go back to my life. Well, it didn't work." Mallory sniffs. "I was dragged back in when Brian Gogh called to say Richard was dead, and I needed to go to the AC, uh Atlantic City. I panicked. I knew Richard's brother and sister-in-law were there, and I figured they had met Greta—or at least seen photos of her. I got lucky when I learned they had never met her. The rest is . . ." Greta shrugs, signifying she is finished.

"Is that all?"

"I think so."

Pierce puts down his pen. "A federal prosecutor has your case, and your crimes fall under a couple of federal statutes—namely, identity fraud, mail fraud, and financial institution fraud. I'm still hearing rumors more charges are coming . . . six counts of murder one, at least. So far, they've placed you in every city at the time of the other murders. And you had that knife in your bag, which they are analyzing as we speak. Should I be worried about that?"

"Why would you be worried?"

Pierce sneers. Mallory ignores him.

"I didn't kill anyone." She says this with waning conviction, realizing it may not matter what anyone thinks. If the authorities don't find someone else with as strong a motive to kill these people—like a billion-dollar motive—the charges against her will be filed soon. No one believes her. No one truly knows her. Fleetingly, she thinks of Brian. But just as quickly, hopelessness creeps in and strangles her as his face disappears from her mind.

34

The Third Monday

After checking Greta Goldman into a seaside hotel yesterday for the duration of her visit, Brian picks her up for their journey to the next location on Richard's list—the home of Richard's personal assistant, Gregg Morse, on North Carolina Avenue. Brian called Gregg yesterday to confirm a short meeting rather than an extended overnight stay, and he's concerned about the guy. Brian knows he's grieving Richard's death, and those feelings seem to be manifesting as anger. Gregg, in no uncertain terms, expressed his displeasure that Richard left his great-niece, whom he hardly knew, in charge of his entire estate. Why she gets to make these decisions and keep or distribute his money is beyond Gregg's comprehension.

"After all," Gregg had complained, "no one even knew who the true Greta Goldman was!" Brian silently agrees. It's a valid argument, but it was Richard's wish to have it this way. Aside from Edith Moore, and perhaps Dawn, Gregg knew Richard best, but Brian is in no position to fuel Gregg's anger and make things more complicated by overtly agreeing with him.

Because of Gregg's blatant hurt and rejection, Brian reduced the visit to an hour and hopes it all works out okay as Antonio pulls the Cadillac up to Gregg's house.

The two-story white-painted house is hidden behind two flowering dogwood trees in full spring bloom. There is a white fence bordering the property, and the two open the gate to access the walkway to the house.

"This is cute," Greta offers as they step onto the sidewalk.

"Yes, springtime in New Jersey is the best time of the year," Brian agrees.

The door to the house opens as they climb the four steps to the covered porch where two weather-worn rocking chairs sit off to the right. When Gregg appears in the doorway, Brian stops—an instinctive reaction to the look on Gregg's face. The fifty-two-year-old's brown hair, is disheveled and his shoulders slump into a forward curve. His bloodshot eyes focus on Greta.

"Gregg?" Brian says, grabbing Greta's hand to pull her back toward him. "Everything okay?"

"Okay?" Gregg spits. "No. Richard is *dead*. And this *person* . . ." he says, emphasizing the *p*, "didn't even know him." He waves toward Greta.

"Maybe we should leave." Brian faces Greta.

As Greta thinks about her response, Gregg jumps in. "No." He sighs and closes his eyes. "I'm sorry. It's fine. I'm fine. Let's just sit outside." He nods to the two rocking chairs. "I'll be right back."

Brian and Greta look at each other, silently questioning the wisdom of sticking around.

"It's okay, Brian. Maybe talking to me will help," Greta whispers into Brian's ear so Gregg doesn't hear should he return.

"If at any point you want to leave, just give me some type of sign."

Greta chuckles and agrees. "Will do." She makes the "okay" signs with her hands, spins them upside down, and holds them up to her eyes. Caught off-guard by her humor at a time like this, Brian can't help but laugh.

A few minutes after they sit in the chairs, the front door swings open. Gregg carries a small straight-back wooden chair in his right hand. In his left, he has a black and white composition notebook.

Once seated, he finally speaks. "I'm sorry. I'm having a rough time accepting Richard's death and the fact I wasn't the one to decide his estate, given I've spent my entire adult life working with him." Another sigh. "I know I'm not family, but I knew everything he was into, who his friends were, what his aspirations were, and even when he needed a vacation." Gregg crosses his arms like a toddler in pre-meltdown mode.

"I'm sorry," Greta says. "I know this must be difficult. And you're right. I didn't know him well. I hope to learn more about him, though."

Brian glances between Gregg and Greta. Each is staring at the other. "Does that notebook contain something you wanted to share?" Brian asks to dispel the stalemate.

"Yeah." Gregg picks up the notebook and flips past the first few pages. "Richard wanted me to write down the quotes and choices he made that impacted me through the years. This is just one of a dozen notebooks. Now that I think about it, it was a pompous thing to ask me to do, but that was Richard. You didn't even realize when he was being arrogant because he was just so gosh darn kind while doing it." He holds it up for them to see. "I'd like to read a few."

Brian and Greta nod. Greta uses her feet to rock her chair back and forth, hoping the rhythmic movement will ease Gregg's anguish.

Gregg begins, "People who only focus on themselves are not only incapable of loving others well, they are incapable of loving themselves well."

Greta stops rocking. *This is deep stuff.*

"Nothing strengthens a heart like the heavy lifting it does when you raise people from their deep, dark pits.

"Today, if everyone decided to forgive the person who hurt

them the most, the world would be filled with peace and joy instead of hate and violence. . . . That last one, given Richard's manner of death, hits particularly hard. I often wonder if the guy who killed him knew him. Knew what he meant to this city. Knew what he meant to so many people. If they knew him . . . If they *really knew* him, I can't imagine they would have taken his life. Even Richard's enemies loved him."

Brian thinks of Sofia DeMarco and her family and how they did not love Richard. The thought of Sofia creates a red-flag warning in his brain and catches him off-guard. He mentally shakes the thought from his head. *Not now.*

"I'd never say Richard didn't have flaws—he didn't take care of himself much of the time. He ate a lot and was obviously overweight. And he was nosy, even over-bearing." Gregg offers a sad smile at his memories of the times when Richard made someone else's business his own. "But even with those weaknesses, he was the greatest friend, the greatest person I've ever known."

Brian nods. He knows all of this and loved Richard too.

"I don't know what to say," Greta whispers. "I'm sorry I didn't know him. I only saw him at my parents' funeral but never spoke to him and only truly met him at my graduation. But during those two days in Charlotte, we had fun together. I should have reached out to him over the years."

"I know he tried to keep contacting you," Gregg says, "even after you stopped taking his calls." Resentment fuels his statement.

"What do you mean? I haven't spoken to him since my graduation. I've been living in Greece."

"Well, he talked to someone, said it was you."

Greta looks at Brian. Neither understands exactly what Gregg is talking about, but Greta guesses what must have happened. *Mallory.*

As he, too, puts the pieces together, Gregg's anger resurfaces like hot lava bubbling up from the earth. His eyes narrow, and he stands up, knocking the wooden chair backward onto the porch.

"I think it's time you leave," he spits out between grinding teeth.

"Of course," says Brian. "Thanks for your time and for sharing some of Richard's more poignant quotes. I loved him too. And I miss him every day." Brian reaches for Gregg's arm to give him a compassionate squeeze, but Gregg steps out of reach.

"Come on, Greta. Let's go," Brian murmurs.

She follows Brian down the porch steps and toward the waiting Cadillac. Once on the sidewalk, she peers back over her shoulder at Gregg, who hasn't moved.

"Mallory, you have a visitor." The guard motions for her to back up, then opens her cell door.

She wonders who the visitor could be, part of her hoping it's Brian, part of her hoping it's not. She's not sure she can face him right now. Her gut twists inside her abdomen, the guilt making her nauseous.

When she reaches the visitor's room, she sees several square tables and matching chairs scattered throughout the space. At a couple of the tables, inmates sit dressed in their khakis as their visitors relax across from them. Mallory watches one man reach for the woman's hands in front of him. A guard yells out, "No touching!" and the inmate promptly pulls his hand back.

Mallory spies one table with a sole occupant.

Precious.

As Mallory sits down, Precious smiles. "You losing weight?"

"Probably. What are you doing here?"

Precious leans as close as she can to Mallory's side of the table without receiving a reprimand from the guard.

"I know you didn't do it."

"Do what?"

"Kill Richard. And all those others." Precious leans back and crosses her arms across her chest.

"Why do you say that?" Mallory's curiosity tingles.

"I can read people. And you ain't the type. You have no real motive for anyone other than Richard. Why kill all those people?"

Mallory chuckles. "I had no *real* motive for any of them. But I guess I could have killed the others to make Richard's death seem random. The police think I had the opportunity for all of them . . . I was staying nearby that night the woman was killed—at Richard's brother's house."

Precious tilts her head at Mallory's strange response but is undeterred. "I'm just sayin'. Something doesn't add up."

"Why are you so interested in helping me?"

"You seem like you've been caught up in things not about you. I know you stole the Goldman name—it's all over the news. And I'm hoppin' mad about that, Miss Mallory. But like I said, I can read people. I think you probably have an okay heart. I think they got it wrong. Mostly, though, I loved Mr. Richard, and I want to find out who did this to him." Precious's lenses fog up, and she removes her glasses to wipe them down with her shirt.

"I don't know what to say," Mallory offers in place of an apology. She wonders if Precious has been watching too much crime TV.

"Are you sorry for what you did do?"

After a slow nod filled with running thoughts, Mallory says, "Of course."

Precious nods back, a slight grin creeping across her face. "I know you are, Mallory."

Missing the turn in the conversation, Mallory has one question for her visitor. "Have you seen Brian Gogh by any chance?"

Precious gives Mallory a sad smile this time. "No, honey. I haven't."

A FEW HOURS LATER, Mallory is again summoned from her cell.

Pierce, dressed in more casual attire today with his blond hair pulled back in a man-style bun, waits in his usual chair. He looks like a child masquerading as an adult in his business-casual pants and short-sleeve plaid shirt, with polished shoes that seem too big for his body.

Mallory doesn't know why she's so critical of Pierce. Precious was right. Her hair is a little more straggly and her face gaunter than just yesterday. She can feel her body shedding weight with each passing day, her appetite refusing to return.

Pierce cuts to the chase once she's seated in front of him. "You're no longer a viable suspect for the murders."

Her first thought is that Pierce must be joking, some extra rib to get under her skin. He oozes that kind of personality. Even though April Fool's Day has passed, she's waiting for the "just kidding" to escape from his cruel mouth and his eyes to betray the lie.

"I'm serious. They are putting a hold on the pending murder charges—for now." Pierce shifts in his seat. It seems he's uncomfortable. *He must want a headlining case to try. I bet he thought I'd be his ticket to the big leagues.*

She opts to respond with as few words as possible. "Why?"

Mallory's question elicits a hearty laugh from her attorney. "Let's just call it a 'get out of jail free' card. The knife they found in your possession wasn't a match to the weapon the killer is using, though they acknowledge it doesn't have to be. You could have ditched the murder weapon, but they *are* still looking for it at all the places you've been. They have only circumstantial evidence right now—motive. And opportunity."

"So they don't have evidence that it's someone else, just not enough to say it's me?" Mallory shifts in her seat to mirror her attorney. "Could they charge me later?"

The questions throw Pierce off, and he looks into Mallory's eyes, wondering what it is about her that is so different. Mallory, used to others' stares, doesn't blink, despite his intense gaze. As a kid, she used to look right through people, not at them, allowing her to engage in childish stare-downs and blinking contests. "They didn't elaborate. . . . But yes, because you were never officially charged, they can change their minds at any time. They are still reviewing the video from the hotel. It's grainy. The killer looks like you, but the height is off by an inch or so. . . . So it's not you?"

"Nope."

Pierce nods, unsurprised by her short answer. "You're still looking at ten to fifteen years for identity fraud. You're pleading guilty, correct?"

Mallory nods. She finally looks toward her lap, and Pierce sees the corners of a smile on her face, a smile she's trying to hide. When she looks up, it's gone.

"What was that?" he asks. "Something funny?" Goosebumps pop up on Pierce's skin as he wonders what his client is hiding.

"Oh, no. Not at all. It's just that when I get stressed or anxious—or relieved—sometimes, it comes out . . ." She is going to continue her explanation, but Pierce seems horrified and unforgiving, so she shuts her mouth. *No one gets it. No one gets me.*

Pierce shrugs, having decided he's content to let it go, and stands up. He gathers his things and walks toward the door. "See you later, Mallory."

"Bye." She sighs and drops her face into her hands, which are still handcuffed.

35

The Fourth Wednesday

Early on Wednesday morning, Greta Goldman wakes up in the small boutique hotel at the south end of Atlantic City, the one with standard rooms—a king-sized bed in hers—that overlook the ocean. She's always felt pulled to the water, whether it be a lake, an ocean, or a river. Something about the movement, the mystery, of this force of nature makes her body and soul feel both alive and at peace. A dichotomy that leaves her deeply happy. Her favorite part of any trip to the beach is when she crosses the bridge from the mainland to the isle or stretch of land between the inlet waterway and coastline. For her, it's as if someone has lifted a ruck pack from her spine and shoulders, setting her free. It's why living in Chios has been so good for her. The quiet life she's led for eight years has been upended, and she looks forward to resolving what she never asked for.

Greta looks out the windows at the water and takes a few deep breaths as she stretches her arms overhead in the bed. Bending her elbow and peering at her smartwatch, she sees she has four hours before Brian and Antonio will arrive to take her to whatever landmark Richard wanted her to visit on Pennsylvania Avenue.

She throws on a pair of running shorts and a sports bra and laces up her running shoes. After guzzling some water, she grabs her keycard and slips it inside her bra. Within minutes, she's striding along the packed sand of the beach, a few feet from the rolling tide. Now in her element, her legs pump faster as the blood flows.

After six miles, she returns to her hotel room to shower and eat something from the continental breakfast before the hotel closes it down.

GRETA SLIDES into the back of the Cadillac feeling content, even excited. The list is getting shorter, and for a moment, she feels a small measure of empathy for Mallory, who had endured most of the locations on Richard's long requirement. Appreciative, even.

"What are your thoughts about tattoos?" Brian asks after a quick greeting. He's ready to move on with his life as well. It's been a long and painful month.

"What? Tattoos? Why?"

"We're heading to a tattoo shop. Richard helped the owner in a pretty specific way, and I just wondered what your opinion about them is." Brian is simply making small talk.

"I'll tell you, but first, what do *you* think about tattoos?" Greta replies.

"I don't have any, but I don't mind them," Brian answers. "Never something I had any interest in getting, but my late sister had one. Hers was pretty cool—an elephant on her forearm and part of it looked like puzzle pieces, some not part of the bigger picture, kinda floating off to the side. We used to love doing puzzles together as kids, so it was meaningful to us both."

"That sounds amazing. I like tattoos. I have one. They say you can't have just one, but I'm living proof that you can."

Brian's left eyebrow goes up. "Oh? What is yours? And

should I even ask where it is?" His eyes dart across her seated frame in a reflexive response, and instantly, he regrets it. "Sorry. None of my business."

"I don't mind. It's an octopus. On my rib cage. I'm a fan of marine life and the ocean, and octopi have always fascinated me. I like that they have so many tentacles, kind of like me—into a lot of things." Greta doesn't make any offer to show Brian her skin art, and he doesn't ask. He doesn't want to get too close to Greta Goldman—to any client ever again. He did that once and was burned and is still looking for relief from the scorching pain.

The SUV pulls up to a hole-in-the-wall business, and Brian and Greta exit the vehicle. After they walk through the doors of the tattoo parlor, Greta turns in a full circle, taking in every inch of the space: the images of the artists' past work on the walls, the blue vinyl tattoo chairs, and the sound of electric needles stirring the air, making it seem alive. And she gets an idea.

"I want to get another tattoo," Greta says.

"Really? Just like that? What about being 'living proof' of someone satisfied with just one tattoo?" Greta's impulsivity shocks Brian; it seems uncharacteristic of her, but after a beat, he shrugs his shoulders. He's happy to sit and watch while the owner tells Greta about Richard's impact on this place and carves something into her skin. It'll make for a great story he can share with Antonio, and maybe Brent, later.

Greta nods. "I want a top hat . . . right here," she says as she points to the space behind her left ankle bone. "In honor of Great-Uncle Richard." Greta, pleased with the idea, pulls out her wallet and looks around.

"I'll get the owner. His name is Mac." Brian takes off for the main counter in the corner, shaking his head at the always positive, upbeat woman with the freckles.

When Mac arrives at the front of the shop from a back office, apart from his dark, close-set eyes and narrow chin, Greta notices the unique tattoo scaling the thirty-something-year-old's forearm, arching toward his shoulder, until it disappears beneath his T-shirt. The black and gray tattoo is that of railroad tracks, which fork at his elbow into two sets, with trees lining the edges.

"Hi, Greta. Nice to meet you," Mac says as he shakes her hand and leads them to his workstation.

Brian sits in the side chair and pulls out his phone to check his email.

"Sorry to hear about Richard. He was a godsend to me and this place." Mac offers his condolences to Greta.

Curious about his statement, Greta asks why as she sits in the chair.

As Mac eyeballs her ankle and then sketches the top hat onto a piece of paper for her approval, he tells her how Richard rescued him from a gang in Trenton when he was eighteen. "Can you believe I actually tried to mug Richard?" Mac says with a laugh. "And when I was unsuccessful, he sat with me in his car for three hours, talking to me!"

Transfixed by the start of the story, Greta nods her approval at his sketch, and he continues. "He told me his story—about being homeless and how a woman cared enough to give him a chance. He said he wanted to do the same for me. I explained to him you can't just leave a gang, you know? You're in it for life, and I didn't want my life shortened—you know what I mean?" Mac prepares the needle and ink. Greta rotates her leg to give him access to the outer side and braces for the pain she knows is coming.

"Yes, I understand."

"Well, he moved me to Atlantic City, put me up in a hotel for three months, scheduled some therapist to meet with me, told my parents I was safe, and kept on top of me. When he realized I liked to draw, he asked what I wanted to do with my life. I didn't know. He looked me up and down, staring at all of my tattoos, and the idea came to him—clear as can be." Mac shakes his head and finishes the border of the top hat. Greta takes a deep breath as he readjusts his equipment to do the shading. The pain isn't nearly as bad as what she endured for her rib cage tattoo.

"He asked if I wanted my own tattoo shop. He said he'd send

me to business classes and put down money for a place that I could start with . . . that I could pay him back whenever I was ready. A year later, Inked For Life opened, and I've been here for twelve years. I paid him back in full after five years, though he almost didn't take the money." Mac shakes his head. "I couldn't be more grateful for his generosity and faith in me, a street kid from Trenton." Mac laughs. "The last three years, we've been voted best tattoo shop in all of New Jersey." Mac's pride is contagious. Brian looks up from his phone and smiles.

Greta looks around the shop again, noticing half of the chairs are full at eleven o'clock on a Wednesday morning. "That's incredible. I'm so happy for you. And the gang let you go?"

"Well, Richard may have offered them something in return. I don't know what, but they never bothered me again." Mac finishes the tattoo and Greta takes a peek.

"I love it!" she exclaims.

Brian puts his phone away. "Looks fantastic." He still can't believe Greta became a customer.

Greta holds up her wallet, but Mac shakes his head. "No way. You're Richard's family. I ain't taking money from you. I'm glad you have this to remember him by," he says as he nods at the tattoo. He hands her some instructions for the after-care, but she waves him off.

"I know what to do. This is my second tattoo," she explains.

After a few more words about Richard and a quick goodbye, Brian and Greta walk out of Inked for Life. Greta is thrilled with her new ink.

36

The Fourth Thursday

Mallory awakes early in the morning to the thought that has been crashing through her brain all night long. Precious was adamant about finding out who killed Richard. *Her energy must have rubbed off on me.*

After brooding for hours, Mallory thinks she might want to write about Richard's life—a memoir of sorts, with permission from Bill and Jean, of course. *Though,* she thinks, *that won't be a small ask. They may never want to speak to me again.* Mallory believes, through her research, she could stumble upon who killed him as she crafts his life story.

She knows she'll be a convicted felon, but it would feel good to do something helpful, noble even, to make right some of the wrongs she's done. And as crazy as it sounds, maybe Precious could assist her from the outside, like a research assistant. Mallory is sure she'd say yes. Maybe Dawn could help too. *Dawn.* She's surprised by the emotions that surface while saying her new friend's name and wonders what her *mommother* thinks of her now.

Good grief. Stop it, Mal. Everyone hates you. And they should. Move on.

As sleep drifts further away and lights start popping on in the correctional facility, Mallory shakes her head at the absurd idea of writing Richard's memoir, dismissing it as quickly as it had come to her.

AT NOON, Greta rejoices with Brian in the back of the Cadillac, something Brian figured was an impossibility nearly a week ago. They are traveling to the final destination on the list: Park Place. The Claridge Hotel, to be exact.

It's been a whirlwind few days between the jetlag, the DNA test, confronting the fact her identity was stolen, meeting family, and visiting the last few locations on Richard's list. Greta is feeling the weight of all of it, evidenced by her heavy eyelids and stiff joints. She didn't have time to run this morning, a religious activity she usually engages in daily before the sun comes up.

She has enjoyed getting to know the late Richard, the great-uncle whom she'd only spent time with once, and Bill and Jean, who hosted her for dinner two nights ago. A sweet couple, she thinks as the Cadillac slows.

The Claridge, a historic hotel built in 1930, looms ahead. Greta is curious why Richard put this on the list. The full-brick building with gold awnings atop the lobby windows, which showcase its notoriety, occasionally serves as the place for celebrities to stay and lay their heads, including Marilyn Monroe several decades ago. Greta knows Richard doesn't own it.

"Here we are," Antonio says over his shoulder. He expertly parks, and the car idles while he jumps out and runs to Greta's door. She giggles and Brian smirks at her. "He loves doing that," he says. "I can't remember a time he didn't make it to the passenger door in time." As soon as he finishes speaking the words, he wishes he could take them back. There were two times —with Mallory, he remembers.

Brian and Greta stride toward the ornate lobby doors tucked beneath the glass-covered entryway. As Brian opens the right-hand door for Greta, he announces, "We aren't meeting anyone. Richard wanted me to bring you here to tell you a story. Should we find some seats? Do you want anything to drink?" He's rambling and inwardly curses himself. He knows he has to move on with his life.

"I'd love something. What are you having?" Greta asks, not wanting to drink alone but also hoping Brian will celebrate the end of the journey with her. She narrows her eyes and nods toward the bar as if the two are already in cahoots.

Brian, forever a relationship-builder, gets the hint. "How about a couple of gin and tonics? It's five o'clock somewhere, right?" he asks with an arched eyebrow. Greta notices his dimple as he speaks.

"Perfect!"

Brian strides toward the bar, weaving between the growing crowd. The official start of summer is closing in. Tourists are filling the Atlantic City hotels by the day. As Greta gets comfortable on a leather sofa in the lobby where everything is gold, including the hotel's name stamped into the marble flooring. Once she's tucked away in the corner of the grand space, she pulls out her phone and scrolls through a list of destinations she's made over the past few days.

Brian arrives with two glasses, each sporting a gold line circling the top, both filled with clear, bubbly liquid and finished with limes. He sits in a side chair across from the couch.

"Thank you. Figure we're not driving, right?" She winks at Brian who internally flinches. It reminds him of his conversation with Mallory weeks ago about the comradery of winking, and he sighs.

"That's true. We should definitely enjoy an early start to the weekend." He raises his glass, then takes a slow sip. "Do you know the Claridge's nickname?" he asks Greta as she crosses her legs and leans back for the story.

Greta shakes her head. "No, what is it?"

"The Skyscraper by the Sea. Obviously, it came from the hotel's tall and slender appearance," Brian explains.

"I love it," Greta says, wondering where this is leading.

"Richard came up with the name. He had booked a room here for one of his friends, who happens to be a celebrity—Casey Applegate."

"Oh, wow! She was huge in the eighties."

"Yeah, he met her through a mutual friend while she was shooting a film here in the late seventies. They hit it off and stayed in touch. When she was scheduled to come back to do a commercial for Atlantic City tourism, she immediately called Richard, who made her a reservation here. When he met her here, they were standing outside, and he mentioned he thought it looked like a skyscraper."

Greta nods. "Yeah, it does."

"Then he kept talking through it, and it became the *Skyscraper by the Sea*. Later, Casey referred to the hotel by Richard's nickname, and it stuck. As a celebrity, the hotel was ecstatic that she was talking about her stay and that she'd given their hotel such a memorable nickname. She tried to give the credit back to Richard, but that part of the story never went very public. But he didn't mind—"

"That's funny. That sounds like him . . . not to mind," Greta adds. She looks up at the ceiling, then around at the fancy lobby and shakes her head. "It is magnificent." Greta readjusts her position on the couch. "So, Brian, is there any progress in the investigation into his murder?"

"I don't know. I haven't heard. I do know they'll release his body to Bill tomorrow. My guess is he and Jean will plan a funeral and lay Richard to rest in the coming week or so."

"I see. That's too bad. . . . You see, I can't stick around."

Greta's face falls as she tells Brian she can't stay for the funeral. "Bill and Jean are so nice, and I hate to leave so abruptly."

"Yes, they are great people. So was Richard. I miss him a lot, even his top hat. No one could pull that off but him." Brian chuckles, but his heart aches.

Greta uncrosses her legs, reminded of her tattoo with the mention of Richard's top hap, and leans toward Brian. "I don't want to make this awkward, but what happens with his estate now?" She grimaces, fully aware of how awful her question must sound to him.

"Well, you have to decide what to do with each holding on that list," Brian nods toward the rolled-up paper in her lap. After three weeks, the paper reveals the wear and tear of being carried throughout the city by multiple people. Brian had retrieved it from the FBI after Mallory's arrest, once they made a copy and cleared it as potential evidence. Evidence for what, he's not sure. "I know you weren't able to see everything or hear all about Richard from his friends, but I hope you'll consider everything he was aiming to do, even in death." Brian looks down at his lap. He doesn't want to press her. She's been through a double trauma—they all have—and she doesn't even live in the United States anymore.

"I appreciate that. I have been thinking about everything. I think I'd like to donate $50,000 to the pediatric wing over at the hospital and another $50,000 to childhood cancer research. Otherwise, I'm sorry to say, I'm going to liquidate everything Richard owned and stop all the payments he was making."

Brian nods as he feels an immense sorrow permeate his soul. Richard's empire, his philanthropic legacy, is over. He thinks about The Hope Floor, and how they will have to fundraise to keep it open, and the Virginia Arms Apartments, likely destined to a developer who will build something more commercial. Then he thinks about ABCC and his sister and her memory. Brian will keep her grant going through his own means, but sadness flows for any future funds Richard's heir could have invested in and supported. He briefly squeezes his eyes shut in defeat. This is not what Richard ever anticipated.

"Okay. I'll draw up all the paperwork, and we can meet soon for you to sign everything."

"The sooner, the better. My shop in Greece has been closed for a while now, and I need to get back. I have a flight booked early tomorrow evening. I hope you understand." Greta frowns. She knows she's rushing a delicate process. But her life must go on.

THAT EVENING, Brian knocks on the door of the yellow house on St. Charles Place. He has been both dreading and looking forward to this dinner with Bill and Jean. *Billie Jean*. He remembers Mallory's play on words and the pain burrows deeper into his gut, making him queasy.

"Brian, so glad you're here," Jean says as she opens the door and invites him in. The smell of garlic bread mixed with apples and cinnamon makes Brian's voice catch. *Jean's apple pie.*

"Thanks, Jean. Good to see you too." His smile fails to reach his eyes as he hugs her.

Bill joins them, and they take their seats around the dinner table. Each adult slowly picks at Jean's homemade vegetable lasagna as if they are children staring at too many green veggies. Brian works through his thoughts. Once his courage hits some unmeasurable threshold, he begins: "I know this has been an incredibly difficult time. I have some news, and I'm afraid it's disappointing."

Bill and Jean set their forks down in unison. Bill's head tilts up in a show of strength; Jean sighs.

"Greta has decided to sell everything." He eyes the couple, a frown forming on his face. "She supported the St. Nick Wing and will donate some money to a charity that supports childhood cancer, but she's keeping most of the profits of the sales." As he speaks, Brian's voice grows softer, his energy zapped by the look on Bill and Jean's faces. "I'm so sorry," he finishes.

"Brian," Bill says. "It's okay. It's not your fault. This is what Richard wanted—for her to decide." Jean nods in agreement with her husband.

"How are you doing?" Jean asks. "Did you love her, Brian?" Everyone knows who Jean is referring to. Images of Mallory's cobalt-blue eyes, and how they nearly closed every time she laughed, storm Brian's brain. From anyone else, the question would be a prying one, but from Jean, it is grace. Brian can't form the words to answer her, fearful the sob sitting in his throat will be the sole outcome. He'd taken a chance and gotten hurt. His chin touches his chest.

"Oh, Brian. We're so sorry." Jean's face darkens, the only show of anger the woman can display. She reaches across the table to squeeze his hand, which is fisted into a tight ball.

"I still can't believe it," says Bill. He refills Brian's wine glass before turning the open bottle of Merlot toward his own. "I'm just thankful she wasn't the one who killed Richard, or anyone else." Brian's head pops up. Bill continues, "They aren't charging her. She's not the killer, Brian."

Brian, stung by the information that she had been a suspect for the murders at all, shivers. He did not know about any of that.

Bill, oblivious to Brian's ignorance, keeps talking. "We liked her. And I can't believe I can admit *that* even with the anger I feel toward her."

Brian takes a breath and moves his shock to another place to deal with later. "I guess we need to talk through the funeral plans. I understand it's set for next week. Friday, right?" Brian changes the subject. He just can't discuss Mallory anymore. "Is there anything I can do?"

"Oh, no, no," Jean says. "It's all been taken care of. Dawn will give the eulogy. Bill will speak for a short bit. You just need to be there."

"Of course. Thank you," Brian says. He wonders how much

of all this Dawn knows. He hasn't had the time to call her—or the will to even do so. "Bill, have you talked to Dawn about M-Mallory?" Her name gets stuck on his tongue.

Bill nods with pursed lips. "She says she's sorry."

The three finish their meal in near silence, then embrace in long hugs as they call it a night. Brian walks through the front door, leaving behind the safest, most wonderful yellow house in all the world.

37

The Fourth Friday

Brian and Greta sit on a wooden bench toward the end of the Atlantic City boardwalk, facing the ocean. The late-May breeze blows Greta's shoulder-length brown hair, and she reaches up and grabs it, stopping it from tickling her face. The sun trends toward the horizon after a hot day, with stripes of orange and pink streaking across the darkening sky. Seagulls, screeching at each other, *kya! kya!*, circle off in the distance, then dart closer. A couple of young boys on the beach are throwing bread into the air and giggling as the birds snatch it in mid-flight. Their parents sit nearby in beach chairs, holding hands, and enjoying the approaching dusk. Next weekend, many hundreds more families will descend on Atlantic City for the official summer season.

"This is it," Brian says. "Just sign these last sales and estate documents, and you're free to start the next stage of your life." He looks over at the woman sitting next to him. She's wearing brown sandals, navy linen pants, and a white tank top.

For the first time, Brian notices the impressive muscle definition in Greta's upper arms and shoulders. A pang of regret and melancholy pierces him as he remembers Mallory. Part of him still wishes this was her sitting next to him. The two women could not be more different. Greta is self-assured and approachable, an impressive combination for anyone. There is no doubt; she takes after Richard. And Mallory is awkward and sensitive. *Greta, honest. Mallory, a liar.* Brian continues to succumb to the emotional war raging within.

"Awesome. I'm looking forward to moving on and becoming anonymous again," Greta says with a lopsided grin at the end of her sentence. She shrugs at her poor joke. Her freckles dance on her cheeks as she continues, "And the money?"

"It'll all be transferred to your account tomorrow morning. We've liquidated everything to the bank. I'll complete the rest of the process tonight," Brian replies. "One point eight billion after the taxes." He slowly shakes his head, wishing the story was different, that she would have kept some of her great-uncle's holdings or that she would have supported his efforts to serve others in Atlantic City. Though, on one level, he understands. She wasn't privy to Richard's heart through the tour that Mallory had embarked upon. Greta's life is in Greece, not here. "That's quite a sum of money. Do you have someone in mind to help you manage it? I'm not asking for my benefit. I can refer someone."

"I'm good. Thanks for your help," Greta says. She takes the pen from his outstretched hand and scribbles three signatures where the yellow arrow stickers mark the pages. Then she rises from the bench.

"Bye, Brian Gogh. Nice to have met you." She offers her hand to solidify the deal, then turns and walks away. Brian watches her retreat down the boardwalk, her hips swaying side to side as she walks. She looks over her shoulder and waves. He waves back. As he rocks forward and stands, he coaxes himself out of the past and aims for the future.

Brian strolls in the opposite direction from Greta and toward Antonio, who is waiting with the Cadillac. He had promised Greta he'd file the paperwork, finalize the sales, and get the transfers set up as soon as possible. So that's what he's going to do.

As she stands on the beach a few blocks away from the busy boardwalk area, Greta smiles at the inky sky over the ocean and the white tips of the crashing waves. Their energy is coursing through her as if she and the waves are one. Her toes curl into the sand as she holds her sandals. Her tattoo is still sore, but she doesn't mind. The pain is a good one. Greta takes in the heavy, pungent smell of fish and brine, and her shoulders relax.

Her life is not what she pictured it would be when she was a little girl. Her parents are dead. Now, her great-uncle too. She's not an architect, as she had assumed she'd become. She isn't married. And she has no kids. Rather, she is quite alone. But by her estimation, her life is now infinitely better than she could have ever imagined. She can go wherever and do whatever she wants. *I can't believe I'm now a billionaire. Thank you, Uncle Richard.*

She pulls out her phone and opens the Uber app, ordering a ride to the airport. Then she walks through the sand, up and over an eroding dune, to the light-gray asphalt of the beach street before putting her sandals back on. As she moves, she relishes the feel of the soft crystals between her toes as she envisions her new life—one she knows will include a lot more sand and surf. Though, she has decided that her new life won't be in Greece. She believes she's found herself now, after eight years of searching. This thought serves as a reminder, and she deletes a saved text from a family-owned pharmacy in Chios, notifying her that her prescription refill is ready for pickup. *That season is over.*

After the black Chevy Blazer arrives and Greta checks it matches the information on her phone, she slips into the leathered seats in the back. She breathes deeply and notices the faint smell of the black-ice-scented car freshener hanging from the rearview mirror. *Nice touch,* she thinks as she takes another deep breath. Greta looks at the Uber driver, a woman wearing a hoodie and black joggers. The woman hasn't turned to greet her.

"How long to the airport?" Greta asks.

"Just a few minutes," comes the terse reply as the driver pulls away. Greta finds it odd the woman's hood is up, covering her face from view. She spies auburn-colored hair peeking out the front of it and tries to glimpse her face in the rearview mirror, but the mirror is angled the other way.

"Everything okay?" she asks.

"Yup."

Greta dismisses the rude driver with a shrug of her shoulders. She opens the Uber app and adds a proactive $200 tip, just for fun. Smiling to herself, she sleeps her phone screen and leans back into the cozy seat, watching the beach disappear from view. *I'll see you soon,* she mentally says to the ocean.

She doesn't bother retrieving her bags from the hotel. In a few hours, she'll be a billionaire, and she can buy whatever clothes, shoes, and accessories she wants. Plus, the one thing she doesn't want to leave behind, she already has with her.

It's a small tactical knife with a wood handle, hidden on a thigh strap underneath her dark blue linen pants.

Finally got past Gogh.

38

Greta Goldman, now *Fiona Campbell,* according to this passport, sits in first class. Her wig—the long, straight ginger-dyed number—is a color not unlike the Uber driver's hair. She had flown from Atlantic City to La Guardia, where she changed her appearance and switched out her passports in a restroom stall after retrieving everything from an airport locker she had rented a month ago.

Now, she is on her way to a tropical location on the other side of the globe, a place where she can finally let her natural, toffee-brown hair grow back as long as she wants. After all, it matches her freckles perfectly. As the plane arcs through the early morning hours, Greta is unaware the murder charges against Mallory were paused. She doesn't know Mallory had carried a knife to Atlantic City, one that didn't match the murder weapon, infusing doubt into the authorities' minds and removing a piece of key evidence they thought they had secured.

Greta, stretching her legs out in front of her, proudly reflects on how her plan unfolded over the past four years.

While living in Greece, Greta was none the wiser about Mallory's fraud until she stumbled on one of Mallory's books in a quaint corner bookstore in Athens. The author had the same name as her, so she opened the book to the author's biography page. She couldn't believe the words as she read, anger racing through her. She'll never forget how it felt to have someone steal something so personal, so *her*. The heat inside her grew with every piece of information she gathered about how this woman had been impersonating her and hijacking her family name . . . assumingly, with her long-range eyes set on Uncle Richard's entire estate.

The betrayal triggered Greta, not changing her from the inside out, per se, but unleashing a dormant wickedness she had inherited from her great-great-grandfather and harbored since childhood. A wickedness fed and perfected by the rigid parenting styles of her deceased mother and father. Greta had barely survived her childhood, one fraught with rules upon rules and punishment after punishment. Perfectionism was expected. And when she wasn't perfect, there were consequences. Her parents had locked her in a basement prison more times than she could count.

Well, she had solved that problem. But after her parents' "accident," Greta had raged for months when she discovered they had left her with nothing, no inheritance to speak of. Greta's anger morphed into hatred. Hatred had spurned evil, and evil had won. But evil isn't easy. And she wouldn't make it easy for Mallory, either.

Rather than go to the police about Mallory's crime, something any sane individual would do, Greta crafted a deadlier strategy to reap her revenge. She wanted this woman to pay—and pay deeply. *A few years in jail is too kind of a punishment for her.* She wanted Mallory to rot in prison forever, if not be condemned to an unjust death. Because that's what Greta had felt. The injustice. And she solidified her plan to frame Mallory as a killer. *This'll be fun,* she had thought.

She fired her Greek psychiatrist, an impish man she doesn't miss. He would have thrown her into an asylum for the mentally ill had he figured out her scheme. He would have understood that her neural roots and moral roots had become deeply entangled, with no chance for change.

Greta was patient, biding her time to enact her revenge. It became her full-time obsession while she ran her seaside store in Chios, including hours spent researching ways to quickly and quietly end someone's life. As she worked out her extravagant plan and researched the people involved, she discovered Uncle Richard had recently willed everything to her instead of his brother, Bill, or even Dawn Marshall. Visions of money and all that it could buy soothed Greta. That's when Uncle Richard joined the list of victims. Greta wanted her money. Her family owed her.

Sure, her visit with Uncle Richard during her college graduation had been *fine*, but he served no purpose to her alive. Greta barely knew him. She had inherited his brains, not his heart. What she realized, only after visiting Gregg Morse with Brian, was that Richard had reached out countless times to build a relationship with her, to not just be extended family on paper but family in real life too. Greta didn't know he would have supported her and loved her before she killed him.

Love.

That had been what was missing in her life, except she didn't know it. Couldn't define it. Psychiatrists through the years told her she wasn't able to give or receive love. She blamed her parents for that too. With her parents' loveless parenting style, she had received no affection, never knew its power. If regret or empathy were possible, she might harbor some about killing Uncle Richard. But they're not possible. Instead, she impulsively got the top hat tattoo to memorialize her entire plan. *In memorandum*, she thinks, satisfied.

Once she had dug around a little more, Greta discovered Mallory's real name through her former tenants in North Carolina and researched Mallory's real past—as someone who had bounced around foster care. She discovered a domestic complaint against one of her foster fathers and further formulated her plan. Her foster dad was an affluent man who seemed to have paid his way out of the charge. Greta had found a motive that fit Mallory. The idea of pinning the murders on a person who already despised the wealthy fell into place. It only helped that Mallory was a woman with no family to call her own, had grown up as an orphan, and was now a loner, if not someone with some sort of mental illness. Greta doesn't even consider the irony of that last statement as a sociopath herself.

Starting with the film director in Tennessee, Charlie Garrison, she chose her victims for one of two reasons: they fit Mallory's contrived motive or lowered Greta's chances of getting caught. Uncle Richard and Charlie Garrison had met about doing a documentary about Uncle Richard's life, something about "from rags to riches," she'd learned. She couldn't let that happen. It would have ruined her long-range plans. When Mallory planned a trip to Nashville for a writers' conference, Greta knew the timing was perfect, and she booked her flight and bought the long black wig.

Victim two expired the following year—a professor at the University of North Carolina-Charlotte. Greta and he had been involved in a purely physical relationship while she was enrolled to study architecture, so she was sure he'd know Mallory was a fraud if Uncle Richard ever visited or a movie was made. He had to go too. His was the only death not attributed to the "Millionaire Club Killer" as the media and authorities had dubbed her. Somehow, his murder in Charlotte, though handled similarly, with a poke to the brain—but through the ear canal as he slept—fell through the cracks of their investigation. *Here's to shoddy police work.*

Then she moved her spree to *the AC* where Richard's life ended on the beach.

That threw Mallory into the fold, solidifying her *opportunity* for the remaining murders. Greta smiles as she thinks of the nickname Mallory had given the city. *That's the one thing I agree with you on, Mal.*

One of the more recent victims, Gabe Riley, had been an art dealer. Greta had learned of Mallory's interest in art, making him and his life even more connected to Mallory's life.

And the billionaire motorcycle enthusiast in Pennsylvania . . . *What was his name? Oh yeah, Roland.* Roland Warren and his company of geniuses had just developed an eye scanner that could match family members. Very cool but, unfortunately for him, he fell right into Mallory's make-believe motive of not wanting people to discover she was a fraud—and he had been a very wealthy man.

It had been pure luck when Mallory decided not to invite Brian over to spend the night at the Virginia Arms Apartments. Greta had been following them that day—after they'd left Bill and Jean's house. She watched the exchange from the street, holding her breath when Brian entered the apartment building with Greta after he had told Antonio they were going to grab his things and bring him back. Greta was ecstatic when Mallory chased him down and told him she'd like to be alone that night instead. *Perfect,* she had thought. *Home all night. No alibi. Enough time for her to hop over to Paoli and back.*

Greta was most proud of how she disguised herself throughout the plan to look like Mallory, even wearing a pair of short stilts under her pants when she knew she'd be on camera, like at the Ocean Casino & Resort. Height was a key part of the frame job, but she was just a few inches short. Training to walk on those stilts had been a blast, especially on the beach. She smiles at her accomplishment. And of course, the wigs were amusing for a while too. Though they had gotten hot and itchy in the New Jersey spring warmth.

There had been only one hitch in Greta's multi-year scheme, but she had taken care of her, and it had worked out better than expected. When everyone had descended on Atlantic City in the last few weeks of the plan, Greta learned that a woman from Chios, Greece was visiting the beachside gambling town for a couple of days—a stopover on her way to Texas, where her main holiday would unfold.

Madalena Kontos had no idea the meaning of her Greek surname would define her life. *Short.* Madalena had been a frequent patron at Greta's boutique shop and, therefore, could not only have recognized her, but could have confirmed that Greta had closed her shop in Chios over two months before she arrived in New Jersey. Madalena was simply in the wrong place at the wrong time. After her death, her car, which Greta had expertly jumped out of while it was still moving, crashed into a utility pole, sending a portion of Atlantic City into darkness. *Nice touch,* she had thought. Mallory had no alibi for the middle of the night. Authorities believed she had snuck out of Bill and Jean's home without their knowledge.

Then she had targeted Brian Gogh, the wealthiest attorney in the AC and someone Greta had more than enough access to harm. Greta had a personal vendetta too. Brian had called the wrong woman when Richard died. When the brakes in Brian's car didn't fail at the right time, injuring Antonio but not Brian, she considered killing Antonio. Mistakes and unfinished jobs irritated her. But seeing Antonio lying in that hospital bed . . . well, she decided it didn't fit with what Mallory would have done. He wasn't outrageously wealthy. Realizing it would be mistake number two, she left the room almost as soon as she had arrived and tossed the robe and shoes in a dumpster.

Greta left town for a bit after that so she could fly into the airport as herself (except for her drab-brown wig, of course), completing her four-year journey toward redemption. And putting an exclamation point on her contrived narrative built for revenge.

THE FOLLOWING WEEK, *Fiona* sits in her new Japanese-style modern mansion—her favorite style from her time in architecture school—which overlooks the blue-green waters of the Pacific, content in all things. That Mallory likes modern styles, too, feels apropos.

Fiona raises a glass toward the ocean, celebrating her apparent victory.

39

Fort Dix Federal Correctional Institute, New Jersey,
ten months after her arrest

"Mallory, you have a visitor."

Briefly, Brian's face appears in Mallory's mind's eye, and a small part of her pleads to the God she doesn't believe in that it's him. She often dreams about reconciliation, a reunion, or even a rekindling of their love of nearly a year ago. *Or are these simply nightmares?* she thinks as she walks in front of the guard to the visitation room in the new, low-security facility to which she was transferred after her guilty plea several months ago.

Through the square window in the door, Mallory spies her literary agent, Roz, sitting at a table. Her heart drops with disappointment. Roz beams as Mallory shuffles inside. It's "pub day" as it's called in the book publishing industry, and Mallory assumes Roz is here to congratulate her. But she's not feeling any desire to rejoice, given her current residence.

Before Mallory can sit in the hard chair, Roz dives in. "Mallory, your novel opened at number one on the *Wall Street Journal* best-seller list today! And you're number seven with the *New York Times*."

The courts had allowed Mallory to use both names since her readers had identified with her in her previous books as Greta Goldman. But there was a catch. On the book cover, it had to read, "Mallory Jones, formerly known as Greta Goldman." The latter part—*formerly known as Greta Goldman*—was designed with an extra-fine, small-print font and placed on the bottom. And her own biography graced the back matter. It had still been a win in her mind.

"*Give or Take* is getting outstanding reviews! Everyone loves it, even the most discerning critics. Way to go, Mal!" Her agent grins.

Shock washes over Mallory. She had expected new readers and old fans alike to boycott her book, given her crimes. Truthfully, she also worried the story wasn't good enough, that she had missed the mark. "Seriously?" she asks Roz.

"Yes! Can you believe it?"

"No."

For the next sixteen weeks, *Give or Take* stays at the number one spot on all the big lists. A production company executive picked up the novel and loves it. Mallory's publisher and she agree to release the story to be optioned and produced as a feature film. And a documentary about Mallory's life—and her crimes—is in the works.

Across the world, sipping on a daiquiri in a lounge chair by her infinity pool, Fiona Applegate is sucker-punched by the news as she scrolls the US entertainment headlines. She knows her real name is still on the cover. She had seen that court ruling months ago and, in a rage, had broken her favorite vase. Now, her fury over the past several years erupts again.

I'm going to kill her, Fiona thinks.

She throws her cocktail glass on the ground, causing it to shatter into dozens of pieces, which glisten in the mean Pacific sun.

Nineteen months after her arrest, Mallory officially crosses the threshold of "multi-millionaire," her revenue climbing with the film—which has already been shot and is now in editing —and her consistent book sales, which haven't waned as book clubs all over the world choose *Give or Take* and revisit her first two books.

As Mallory's agent shelters her royalties and earnings in a special account, Mallory plots what she's going to do with the money once it's released to her. Though it's tied up now, inaccessible to her while she's incarcerated, she hopes that because of her altruistic intentions, the state will allow her early access to it.

Sitting in her cell in the dark early morning hours, Mallory thinks of Brian as she strategizes her financial future and someday freedom. She tries to recall every day she spent with him, particularly the dates they had—the time on the beach, the dinners at Villain and Saint and Landry & Sons, and the night at his house. Her eyes fill with liquid regret as she realizes her feelings for him have not waned.

I'm sure his have.

Until now, she has forced herself not to think about him, not since her sentencing. The stabbing pain in her heart has been too great, her shame keeping her awake on countless nights. She wonders what he's up to . . . who he's with. She thinks about Leah in the mayor's office and ponders whether anything transpired there.

Does he think about me at all?

She speculates with more remorse than her conscious mind can hold. So she opens her notebook, one of the few personal items she keeps with her, and sketches, a distracting hobby she's picked up while incarcerated. After a few minutes, she lies down on her bed, drops her notebook onto the concrete ground, and weeps.

40

After months of back and forth, the courts finally approve Mallory's plan, and she's granted limited access to her growing wealth.

Nearly three years after her journey through Atlantic City with Brian Gogh, Mallory Jones, inmate number 47983-050, becomes the second-largest donor to The Hope Floor in the Ocean Resort & Casino—second only to Richard M. Goldman.

The owner who took over the Virginia Arms Apartments after Greta Goldman sold it to the bank, much to Mallory's relief, had done nothing with it and put it back on the market. She gladly makes an offer and secures it for the future remodel—with the industrial loft décor Richard had in mind.

Next, she creates a scholarship for future ABCC students who want to pursue education or creative writing degrees. *Creative writing*—her primary passion. Mallory thinks of Dawn Marshall. "What makes you so excited that you could dance?" Dawn's words float inside her mind, and she can't help but feel the joy she saw in Dawn's life.

She also donates another original Dali to ABCC's main offices in honor of Brian Gogh and hopes he doesn't hate her for it. Being an art connoisseur herself, she knew right away when she saw the first Dali that day with Brian who the artist was and how much the piece was worth. And Mallory knows Brian's affection for quality art too. *I miss you, Brian.*

Then Mallory donates fifty-one thousand dollars to the hospital, specifically to the St. Nick Wing, even though she never had the privilege of seeing it. It's one thousand more than Greta had donated. She knows it's a petty act but doesn't care. When she'd heard that was all Greta had done with Richard's billions, a mix of sadness and anger had overtaken her. Now, she asks for the money to be used to buy Christmas gifts for the next two years for the children on the floor and the staff who work on that day as well.

And the fire station. *Jason, I won't forget your kindness.* She sets aside another one hundred thousand for the firehouse to use at their discretion.

Finally, Mallory pens a letter to Dawn that includes her intentions of setting up a growth fund, honoring Richard, to which Dawn will have unbridled access to distribute cash to The Community Chest in Atlantic City whenever needs arise.

After her philanthropic giving, Mallory secures the remaining money in a trust sponsored by her agent. It will be just enough for her to live comfortably, definitely not extravagantly, once she's released from prison. She hopes that day comes soon. She has a parole hearing in a few weeks, and she thinks her odds are fairly good. Despite her quirkiness, she's been a model inmate. The guards and prison staff have appreciated the odd conversations they've had with her, entertaining as they are, given the only things inside to look at are gray walls and iron bars. Everyone around her is watching her transformed heart on full display.

As Mallory lies awake one night, listening to the whispers of neighboring prisoners, she thinks about her past. Then she thinks of Dawn again. She can't get her out of her mind. As her throat grows thick, she pulls the worn King James version of the Bible from its place on the twelve-inch shelf afforded to each cell. She's never touched it in all these months. At times, she stared at the words etched in gold along the spine, but she could never bring herself to open it.

She doesn't open it this time either. Slowly, Mallory places the Good Book on its original perch. Then she lays her head on the flat pillow and falls asleep.

A WEEK LATER, just before the dinner hour, a guard approaches her cell and stands in front of it. "Mallory, you have a visitor."

"Right now?"

"Yep. Let's go." His straight face and the odd visiting hour unnerve her. She steps back so he can open her cell door. It squeals on its hinges, in dire need of WD-40. The guard ignores the metal door's complaint and nods for her to exit.

As Mallory makes her way to the visitation room, the guard, who is walking behind her, pushes her in the lower spine. "Hurry up," he barks.

"Okay already. What's going on with you today?" She wonders why the guard is acting so rude when normally, the cell-block guards and she get along well.

When the door to the room opens, Mallory's breath catches in mid-inhale.

Sitting at a two-top is Brian, his lips forming a straight line of anticipation across his face. She turns to the guard behind her, who now has a wide-open smile. The guard winks and shuts the door.

Mallory practically runs to the table. Brian stands, and from across the room, another guard yells the reminder: "No touching!" Brian bows slightly and shrugs his shoulders. Mallory watches his chin dimple deepen. He's wearing jeans and a button-down shirt. His blond hair seems lighter, as if he's been spending time in the sun. *He looks so good,* Mallory thinks, but she can't find any words to say out loud. She opts to sit.

Finally, after a long pause, she opens her mouth. "I'm surprised to see you."

"Yeah, I know. It's been a long time. You look good—great—by the way." He gives her a small smile.

She shakes her head, knowing almost three years in prison doesn't make anyone look *great.* "You too." Her eyes are glued to his, and memories bounce back into her head all at once. Feelings she thought were long-dormant—even gone—flood her heart. "Brian, I'm so sor—"

He waves her off. "Can I start?" She nods, suddenly cautious. A tiny wall erects itself around her heart in anticipation of needing protection.

"I want to apologize for not coming sooner. I just . . . I was just so angry and hurt. I needed time. A lot of it, I guess. I love the Goldman family, and what you did with . . . well, anyway. I know you didn't realize how deep you'd get into it. I understand Richard's passing was a surprise, and I know you meant no harm. And I realize you didn't plan to inherit his estate—probably never even thought about it when you took Greta's name." Mallory shakes her head back and forth as confirmation of what Brian is saying. "But I haven't stopped thinking about you. I've missed you . . . Mallory." Saying her real name causes Brian's mouth to bend into a slight frown, but he blinks and recovers.

Rivulets of both guilt and relief slide down Mallory's cheeks. She can't speak. She clasps her hands together and tries to keep from shaking. A small sob escapes her lips, but she prevents the full release by biting the inside of her cheek.

"And," Brian says, "I heard about the Dali you donated to ABCC in my honor." He chuckles. "Thank you. I think that's what made me realize I didn't want our relationship to end the way it did."

Mallory's eyes dart to the table. *Is he going to end it now? Here, in person? Did he come just to bring closure?* Her lungs refuse to breathe.

"Okay. That's all I wanted to say. Oh, and . . . I forgive you."

Mallory can't hold in her crushing feelings any longer. Her hands come to her face and turn wet as her shoulders convulse with emotion.

Brian looks at the guard, a silent plea for permission to comfort Mallory. There is a slight nod, and Brian jumps up and grabs Mallory, bringing her to her feet for a hug.

The fir balsam and coriander scent of his cologne makes her knees buckle, but he holds her up.

"I'm so sorry, Brian," she bawls.

"I know."

"I never wanted to hurt anyone."

"I know."

The guard clears his throat, and Brian releases Mallory and guides her to her seat. He sits down in his chair opposite her once again. The short but sweet contact he was gifted by the guard courses through him like lightning. She felt good in his arms.

For the remaining minutes they have together, Mallory tells Brian about her upcoming parole hearing and about Precious and the idea of partnering with her to write about Richard's life. Brian, his compassion swelling as he realizes how much Mallory has grown, agrees to help.

A minute of silence follows, and Mallory stares at Brian, the unasked question of any future relationship hanging between them. Brian smiles, and his dimple deepens. She holds her breath.

Then he winks at her.

And Mallory's heart fills with hope.

THE FOLLOWING WEEK, Mallory begins to write short pieces about her past—specifically, her tumultuous childhood bouncing from one house to another and her adult choices, with the themes of identity—how we become who we are—and altruism weaved throughout. She thinks of Dawn as she writes, and her entire body aches over her lost friend. She's had no contact or communication with her fairy *mommother* and wonders if she ever will.

At Dawn's house the night before Mallory was arrested, Dawn spoke of her past as if she had let it all go. The pain. The heartache. The abandonment and neglect. It was clear to Mallory: the weight of Dawn's childhood trauma no longer held her down. She remembers the look on Dawn's face and the sound of her voice as she shared her story. There wasn't a trace of resentment. In its place sat peace . . . and redemption. As Mallory's mind tosses the idea of redemption—true emotional freedom—around, she is reminded of the Howard Family on The Hope Floor. And the Rodriguez Family, who owns the alcohol-free bar.

Mallory smiles.

There is hope in the stories and people she had the privilege to meet. *Some good did come of my crimes.* She's determined to find that hope and peace for herself.

Finally, she writes about wealth, privilege, and the dark secrets she kept tucked into her wounded psyche from her childhood experiences. Though she never provides the names of her abusers, she describes the pull money and power have on people and how, as a society, we could all do better not to succumb to that power. To not keep the secrets. To not cover up and protect the guilty.

On a sunny day three weeks later, Mallory meets with Roz, her agent, one more time. After glancing out the small window and seeing the clear blue sky, she takes it as a positive omen and hands Roz the articles and essays she's written.

"I don't know if they're any good," she tells her agent. Even though her words reveal her self-doubt, Mallory understands these also might be the most meaningful pieces she's ever written. Roz grins and takes the pile of lined notebook paper. Later, she will type them out and post them to Mallory's new blog, one that will soon garner a hundred thousand readers within the first few days.

"When is your parole hearing?" she asks Mallory. "It's soon, right?"

"Next week." With those words, Mallory's heart flaps in her chest. She hasn't realized until now how close the date is—how close physical freedom may be.

With the court's permission to give away most of the money she's earned with the book sales and movie, Mallory hopes the "powers that be" will be lenient during her parole hearing. *Not that I deserve it,* she thinks. *But I want to go home.*

On a rainy Wednesday, the day before her hearing and for the first time in three years, Mallory sits in her cell and considers her future with Brian. She recalls the wink from a month ago that signified his readiness to forgive and start anew. Since then, he's visited her several times, and they've fallen back into the flirtatious relationship with which they had left off.

During the last few years, Mallory wasn't able to picture his face; now, she rolls a movie of them together—walking on the beach, sharing meals, and visiting art shows—in her mind's eye. It's an epic film with a fairytale ending.

Tears spring forth, and she allows herself a good cry. They slide down her cheeks and squeeze themselves through the corners of her mouth, their salty flavor reaching her taste buds. It is a *good* cry.

Tomorrow would be a perfect day to be free.

She can't wait to get back to *Gogh.*

Epilogue

Over the years, no additional murders have been committed—at least of ultra-wealthy men in the United States. The investigative authorities have yet to determine who the serial killer was, and the scant evidence they have collected, which comprises loose connections a few of the victims had to Mallory, sits in a cold-case box in the evidence vault at the FBI field office in Philadelphia. Many still suspect Mallory, especially since the spree stopped with her incarceration. But the multi-millionaires and billionaires of the country all breathe a collective sigh of relief as they continue to live out their extravagant existence, moving their life pieces around, and positioning themselves for greater success while amassing more money, real estate, and possessions along the way.

Acknowledgments

The Billionaire's List was a multi-year labor of love. Like life, the writing process is a journey, one meant to be savored, and for this author, it was more about the pilgrimage than the destination. There are many to thank for this particular journey:

First, I thank God for making me part creator, part word nerd. He is my everything.

To my husband Marc, my best friend. I'm so glad we're giving this life a whirl together!

To my friends and family who encourage me daily, especially those who were beta readers for this novel: Dana Horne, Coe Sherrard, Jaye Soss, Barbara Zerfoss, and my parents, William and Dona Trull (the real Bill and Jean).

To Jane, a former FBI special agent, for her expertise in helping ensure the parts of the story related to the Bureau's procedures are plausible.

To fellow author Janey Pitts and former physical therapy colleague Katherine Huffstickler for their contributions. Their proposed character names won in a fun social media survey during the writing of this novel. Special Agent Kat Turner and Mallory Jones thank you too.

To Hasbro, your Monopoly board game kept my family busy during the 2020 COVID-19 lockdown and inspired creative juices I didn't believe I had. It's a game I've always respected, one that taught me how to save as I stuffed half of my earnings under my tushy until the end of the game, only to pull it all out and surprise everyone with my secret savings account. Thank you.

Points of Interest

Villain and Saint

This modern gastropub, located in the Oceans Casino Resort in Atlantic City, New Jersey, has every bit of the rock-n-roll vibe described in *The Billionaire's List*. It has won awards for entertainment and features live music and draft beers from around the world.

Virginia Arms Apartments

The Virginia Arms Apartments is located in Atlantic City, New Jersey. This renovated apartment community was built in 1920 and has four stories with thirty-eight units.

The Civil Rights Garden

The Civil Rights Garden is a hidden gem in Atlantic City, New Jersey. This memorial is a beautiful and tranquil place tucked among the casinos, beaches, and boardwalks. The project was the first large-scale civil rights park built in the North. On the top of a pillar in the back of the park is a hand, which represents the right to vote and is paired with a quote: "The first step towards liberation for any group is the use of the hand. And the power in hand is the vote." (Hellen Gahagan Douglass, 1973) If you enter the garden, you'll also find quotes from Edward Bellamy, Austin Steward, and Harriet Tubman covering the first granite pillars. Ten of the eleven pillars have uncompleted sections meant to signify the journey toward full civil rights for all is ongoing.[1]

Marven Gardens

Marven Gardens Historic District is a sixteen-acre historical district in Margate City, New Jersey, not in Atlantic City. On the original Monopoly game board, it is the only stop *not* located within Atlantic City limits (though in this story it is!). Interestingly, it's also misspelled as *Marvin* Gardens. Charles and Olive Todd misspelled it when they taught the game to Charles Darrow, its eventual patentee. In 1995, Parker Brothers, who owned the game at the time, acknowledged the mistake and formally apologized to the residents of Marven Gardens for the typo.

Claridge Hotel

This famous Atlantic City hotel opened in 1930 (during the Great Depression) and was once known as the "Skyscraper by the Sea." The Claridge Hotel stands twenty-four stories tall and radiates a certain charm. It's located a few steps from the Atlantic City boardwalk, and over the last century, guests have included celebrities and star athletes, such as Marilyn Monroe, Martin Luther King Jr., Mickey Mantle, and Frank Sinatra.

---

1. Christian Hetrick, "Civil Rights Garden: A 'Little-Known Secret' in A.C." Atlantic City Press. February 21, 2016, accessed June 11, 2022, http://www.-pressofatlanticcity.com/news/breaking/civil-rights-garden-a-little-known-secret-in-a-c/article_06832fe0-d914-11e5-b6aa-c7b83dd3bd34.html.

About the Author

Cortney is a hummingbird-watching marriage lover. She owns and is the principal writer at vocem LLC and serves as the associate publisher of Fiction for Morgan James Publishing. While she has ghostwritten more than ten books—including a couple of best-sellers—there are two others she can call her own: a memoir titled *Clay Jar Cracked: When We're Broken But Not Shattered* and *The Outlier's Choice: Why Living an Uncomfortable Life is Worth It*, written with co-author Becky Huber. Cortney lives in Charlotte, North Carolina, where she enjoys board games (of course!), paddle boarding, hiking, and escaping to the beach with her husband, Marc, and their teenage kids.

Made in the USA
Columbia, SC
01 November 2022

70343840R00163